CHERRYBROOK ROSE

Recent Titles by Tania Crosse

MORWELHAM'S CHILD
THE RIVER GIRL
CHERRYBROOK ROSE *
A BOUQUET OF THORNS *

available from Severn House

CHERRYBROOK ROSE

Tania Crosse

This first world edition published 2008
in Great Britain and the USA by
SEVERN HOUSE PUBLISHERS LTD of
9–15 High Street, Sutton, Surrey SM1 1DF.

British Library Cataloguing in Publication Data

Crosse, Tania Anne
  Cherrybrook Rose
  1. Dartmoor (England) - Fiction 2. Great Britain - History
  - Victoria, 1837-1901 - Fiction 3. Love stories
  I. Title
  823.9'2[F]

ISBN-13: 978-0-7278-6628-8   (cased)
ISBN-13: 978-1-84751-062-4   (trade paper)

All Severn House titles are printed on acid-free paper.

Typeset by Palimpsest Book Production Ltd.,
Grangemouth, Stirlingshire, Scotland.
Printed and bound in Great Britain by
MPG Books Ltd., Bodmin, Cornwall.

For my mother-in-law Wyn.

And as always for my husband for his patience and support.

Acknowledgements

First of all, a huge thank you to my wonderful agent and everyone at Severn House for bringing this novel to fruition. Also my deepest gratitude, as ever, to my good friend Paul Rendell, Dartmoor guide and historian and editor of *The Dartmoor News*, who is always so willing to share his extensive knowledge of the moor with me. Particular thanks go to Dartmoor Prison historian Trevor James for all his support and time spent providing precise historical detail. I must also thank our long-standing friend Colin Skeen, barrister and magistrate, for his research into the history of the legal system on my behalf. Others who have contributed information are Tavistock historian Gerry Woodcock, retired physician Dr Marshall Barr and the British Army Museum. My sincere thanks to you all.

Author's Note

George Frean was the real-life proprietor of the gunpowder mills. Research showed him to be a just and kindly gentleman and he is portrayed thus in the novel.

Anyone who trespasses on the powder mill ruins does so entirely at their own risk.

One

It *had* to be Rose Maddiford, didn't it?

Ellen Williams poked her severely groomed head out of the open door of her grocery and draper's establishment, and her neatly contained bosom exploded in a sigh of exasperation. A pall of dust had been lifted from the parched surface of Prison Road by the clattering hooves of the charging horse, and Ellen quickly shut the door against it, for she hardly wanted the insidious layer to settle on *her* goods and products! But she could not resist sidling into her immaculate window display and pressing her nose against the glass so that she might have a better view along the street towards the prison, not that she could see the bleak and daunting edifice from her shop in the centre of Princetown. Sure enough, the billowing cloud had come to a whirlwind stop outside the Albert Inn, loose stones scattering in every direction as the rider brought the stampeding animal to a violent halt. The creature reared in protest with a bellicose neigh, its forelegs pawing furiously at the air before it dropped swiftly on all fours once more. The figure on its back, however, kept its seat as if glued to the raging beast and proceeded to turn the demented steed in tight circles until its bunched haunches relaxed and with a snort of disgust the sleek young gelding bowed its head in submission. One long, shapely leg was swung over the hairy neck, two well-shod feet landed lightly on the ground, and taking the reins behind the foaming mouth, the rider led its mount, meek as a lamb now, towards the stables behind the Albert Inn, and out of Ellen's view.

The older woman pursed her lips, her grey eyes steely with disappointment that the moment had passed without grave mishap. Her sharp features instantly hardened into a forced smile as she realized that two gentlewomen who had paused to witness the feckless rider's progress had now turned their attention to her window and were staring at her from the other side of the glass. Ellen Williams was not about to lose a sale by gaping rudely at potential customers, and moving with as much grace as her short, stocky form could muster, returned to her station behind the counter, tutting reproachfully with her tongue.

Someone really ought to take that girl in hand! She and that fiendish monster on whose perilous back she galloped all over the moor, well, they were as bad as each other, in Ellen's opinion. What on earth did the girl's father think he was at, allowing her such behaviour? But then it was well known that Henry Maddiford, manager of the gunpowder mills three miles away at Cherrybrook, doted on his only child and had apparently done so ever since his dear wife had sacrificed her own life bringing her into this sinful world. And it hadn't done her any good, had it, being spoilt like that? Just *look* at the girl! Riding *astride* if you please! And beneath the full riding skirt, her legs were tightly clad in breeches as if she were a young man! Ellen had glimpsed them quite clearly as the hussy had dismounted, as if she hadn't seen them often enough before! And what rankled Ellen's sensibilities more was that the little madam had sewn the outrageous riding outfit from a distinctive material bought in *her* shop and which had been prominently displayed in *her* window, so that everybody would know she was prepared to serve the wayward wench!

Ellen's mouth wrinkled into a mean knot as the two women moved on down the street. Well, beggars couldn't be choosers, could they? She couldn't afford to turn down a sale, and Rose Maddiford *was* a good customer, for both groceries and material, and always sewing her clothes herself without using the services of one of Princetown's dress-makers. And she was a good seamstress, Ellen had to give her *that*. And she supposed that, for a lively and wilful young girl, living at the isolated powder mills – slap in the middle of the great wilderness of Dartmoor and even lonelier than the grey community of Princetown – was hardly ideal. Life wasn't always what you wanted, no one knew better than Ellen herself.

Her father had been a miner, his health broken as a young man by breathing in the choking air and dust deep beneath the surface of the earth, until the mine surgeon had told him if he didn't change his occupation he would be dead within the year. The re-opening in Princetown of the defunct prisoner-of-war depot as a convict gaol in 1850, revitalizing the remote, decaying village, had been his salvation. Once the convicts arrived, the settlement had begun to flourish again as no less than a hundred warders and their families were gradually drafted in. John Williams, his wife and ten-year-old daughter had opened up the grocer's shop with what meagre savings they had. They had worked every hour God sent and built up the thriving little business to what it was today, the beginning of September 1875. Ellen's parents had now passed on, leaving her comfortable, though not wealthy. But at what cost?

At first, it had been army guards, and soon afterwards army pensioners, and finally in 1857 – when Ellen had been a fresh-faced girl of seventeen – younger men from the Civil Guard who had constituted the armed escorts for the convicts labouring outside the massive prison walls, assisting the warders who worked both in and outside the gaol. The warders were usually older men, burly miners or farmers, used themselves to the harsh discipline of the moor. It was a condition of their employment that they lived in Princetown so that they could be quickly summoned to assist in a riot or to search for an escapee. But for their families it was purgatory, incarcerated in the forlorn town, fourteen hundred feet above sea level on the desolate moor, exposed to lacerating cold and deep snowdrifts in winter and miserable, rainy summers, imprisoned just as securely as the felons within the gaol itself. Any son of a warder would be off to better climes to make his own way in the world just as soon as he was old enough, that was if his entire family hadn't had so much of the place that they had already upped sticks and moved away somewhere more hospitable.

So where had that left girls like Ellen? On the shelf, of course. She hadn't been unattractive, she considered, but there simply hadn't been enough suitable young men in the restricted vicinity in which she had been trapped. They were always snapped up by any girl whose beauty easily outshone the common crowd.

Girls like Rose Maddiford!

Ellen's jaw clamped fiercely as the swirling jealousy threatened to choke her.

Ned Cornish looked up with a cheeky grin as he paused in his labours of shovelling the pile of steaming horse dung into the heavy wooden barrow. Stable work was all he had ever known in his young life. And if it meant he came into close contact with Rose Maddiford whenever she swept into Princetown and needed to leave that confounded animal in his care for a few hours, then he blessed the morning his father had deposited him at the door of the Albert Inn to do his first day's work at the age of nine, for his family needed his wages to survive.

That was years ago, and now he was a strong, bulky youth with a wicked sense of humour and an eye for the girls. His secluded room above the stables behind the inn had seen more than one maiden willingly deflowered. But Rose Maddiford was not amongst them, and never would be.

She came towards him now, her cheeks flushed with the exhilaration of the gallop across the moor, her bouncing ebony curls rippling wildly down her back in a shining cascade from beneath the apology of a hat that sat, somewhat askew, like a frilly pancake on the top of her beautiful head. Her slanting violet-blue eyes danced, and beneath the jacket of her riding habit her straining breasts heaved up and down above her slender, pliable waist.

Ned watched them. And smiled.

'Good afternoon, Ned,' she greeted him in her habitually friendly manner. 'How are you today?'

Ned's heart beat faster. 'All the better for seeing you,' he answered truthfully, leaning on the handle of the spade to contemplate her willowy figure. She was of average height, but her slight frame made her appear taller than she was, and her halo of unruly hair gave her at least another inch.

Her full red lips broke into a short laugh. 'Flattery will get you nowhere with me!' she chided playfully.

Ned sniffed. She was certainly right there! He had never got so much as a harmless kiss out of Rose Maddiford. It was as if she was unaware of her tantalizing charms. She was devoted to one man alone, and that was her father!

'You off to visit young Molly?' Ned asked, his chest giving

a little jerk of jealousy as his generous mouth curled at one corner.

'*Miss* Molly to you!' Rose grinned. 'But, yes, I am. So you will look after Gospel for me, won't you? There'll be sixpence in it for you, as usual.'

Ned grunted his displeasure. If it weren't for Rose, he wouldn't have gone near the animal for two guineas, let alone sixpence! Bad-tempered creature it was, at least it was the minute Rose was out of its sight. Black as the devil, and that would have been a better name for it, Devil! Ned thought. As for calling it Gospel, well! When he had questioned Rose on her strange choice, he hadn't quite fathomed her explanation. It was something to do with the monster's dark coat, and the religious chants that the African slaves in the American cotton fields apparently sang to ease their aching spirits. Well, Ned didn't know anything about *that*. He didn't even know where America and Africa were! A long way off, he knew that. But then to Ned so was anywhere beyond Plymouth, which he visited possibly once a year. Back along, there had been American as well as French prisoners of war held in what was now the convict gaol that stood within spitting distance of the Albert Inn. So America couldn't be *that* far away, Ned reasoned. Americans spoke English, so America must be nearer than France, where they gabbled in some incomprehensible language – or at least, Ned imagined they did. But, to be honest, he wasn't really bothered where other countries might be. It hardly made any difference to *his* life, did it? He could write his own name when he put his mind to it, which was more than his parents could, and that was enough for him.

Except when it came to Rose. Then, and only then, did his ignorance trouble him. Rose *devoured* books. She adored Jane Austen's novels – whoever she was – and now she was reading this controversial fellow Charles Dickens. And how she would love to see a theatre production of *Macbeth*. It was set in the Highlands of Scotland, but couldn't you imagine it happening amongst the wild and spectacular beauty of Dartmoor? Ned had nodded cautiously, praying it was sufficient response. He knew she read the *Tavistock Gazette* each week from cover to cover, for it reported not only local news, but national and international events as well, events she evidently discussed at length with her father. It was no wonder she was way out of

Ned's league. *And* out of the league of virtually every young male in the vicinity, although plenty of them wouldn't have minded getting their hands on her virginal figure!

'You can put that nag of yourn in the end box,' he ordered with a disgruntled snort. 'And take its tack off yoursel, if you wants to. *I'll* not go near the brute.'

Rose raised a teasing eyebrow as Gospel nuzzled against her shoulder and she stroked his arching neck in response. 'You're not afeared, are you, Ned?' she asked.

Ned flushed. But he wasn't going to let Rose's clever tongue get the better of him, so he threw back his head with a throaty laugh. 'No. But the marks 'aven't quite faded from the last time 'e bit me, and I doesn't want a matching set just yet.'

It was Rose's turn to look abashed. 'I'm really sorry about that,' she said with feeling. 'Of course I'll see to him myself. I'm just grateful to have somewhere safe I can leave him.' And so saying, she clicked her tongue and led the infamous beast into the stable Ned had indicated, emerging a few minutes later with the heavy saddle, which the youth was pleased to take from her, delighted at the opportunity to show her some gallantry. He lowered his eyes to the gleaming leather with a lecherous smirk. An *astride* saddle, of course. But that was Rose Maddiford for you, wasn't it! And his heart sighed as he watched her stride out of the yard.

Rose hurried down Prison Road with a spring in her step. Not that she had far to go, but the prospect of spending a few hours in the company of her good friend, Molly Cartwright, filled her with happiness. As she left the relative tranquillity of the village behind, a general bustle of activity took its place in the warm, early autumn sunshine. Just beyond the encircling wall of the barracks which was her destination, work was continuing apace on the new accommodation block for the prison warders and their families. Molly's mother was praying they would be allocated one of its thirty flats, each of which was to boast two tiny bedrooms, a small living room and a working scullery. And who could blame her, when two adults – three if you counted Molly, who was nineteen – and five younger children had been squeezed into just two rooms in the decaying barracks for years!

Rose paused for a moment to contemplate the progress on

the new building, which was to be named, most imaginatively, she mocked, Number One Warders' Block. There was some way to go before it was finished, despite the convicts that swarmed over the growing edifice like ants in their drab uniforms with the distinctive arrows. And they *worked* like ants, too, at least they did if they didn't want to feel a warder's truncheon across their back. The term 'hard labour' was somewhat of an understatement, Rose always thought. Inhuman it was sometimes, in her opinion, gruelling, non-stop physical toil on prison buildings that were being doubled or trebled in size from the original prisoner-of-war blocks, or out on the extensive prison lands, clearing them of granite boulders or working up to the waist in cold water as they dug drainage ditches, all to extend the workable areas of the prison farm. If not that, then digging mountains of peat for the new gasworks just outside the prison wall which supplied light for the prison itself and all prison property within the village, or slaving on the public roads or in the prison quarry a hundred yards or so further down towards Rundlestone. It was no wonder a convict would suddenly lose his reason and, in a moment of madness, make a dash across the moor, even knowing the armed warders or Civil Guard who accompanied all outside work parties would shoot him down. Still, if you didn't like it, you shouldn't have come, was the old prison saying. Hardened criminals, most of them, violent, incorrigible villains. Though some were merely habitual thieves or forgers, innocent of any physical violence, but sentenced to a minimum of five years to qualify for Dartmoor's infamous gaol. But what if, Rose's questioning mind considered, you really were wrongfully convicted . . .

She flicked her head as if tossing out the unwelcome thought, kicked the hem of her riding skirt out of the way of her strong, athletic legs, and marched through the gateway of the barracks compound. She braced herself against the coming onslaught from the Cartwright family, and then stepped across the yard, greeting people as she went. A woman was lugging a basket overflowing with laundry to the little hexagonal wash-house in the centre of the compound which served the hundred or more families who were crowded into the eleven barracks. Children too young to attend the new prison officers' school – built and maintained, it went without saying, by convict

labour – played safely outside in the sunshine, amongst them
the youngest of the Cartwright clan. The wife of one of the
twenty-four Civil Guards, younger, fitter men who were all
housed in Number Six barracks, was leaning against a wall,
her stomach jutting with her first child, as she chatted to a
neighbour. Rose hailed them all as she passed, and then bound
up the outside steps to the humble dwelling in Number Seven
barracks.

The small front room was a jumble of garments and linen,
for Molly and her mother were tackling the weekly mountain
of ironing, taking it in turns to do the ironing itself whilst the
other folded the pressed articles and hung them over the
wooden slats of the airing rack which would later be hoisted
to the ceiling. The air was heavy with warmth and moisture,
a strange mix of the freshness of ironing and the acrid smell
of the peat fire that smouldered in the small grate where the
two spare irons were reheating whilst Mrs Cartwright used
the third.

'Oh, Rose! How lovely to see you!'

Molly's naturally pale cheeks were flushed with the afternoon's activity and she pushed back a wayward wisp of light
ginger hair that had escaped from beneath the plain white
muslin cap on her head. Her small but well-shaped mouth
broke into a grin, and above it, her eyes, a distinct feline green,
danced with delight.

'Well,' Rose replied with an exaggerated tilt of her head,
'I'd not seen you for a week and I wanted to make certain
you were behaving yourself.'

A faint smile lifted Mrs Cartwright's work-worn face at
their irrepressible visitor, but with eight mouths to feed and
the apparel of eight bodies to launder, she had no time to stop
and chat. But Rose always brought a breath of fresh air into
their humdrum lives, and was always welcome. Besides, she
was a lady, and perhaps one day some practical advantage
might come of their association and lift Molly from the drab
future she faced at present.

Molly's lips, however, twisted into a mock grimace. 'Behave
myself!' she groaned. 'And what chance d'you imagine I'd
have to do ort else?'

'Well, I don't know! Perhaps one of the new Civil Guards?'
Rose teased. 'There's one particularly attractive fellow . . .

Why don't we walk down to the quarry and see if he's on duty there?'

'Oh, Rose, you'm a real devil!' Molly chuckled. 'But I cas'n. Look at this pile of ironing! The girls'll be home from school directly, and we must get it finished by then.'

'Let me help, then.' And throwing her riding gloves on to the bed Molly shared with the elder two of her three younger sisters, Rose unfastened the jacket of her riding habit, tossed it on top of the gloves and rolled up the sleeves of her shirt. 'Now, what can I do? Or would it be more use to you if I started preparing the meal?'

Mrs Cartwright shook her head. That was Rose for you! Heart as big as the ocean. And it wasn't an empty gesture. The girl knew how to cook, sew and iron, and would work as hard as any of them. And so it was that by the time the three younger siblings arrived back from school the laundry was stowed away on the airing rack, Rose had rescued little Philip from the compound and cleaned him up and a pile of bread and dripping was waiting on the table next to a heap of vegetables prepared by Rose's hand ready for the cooking pot for supper. She supervised the tea, entertained the children and helped wash up, while Mrs Cartwright sat with her feet up, sipping the hot brew from a chipped enamel mug. So that by five o'clock the two young women were able to set out, arm in arm, down the road towards Rundlestone.

Work on the new accommodation block would soon be stopping for the night, and Molly paused to glance ruefully at its progress. 'I do hope as we gets one of they flats!' she breathed with feeling, her full breasts rising and falling in a deep sigh. ''Tis so cramped in the barracks and we're all getting so big.'

Rose looked askew at her friend, her heart torn. It was hard to know quite what to say. She felt so sorry for the Cartwright family, but she didn't want to offend. 'What about Brian? Could he not be moving out soon? He *is* sixteen.'

Molly cocked an eyebrow. 'Too old to be sleeping on the floor in the same room as mesel and Annie and Emma, you mean? I'll not disagree with you there! Though he's usually so tired arter his work, he sleeps like a log. But Annie's got a live-in position down in Yelverton so she'll be stopping school, so at least 'twill be one less squeezed into the bed.

It shoulda been me really, being the eldest girl, going into service. But I've always been needed at home, and it sort of stayed that way.'

'And I'm so glad it did!' Rose beamed at her, patting her friend's arm. Their eyes met, Molly's a glistening emerald whilst Rose's softened to lavender, the bond between the two girls ever deepening.

They had inadvertently stopped to look at the growing walls of the building, and as if of one mind, continued on their walk. It might not do to stop too long. The two pretty young women had already attracted the silent attention of more than one prisoner, and that could cause trouble. And so they stepped out briskly, their eyes averted, as they approached the gaol itself. But, familiar as they were with its grey, stone severity, neither could help glancing at the forbidding complex and the prison farmland that stretched out behind it as far as the eye could see. Within the horseshoe-shaped outer wall, the cell blocks radiated like the spokes of a half-wheel, an ominous backdrop to the workshops, hospital and lesser buildings at the front of the compound. Over them all towered the massive Number Five Prison, the first of the original prisoner-of-war blocks to be rebuilt as a five-storey monster with regimented rows of small barred windows in its unyielding walls. Constructed by convicts with stone from the quarry, it had only opened two years previously, and yet they knew from Molly's father that damp was already seeping into some of the three hundred unheated cells, and prisoners who had been moved there from the old buildings – which had been converted internally with dry, iron cells – wished they were back in their former abode, grim as it was.

Rose shivered as they passed the main gate, for even her own comfortable home with its blazing fires could be cold in the depths of the long Dartmoor winter. She squared her slim shoulders. It had been a glorious autumn day; she should enjoy it whilst she could, and put such dark thoughts aside.

'Amber's still behaving like a lunatic,' she began anew. 'She's very obedient and willing to learn, but the instant anything exciting happens, like a rabbit or something, she forgets everything I've taught her and won't obey a single command!'

Molly's face lit up at the mention of Rose's young dog, far

more of a pet in her opinion than the fearsome Gospel, of whom, like most other people, she was petrified. 'But she's only a puppy, Rose! You cas'n expect her—'

'She's nearly a year old. She should be able to contain herself by now. I want to be able to take her out riding with me.'

'What! And frighten everyone even more than you does already with that monster you calls an 'orse!'

Rose blinked her eyes wide, and then the pair of them fell about laughing as they wandered on down the road. As their merriment subsided, they paused again to gaze on the sheer immensity of the landscape, the prison lands that had been cleared and drained under cultivation to some hardy crop, while sheep or cattle grazed in other fields. And yet what they could see was merely a small patch of the three hundred and sixty or more square miles of spectacular scenery, exposed, rugged hills with impressive outcrops of granite tors, or pretty valleys and sheltered pockets of fertile farmland that made up Dartmoor. A hostile wilderness, and yet a luring sense of peace and infinity . . .

'Get along there, you, six four nine!'

Molly flicked her head with surprised pleasure. ''Tis Father's voice. He must've been on duty at the quarry today. That'll have pleased 'en no end.'

They both turned instinctively to peer down over the low but solid stone wall on their right. Behind them, on the opposite side of the road, was the entrance to the heavily guarded prison quarry, but to avoid the inmates marching down a public road to and from the place of their labour, a tunnel passed beneath the highway, emerging on the other side on to prison farmland and a well-trodden track that entered the gaol by a side gateway in the massive wall. The day's back-breaking toil was over, and sure enough, a line of weary convicts, some – the least trustworthy – chained together with heavy leg irons, were dragging themselves back towards the comfortless buildings that would swallow up their very existence until it began all over again the following day. The track was some twenty feet immediately below the two girls, who watched from their vantage point, entirely unseen.

The line of men in their ugly uniforms and forage caps on their closely cropped heads was lengthening as they were marched out of the tunnel accompanied by several armed guards and even more prison warders, amongst them Molly's father. Jacob Cartwright had worked since a boy in the Dartmoor quarries, his skill and experience gaining him a respected position as the years went by. That was how Rose and Molly had originally met, when Jacob had come to Cherrybrook to order gunpowder for quarry blasting, and for some reason had brought Molly with him. But he wasn't getting any younger, and some time ago had decided, like other of his colleagues, that being a prison warder would be more suit-able employment for a man of more mature years. The Governor had to be careful who he employed, and Jacob fitted the bill admirably: a strong, sturdy local, experienced in directing strong-willed men, and of course his expertise in quarrying was invaluable. He was a fair and just warder, popular with the inmates, for though he would deal toughly with those who deserved it, he was one of the few who found room in his own strictly regulated role to reward good behav-iour with clemency and understanding.

He hurried along now, his sharp eye ever watchful, unaware of his eldest daughter and her friend looking immediately down upon him. The girls would not utter a sound, of course, for they knew his concentration must not be distracted for one second. It filled them both with unimaginable horror, there-fore, when one of the convicts behind him swiftly picked up a heavy stone that happened by some oversight to be lying by the side of the track, and went to smash it over his head.

The scream lodged in Molly's throat, her suddenly weak and trembling knees buckling under her, whilst at her side, Rose's jaw hung open in appalled disbelief. But in that terrible moment, another prisoner bounded forward and in a brief struggle plied the weapon from his fellow inmate's grasp. Before Jacob Cartwright could turn round to investigate the scuffle behind him, two Civil Guards emerged from the tunnel and, spying the second convict with the rock still in his raised hands, rushed at him with a lustful cry. One of them slammed the butt of his Snider carbine into the man's stomach. He fell to the ground, dropping the stone, totally defenceless against the two guards, who became intent upon kicking him into submission with their steel-capped boots.

Molly remained motionless, her muscles incapable of doing

anything more than keeping her upright, but beside her, the indignation swirled in Rose's breast like a rising tide, drowning her senses in unleashed fury. In a trice, she flung aside her riding skirt, vaulted the stone wall and careering down the steep bank, began to pummel the back of one of the guards.

'No, you senseless fools!' she shrieked, spittle spraying from her incensed lips. ''Twasn't *him*! He *stopped* the other one!'

Her fists continued to pound ineffectually at their target, and it wasn't until Jacob's arms encircled her, pinning her own to her sides, that she was forced to stop, though she wriggled like a mad woman, her hat flying from her head and her dark curls whipping across her face like some wild witch.

'Hush now, Miss Rose!' the strong, steady voice commanded. 'And you two, *stop* before you kill 'en, will you!'

His authoritative tone ran like ice through the guards' brains as they ceased their retribution with reluctance. Every man held his breath, his heartbeat quickened, as the tension crackled along the halted line, those that were near enough confounded by the savage but beautiful apparition that even now was desperately attempting to break free from the burly warder's hold, her chest heaving deliciously up and down.

'Is this true?' Jacob asked in his usual calm manner.

'Yes. Of course 'tis!' Rose told him. '*He* was the one who was about to hit you over the head with the stone!' she accused, pointing at the guilty villain, who merely grinned back. '*That* poor fellow stopped him, and those idiots—'

'All right, all right!' Jacob tried to interrupt.

'We saw it all from up there! Ask any one of these men—'

'Rose, do calm down!' Jacob hissed warningly in her ear. 'Never ask a prisoner to cop another! Now!' He raised his voice again as he turned back to the guards, slowly releasing his grip on her as he did so. 'I believe what this young woman says. Six four nine's always been a troublemaker. I'd just that second had to rebuke 'en. The *other* fellow's new. Model prisoner, so far. So, all right, everyone! Show's over! Move along now!'

A general moan rumbled along the line of convicts as they began to trudge back towards their meagre evening meal, an hour of oakum-picking and an hour of reading or writing in their cells, or if they weren't literate under the prison teacher's tuition, before lights out. It had been a rare entertainment, and that untamed, spirited wench . . .

'Yes, get up, you bastard.'

Jacob had already moved on and didn't see the final blow that one of the guards inflicted with his boot upon the prostrate form of the prisoner. But Rose did, and the soldier's shin felt the crack of her own foot as she lashed out at him, her blazing eyes deepening to an outraged indigo. He backed away. He had the feeling he'd seen her somewhere before. She was dressed like a lady in a riding habit, and although she spoke with a local accent, it was refined, and her words were well chosen and articulate. You never knew . . . And he didn't want any trouble.

With a scathing glance in her direction, he bent down to thrust a hand under the criminal's armpit and drag him to his feet. The convict stifled a gasp of pain, one arm clutched across his middle, but he lifted his head and turned to look at his saviour.

The tortured expression on his face was like a spike in her compassionate heart. He was young. At least, fine creases were only just beginning to radiate from the outer corners of his clear hazel eyes, so she imagined he could be no more than thirty. It was difficult to tell exactly, for though his cap had been knocked from his head, his hair had been clipped so closely the scissors had grazed his scalp in places, but a cap of light down was just visible here and there. A trickle of blood was curling down his chin from his torn lip, but the pained shadow of a smile twitched at his mouth and his gaze held hers until the other guard cuffed him about the ear and forced him to stumble onwards.

Rose stood and watched as the rest of the work party was marched past, a strange knot frozen solid in her chest as she fought her way back to reality. A convict. Guilty of some heinous crime. Ah, well . . . He must deserve to be incarcerated in Dartmoor's infamous gaol. Put to some of the most gruelling toil known to man, treated like the scum of the earth. The quarry was probably the most feared and hated of prison work. Not a moment's rest was allowed from the strenuous, crushing labour. Serious accidents were frequent, no care given to the prisoners' safety – except if Warder Cartwright was on duty, for he could not find it in his Christian soul to allow even a convicted felon to be maimed if he could help it. Others were less mindful and as well as paying no heed to other dangers in the quarry would order convicts to pick out by hand any unexploded charges. It was not uncommon for a hapless villain to be blinded or have his hand blown away when the powder went off belatedly.

A whimper scraped from Rose's lungs. And she somehow prayed that the prisoner – whoever he was, but who had possibly saved Jacob's life – never suffered such a tragedy.

She buried the sickening thought somewhere deep in the darkest recesses of her passionate young mind, and retrieving her hat from amongst the grass at the side of the track, scrambled back up the slope to where Molly was waiting.

Two

For once, Rose Maddiford held in check the colossal steed on whose back she rode. It was no mean feat, for the creature was strong and possessed a will of iron. But so did Rose. She kept the reins short in her gloved hands and low down on either side of the gleaming black neck, for she refused to use what she considered the cruel martingale the previous owner had admitted was the only way he could control the beast. She could feel the power now in Gospel's clenched haunches, and she only needed to let her concentration slip for a second before the horse started to pick up its front legs and dance sideways in an effort to escape from Rose's tight constraint. But Rose was not in the mood for their usual mad gallop as they left Princetown behind.

The incident by the quarry tunnel had thrown her senses into some strange confusion. Molly had been like a quivering jelly, wanting to return home at once. It had taken every ounce of Rose's ingenuity to persuade her to complete what was known as the 'triangle', down to the small settlement at Rundlestone, along a stretch of the main highway that cut right across Dartmoor from east to west and finally back up to the prison village via Two Bridges Road, the very same Gospel's hooves were treading now in the opposite direction. Think how your mother will worry if you tell her your father nearly had his head split open by a convict, Rose had argued. Of course, *she* had been upset, too, for she was fond of Mr Cartwright, but there was something else that had gripped her heart with a violence that astounded her. The unmerited beating the prisoner had received at the hands – or more precisely, the *feet* – of the guards had sickened her, but even more than that, when the fellow had looked straight into her eyes, she had felt a curious and unwanted pull on her innermost feelings. He was a convicted criminal, guilty of some appalling act to warrant incarceration in the dreaded Dartmoor gaol, and yet the vision of his anguished face was haunting her.

Some bemused compulsion drove her to glance swiftly over her left shoulder towards the dark and menacing silhouette of the prison buildings outlined against the blinding light as the sun sank in the autumn sky. She wondered what the convict would be doing now, locked in his cramped, damp and lonely cell for the night. But then her attention was snapped back to the road as they crossed the bridge over the Blackabrook by the quaint farmhouse known as the Ockery. It was rumoured to have once been the billet of two French prisoner-of-war officers out on parole, as had been the custom. Gospel had decided to take exception to the tumbling waters and was side-stepping restlessly. But Rose was determined to keep to a walk, her mind locked in a brown study. What was his crime? she wondered. New. A model prisoner, Mr Cartwright had said. He would have at least five years to serve, then, for that was the minimum sentence for Dartmoor. Five years . . .

They gained the brow of the hill and all at once the panorama of the isolated hamlet of Two Bridges lay beneath them, the picturesque West Dart river valley bathed in the apricot evening sunlight. The breath caught in Rose's throat, the beauty of the dell with its old arched bridge once again enchanting her, though she had seen it a thousand times before. The water twinkled merrily as it rushed over the shallow, rock-strewn riverbed in its hurry to be across the moor and down to the sea, length-ening shadows playing mysteriously on the clear, deeper pools. Just one facet of the moor's deceptive landscape, a gentle oasis in the savage wilderness that surrounded it.

Gospel shook his head and snorted impatiently. He knew he was nearing home and the handful of tasty oats the stable lad would feed him. But why was his mistress holding him back? They joined the steep road that dropped into the valley, then sharply up the far side, and the horse took the incline as easily as swishing away a fly with its tail. And then, as they turned on to the road towards Postbridge and the north-east corner of the moor, the familiar surroundings finally soothed Rose's soul, and with a resolute clamping of her jaw, she gave the animal its head.

Gospel's muscles exploded like coiled springs. Rose could feel the strength of his body beneath her as he powered up the hill, stretching every sinew of his vigorous limbs. She kept her hands together now at the base of his thick mane, gripping with her knees as she sank into the one, two, *three*, one, two, *three* rhythm of his pounding hooves, gathering speed until the glorious moment when the canter broke into a gallop and they surged forward as if of one being. She leaned out along his arched neck, her own body rippling to his flowing motion. Her hair streaked out behind her like the tail of some meteor, the wind whipping through her head and driving out all memory of the convict who, for one incomprehensible moment, had touched her heart, but who she would never see again.

On and on, until the extensive site of the gunpowder mills came into view, its sturdy buildings spread out, for safety reasons, on either side of the Cherrybrook valley. She sat back in the saddle, easing gently but firmly on the reins until Gospel was persuaded to slow his breakneck pace, and by the time they reached the first cluster of powder-mill cottages by the roadside, Rose was rising to the gelding's lively trot. The lengthy gallop had hardly made him sweat, and Rose herself would have been happy to continue out over the moor for another hour to expend some of his energy, but the evening was drawing in with that autumnal sting in the air despite the sunny day, and she knew better than to trust the treacherously changeable Dartmoor weather at night.

They left the main road and continued along the powder-mills track to what, if anything, could be called the centre of the isolated community, a large building that served as both Methodist chapel and school, another row of neat little cottages, the manager's house, a substantial cooperage and several other outbuildings. Up to a hundred men had worked at the mills not so long ago, living in the purpose-built cottages including those near Higher Cherrybrook Bridge. Others resided in nearby Postbridge village, whilst some tramped in each day all the way from Chagford, Peter Tavy and even Tavistock. There were not quite so many employees now. Demand for gunpowder had been falling recently with the closure of many of the local mines, though considerable amounts continued to be supplied to the massive Dartmoor quarries, including that of the prison, and also the Cornish slate quarries. The powder was carried by horse and wagon to a growing number of outlying maga-zines or storage sites across the moor, or directly to where it was required. Further afield, it was still exported via Plymouth all over the south-west and as far as south Wales and Gloucestershire, for licensed gunpowder factories were few and far between. But eight years previously, a scientist by the name of Alfred Nobel had invented a far safer explosive called dynamite, and its usage was spreading. Nevertheless, Cherrybrook remained a hive of activity with all its skilled labourers, coopers, carpenters, the blacksmith, the wheelwright and all the wagoners and stable staff. And Rose Maddiford, the venturesome daughter of the manager, knew and cared for every one of them and their families.

She turned Gospel's head to the path that led across the rear of the cottages, and the spirited animal clattered into the small stable yard behind the manager's house. Rose dismounted with her usual flourish as Joe Tyler hurried out of the back door, his young face split with his welcoming grin. At his heels pranced the boisterous Labrador, behaving, just as Rose had described to Molly, like an overgrown puppy, her tail waving furiously to and fro as she bounced around her mistress's legs.

'You'm late, Rose!' Joe chided, his cornflower eyes stepping a merry dance beneath his thatch of straw-coloured hair. 'Florrie's proper vexed at holding dinner back. You'd best look sharp!'

But Rose merely bent for a moment to fuss over the jubilant dog, breathing heavily from the energetic ride and her well-shaped lips parted in a knowing smile. 'See to Gospel for me, would you, Joe? 'Twouldn't do to keep Florrie waiting now, would it?'

Joe chuckled somewhere in his youthful throat. He knew as well as she did that Florrie's scolding would be no more than a mother hen's clucking over her wayward chicks. Joe had served Henry Maddiford, his daughter and their housekeeper for seven years now, ever since Rose had rescued him from the cruelties of his master at a livery stables in Plymouth on a rare visit to the bustling city. He had instantly become one of the family, wrapped in the kindness that was the Maddiford way of life. Rose was now his beloved elder sister, although now he was eighteen he sometimes looked at her in a different light. But Rose was Rose, hare-brained, open, unique in his eyes. Taking your breath away, and filling your heart with exasperated love.

Rose threw open the back door and flouncing up the passage, poked her head into the kitchen. 'Oh, Florrie, that smells delicious, and I'm mortal hungry. I'll just slip upstairs to change, and then I'll be down afore you know it!' And hoisting the hem of her riding skirt up around her knees, she raced up the carpeted stairs two at a time before Florrie Bennett had time to open her mouth.

'Rose, dear!' Henry Maddiford's fading blue eyes crinkled at the corners as his daughter floated into the dining room five minutes later. She paused for just a moment, framed in the doorway, her cheeks blushed a healthy peach as she beamed devotedly at him. His heart lurched painfully, for she was the image of his darling Alice, lost to him twenty-one years ago. Rose had changed for dinner, not into an evening dress, for she did not possess such a thing, but into a simple yet sophisticated affair of burgundy velvet, trimmed with black lace at the collar and cuffs, and with the fullness of the skirt drawn into a small bustle at the back in the latest fashion. All designed and created by her own hand, Henry sighed wistfully. Alice would have been so proud.

'Father, I'm so sorry I was late back!' She bounced forward, depositing a kiss on his balding head before she sat down opposite him at the highly polished table. She put out a stern finger at the young dog which stood beside her, gazing up with expectant eyes, and for once the animal obeyed and reluctantly lay down. 'You know I went to see Molly, and well, the time just flies when I'm with her! And they were doing the ironing, so I had to help so that Molly and I could walk the triangle, and we had bread and dripping for tea, and—'

'Well, I hope as you've enough room left for this yere dinner, young maid! I've spent all arternoon—'

'But of course, Florrie! That looks absolutely mouth-watering! Roast beef, with lashings of juicy gravy and horseradish sauce, and *piles* of vegetables!' she enthused with gusto. ''Tis just what I fancied! I'm starving!'

'Well, I don't know where you put it, I'm sure,' Henry chuckled, shaking his head with amusement as he reached for his starched napkin.

'I only hope as 'tidn spoilt,' the older woman grumbled, trying to conceal the grin that was battling to break over her round face.

'It looks superb, Florrie! But then you *are* the best cook in the whole of Devonshire!'

Her exuberant smile finally won Florrie's heart for the millionth time, for the housekeeper could never be cross with Rose for more than a minute. She had helped raise the child from the day Alice Maddiford had died, her newborn babe in her arms, and Florrie had always looked upon the headstrong girl as her own. Her already ample bosom swelled with pride, not so much at the compliment as at the winning ways of her charge, who could charm the clouds from the grey Dartmoor skies.

'I should think so, too!' she agreed, her cheeks wobbling with laughter now. 'Though I've yerd tell there's a good French chef at the Bedford Hotel nowadays.'

'And I'm sure you're every bit as accomplished as he is.' Henry's expression retained its habitual benevolence, but there was that hint of firm integrity in his voice that made him the respected businessman that he was. 'And next week you'll have another chance to prove it. Mr Frean will be paying us one of his visits, and several of the shareholders will be accompanying him, so I'd like you to put on one of your best luncheons. Some of them are coming from as far off as London, so 'twould be nice to put on a good spread and show them we provincials can produce cuisine as excellent as in the capital.'

He winked playfully at his housekeeper as she wiped her hands on her apron. 'Well, I'd best put my thinking cap on!' she announced.

'Go and enjoy your own dinner first, though, or you'll faint from lack of nourishment.' Not that there was any fear of that, he thought mildly to himself.

'Yes, of course, sir.' She turned to leave the room, but paused with her hand on the door handle. 'But I'll do you proud, I promise.'

'Thank you, Florrie. I know I can rely on you.' The gentle smile remained on Henry's face as his faithful servant closed the door quietly behind her, and then he turned to his daughter. 'So, you had a good afternoon, then?'

'Mmm!' Rose nodded enthusiastically as she struggled to swallow a mouthful of food. 'Oh, this is superb! I don't know how Florrie does it, but I'm certain she'll surprise your visitors next week!'

'Talking of which . . .' Henry cleared his throat, and his

features moved with unusual solemnity. 'I want you to be there as the *perfect* hostess. I know you've flitted around before on such occasions, but this time I want you there as an accomplished young lady, to show them that everything in the garden is rosy, if you'll excuse the pun.'

Rose's fine brow puckered. 'And isn't it?' she enquired seriously now, her eyes meeting his steadily.

Henry slowly pursed his lips, moving his gaze to stare at his wineglass, whose stem he was rubbing between his forefinger and thumb. 'Not as rosy as it used to be. You know so many of the copper mines have closed in recent years, and those that are surviving on arsenic are worked on a smaller scale than before.'

Rose's frown deepened. 'But they're only part of our trade. What about all the quarries on the moor? And the new one at Merrivale? 'Tis proving a good customer, isn't it?'

Henry looked at her again with an anxious grimace. 'Only so-so at present. 'Tis yet to become established as a going concern. And any of them could decide to change over to dynamite at any time. Sad to say, overall, our sales are down.'

'Hence the meeting.' Rose sucked in her cheeks. 'But I can't do anything about the sales. 'Tis the agent's job.'

'I know. But you can help to make a good impression. And,' he hesitated, feeling uncomfortably hot, 'we may need to start making some economies ourselves.'

Rose's complexion paled as she blinked at him. 'But . . .' she stammered in horror, her heart suddenly beating wildly. 'I can keep Amber and Gospel?'

'Of course,' Henry answered her obvious anguish. 'But only if you give up other luxuries.'

'Oh, thank you, Father!' She sprang up from her chair and threw her arms about his neck. 'I'm certain I can find lots of things to do without!'

Henry patted the back of this beloved child who had held his life together, but as he gazed out over her shoulder, he only wished the answer were so simple.

Rose dropped her sewing into her lap with a pensive sigh and bowed her head over her idle hands for a moment before rising to her feet and crossing to stare out of the parlour window. The weather had changed dramatically overnight. Rain had swept in from the west, smiting Dartmoor with a lashing deluge that had driven away the last vestiges of summer. The storm had battered relentlessly against the sturdy walls of the house, refusing to abate until mid-morning, and even when it did, a dampness hung in the air in fat, almost tangible droplets. Rose might have saddled Gospel, though, and followed one of the familiar tracks across the moor, for it would be unwise to venture off the path with the threat of a disorientating veil of mist, even for someone as used to the terrain as she was. But much as her spirit yearned to be away, there were other matters that required her attention. She had spent a couple of hours at the kitchen table opposite Florrie as they planned the luncheon for their guests the following week. And now she was patiently sides-to-middling a worn sheet, a long, boring process but one which allowed her to ponder what her father had said the previous evening, as her dextrous fingers plied the needle with endless small and tidy stitches.

Economies. Well, she was quite happy to make this one, even if it was tedious. Florrie had taught her to sew simple items when she was a young child, and now she only had to study a new style in a magazine and she could create it for herself. All that would have to stop now, if they could no longer afford to buy the material, though there was no reason why she shouldn't alter some existing garment. But so long as she could keep Gospel, she didn't mind. She would do without a fire in her bedroom. A stone bottle filled with hot water from the kitchen range and placed between the sheets at bedtime would be quite sufficient. As a household, they ate well, but cheaper cuts of meat, for instance, could be just as tasty when cooked to Florrie's special recipes. There were numerous sacrifices they could make that were so small they would scarcely be noticed, and all their problems would be solved.

Yes, she decided with satisfaction, as she contemplated the progress along the track outside the house of a small wagon under whose tightly secured tarpaulin she knew would be stowed carefully filled leather-clad one-hundred-pound barrels of gunpowder, or ready pressed cartridges. The horse that pulled the wagon plodded steadily, its coat gleaming and the long hair or feathers at the back of its lower legs washed and brushed, probably by Joe since his main employment was in the powder-mills stables.

The thought of Joe made Rose purse her lips. As long as they all stayed together, nothing else mattered. She had two or three special dresses, such as the one she had worn the previous evening, all made by her own hand in attractive but good quality, sensible materials that would last for years. In her wardrobe also hung a warm coat that fitted over them, and her riding habit. She possessed several hats, not because she liked them, for she would rather go bare-headed, but because it was considered unseemly for any female of even the lowest class to walk abroad without one. She had one pair of dainty shoes to wear with the dresses, her riding boots, and two pairs of strong, sturdy boots for her everyday life on the moor. Generally, as today, she dressed in a simple blouse and skirt without the encumbrance of any bustle, adding a jacket or shawl or extra layers of underwear for warmth, according to the weather. Her father was equally well attired, so she had no need to visit Ellen Williams's shop for anything but groceries for many a long year. They could do without wine on the table except perhaps on Sundays, and with her sewing skills she could always repair instead of replace, as she was doing now. Her father's position as manager brought with it this comfortable, rent-free house, which had been her home ever since she could remember, and a generous salary. If her father had taken a small drop in his wages as she imagined he might have done, well, there really was nothing to worry about.

She dragged her gaze away from the wagon as it trundled on into the mist, and turned her eyes instead in the opposite direction towards the scattered buildings of the gunpowder factory itself. Sure enough, her father was walking past the cooperage next door, dead on time for his luncheon at half-past twelve. Rose smiled to herself as she wondered if old Silas had anything left to eat for *his* croust, or midday meal. The fellow had been a powder-maker at Cherrybrook since the whole enterprise had been started by Mr George Frean over thirty years before, and knew his job so well he was scarcely likely to cause himself an accident. Nevertheless, walking in at the crack of dawn from his home in Postbridge, Silas always ate the midday pasty he brought with him at the same time as his breakfast – just in case he should be blown up beforehand and never get to consume it!

The corners of Rose's coral lips were still turned upwards as she hurried out into the kitchen to make sure everything was on the table. It was cold enough to light a fire in the dining room, where they would normally have eaten, but they might as well start as they meant to go on, so she had ordered a reluctant Florrie to set the meal in the warm kitchen where the range was continually alight. It seemed no hardship to Rose, since she spent most of her time there anyway, and her father was a sensible man and would entirely agree with her logic.

As if to confirm her thoughts, he came in through the kitchen door and raised a surprised eyebrow at the table, which was neatly set with the remains of last night's beef cut into wafer-thin slices, pink in the centre shading to a light brown on the edges, various jars of homemade pickles, butter from Cherrybrook Farm and bread baked by Florrie's own hand. The kettle was singing on the range, and Florrie glanced up apprehensively as she made a pot of tea, for never had she served the master a meal in her kitchen!

She need not have worried. A slow smile pulled at his mouth and the slight doubt in Rose's mind was dispelled as he beamed cheerfully, 'What a good idea! 'Tis good and cosy in here, and that dampness outside gets through to the bones. I can hardly believe it after yesterday.'

'The weather had to change some time, sir,' Florrie observed, for though she was officially a servant, her position as one of the family allowed her to speak freely. 'Now you just get a cup of this yere hot tea down you, and you'll soon warm up.'

Henry obediently sat down at the table, winking a bright blue eye at his daughter as he did so. Rose felt her shoulders relax as she cut slices of the delicious-smelling mouth-watering loaf and passed the plate to her father. They both tucked in, Florrie ensuring they had sufficient quantities of boiling water to top up the teapot, for though they were eating in *her* kitchen, she would not dream of sitting down to her own meal until they had finished, and the master had gone back to work.

It was as Henry was pouring himself a second cup of the steaming liquid that they all heard it. Rose snatched in a sharp breath and held it as her eyes snapped wide, every muscle frozen rigid. Her gaze met her father's across the table, and for a split second, his motionless face was inscrutable.

It was Florrie who broke the silence. 'Saints preserve us!'

she cried hysterically, throwing her apron over her head in what Rose had always considered a ridiculous habit.

She didn't have time to think it now. She and Henry were already on their feet, and Henry had shot out of the door, knocking the freshly poured tea all over Florrie's snowy white tablecloth in his desperate haste. If he noticed it, he did not pay any heed, and neither did Rose as she sped out of the house after him, grasping her shawl from the hall stand as she hurtled past. Horror shuddered through her body, leaving her heart thumping in her chest. She ran behind her father, for though he was turned fifty, he was fast on his feet, and when he stopped abruptly at the point along the track where the numerous stone buildings opened up before them, she nearly collided into his back.

'Oh, God, this is all we need,' she heard him hiss between his teeth, and dragging her eyes from his grey face, she gazed across the gently sloping valley where the Cherrybrook played peacefully along its rocky gravel bed. They were both staring instinctively towards the three incorporating mills high on the opposite slope, spaced well apart for safety reasons but linked by the raised water-launder that snaked from one to the other in turn, and drove the huge central waterwheel in each building. Incorporating, or finely blending the three separate ingredients of the gunpowder, was the most dangerous process and the obvious site for an explosion, but as father and daughter narrowed their eyes at the massive stones that formed the solid walls of the mills, over six foot thick in places and now half shrouded in a dank grey cloak, they could neither of them make out any signs of mishap.

''Tis the corning 'ouse, sir!' someone called, and then agitated men, emerging from every door, began running towards the corning and dusting house on the near side of the river. It was uncanny, unreal, as so many feet made no sound in the muffling echo of the mist, for every man changed his hobnailed boots for leather-soled shoes on arrival at the powder mills each morning, as the slightest spark of metal on stone could cause an explosion. Neither Henry nor Rose could go a step further until they had done the same, and she plunged after him into his office to kick her feet into their special footwear before racing down the track and along to the next of several buildings strung out in a line above the west bank of the river.

Henry came to a halt then, raising his hands so that every man stood still. Rose fixed her eyes on him, her pulse thudding. At close quarters, she could see his face working painfully, but he was in charge, their leader. They looked to him for instructions, and he must not let his heart, which ached to get inside and rescue anyone injured, rule his head.

'No one must go in! Not yet! Fred?' he questioned, raising an eyebrow at his foreman, a giant of a man who stood, arms akimbo, the leather apron he, like every other worker, wore making him look even larger than he actually was.

'I doesn't know what's 'appened, Mr Maddiford, sir,' the fellow answered, 'but no one goes in till we knows 'tis safe. It don't appear too serious. The roof be still on.'

Henry sucked in his cheeks, his eyes travelling keenly over the exterior of the corning house. Beside him, Rose's pleated brow throbbed. Nobody had yet staggered out, though a pall of grey-brown smoke with its distinctive smell had billowed through the glassless windows and was hanging in the saturated air in a choking smog. Was someone lying unconscious inside? Her heart beat savagely, every second an hour as they waited . . .

Edward James stumbled from behind the sturdy structure, half supporting himself on the stone walls, dazed and visibly shaking. In an instant, his colleagues surrounded him, keeping him upright as he struggled to reach his respected boss.

'I only went outside fer set the rollers in motion,' he stammered, and as his knees folded beneath him, his fellow-workers dragged him upwards. His head was rolling on his shoulders, his face white and anguished with his need to explain. 'There were a lump o' cake stuck to the bottom. 'Twere too big fer get out wi' the wooden shovel so I poured a pail o' water over it, an' turned the rollers on fer crush it like we always does, an' the next thing . . .' He shook his head, his eyes wild with shock as he gazed fearfully over his shoulder at the wide doorway. Though the initial acrid cloud still clung to the vaporous mist in long threads, no more smoke had drifted from the interior of the building.

'Were anyone inside?' Henry demanded, his eyebrows fiercely dipped.

'N . . . no,' Edward James stuttered, his teeth starting to chatter. 'We'd just stopped fer eat our croust. Young John'd just . . .'

'Ais, I's all right,' the youth called from somewhere in the crowd.

The taut lines on Henry's face slackened, and Rose felt the blessed relief invade her tense body. She heard her father muttering something under his breath, and then he turned to his foreman. 'Reckon as 'tis safe enough now, Fred?'

The big chap nodded, and as they both stepped cautiously towards the doorway, Rose went to follow, but Henry put a restrictive hand on her arm. 'Not you, Rose. 'Tis too dangerous.'

Rose swallowed hard as she stared at him, her eyes deep, glistening orbs of alarm. 'And . . . what about you, Father?' she croaked.

''Tis my job,' he said levelly, a loving smile touching his lips. 'Now you look to Eddie James. Poor fellow's in shock.'

Rose obediently backed away, biting hard on her lip in an effort to stop it quivering. If anything ever happened to her father . . . Accidents were not a common occurrence at the gunpowder mills. There were strict government rules which must be rigidly adhered to in order to retain the licence, but it was still a dangerous business. Incorporating was the most perilous stage of production, but corning, when the one-inch-deep compressed cake of damp powder was broken down into granules of the required size, could be almost as hazardous. And any incident, even relatively minor, was a sharp reminder of the need for constant vigilance.

She forced herself to turn her attentions to Edward James, sitting him down and pushing his head down between his knees before he was physically sick, which by his face, he was on the brink of being so. But at every moment, her eye was trained on the doorway to the corning house, the blood coursing tremulously around her body until her father reappeared, his face set grimly.

'Right, men, you can start clearing up the mess now,' he instructed. 'And for God's sake, be careful. You carpenters'll have to work day and night to repair the machinery. Let me know if we need to order any extra timber. And in the meantime,' he added severely, 'I want you in my office, Eddie James. I'll have to give Mr Frean a full written report.'

He strode away up the road without even glancing at his daughter, a measure reflecting, she knew well, his worry over the situation. A common practice, one which should have been safe, had resulted in an explosion, albeit a small one, and nobody was to blame. But he was responsible, both for the factory and his men, and sometimes he bent beneath the strain. Rose's heart jerked as her eyes followed him, her dearest, kind, thoughtful father of whom she was so proud . . .

Three

Rose frowned at her reflection in the mirror and smoothed down the front of her bodice. She had chosen the most modest of her special outfits, a soft grey affair in a fine wool, with a simple bustle and a tight-fitting jacket which accentuated her tiny waist. Florrie had helped to twist her hair into a complicated chignon, and she had fixed a small lace cap on to the crown of her glossy curls with a mother-of-pearl pin that had once belonged to her mother. She looked the perfect hostess for the occasion, smart and attractive, yet not frivolous or overly dressed. She wanted to do her level best for her father, who had been worried enough over the shareholders' inspection *before* the explosion. He and his men had been working flat out to repair the machinery damaged in the blast, and have production back on full level by today, and they had succeeded. Nevertheless, he would have been hard pressed to explain the mishap and would no doubt have had to answer some difficult questions during the visitors' tour that morning. So when they appeared at the house for luncheon, Rose was determined to make it such an enjoyable experience that any misgivings about the gunpowder factory would be forgotten.

She took a deep breath as she tripped down the stairs, for her heart was beating a nervous tattoo in her breast. The fire in the dining room was crackling merrily, and the table that Florrie had polished with what she called a good lot of elbow grease gleamed with the best silver and glassware in the house. Now Rose stood back with a satisfied smile. The room looked tasteful and welcoming, yet not overdone, suitable for a competent manager who was paid a reasonable salary yet was not a drain on the company's resources.

'Oh, bless us, they be coming!' she heard Florrie wail from the hallway. 'Oh, Miss Rose!'

'Oh, Florrie, don't you fret none!' She swept out of the

dining room and followed Florrie back into the kitchen. ''Tis all perfect, and I for one can't wait to sit down to this superb meal you've prepared. My mouth's watering just at the smell of it all!'

She beamed radiantly, her eyes sparkling with confidence, and Florrie paused, her hands on her hips, as if drawing reassurance from her young mistress. 'Well, if anyone can sweet-talk them, my dear, 'tis you! So you go out there and . . . and just be yersel'!'

Rose took an instant to throw a last winsome glance at her and then hurried out to arrange herself in the parlour, the correct place for the lady of the house to be installed to receive her guests. She could hear the group of men coming up the garden path now, and a few moments later, voices in the hallway as they removed their hats and coats. She clasped her hands in her lap and straightened her back, then tipped her head with an engaging benevolence on her face as the door handle turned and Henry stood back to allow his guests to enter the room.

'Rose, my dear, how pleasant to see you again!'

Rose got to her feet and dipped her knees in a polite curtsy, as George Frean, proprietor of the mills, stepped across to her and took her hands in his. The elderly man was a fair and respected employer, and had watched her grow from an affectionate child to the accomplished young woman who stood before him now.

'Gentlemen, may I introduce my daughter, Rose,' Henry said from somewhere near the door.

The gentlemen in question were still occupied in the process of crowding into the room behind Mr Frean, whose broad back obscured Henry Maddiford's daughter from their view. He moved aside then, his face lit with a proudly paternal smile as if it were *his* child they were to have the honour of meeting. He was waiting for the effect she would have on the visitors, and he was not disappointed. The amazement followed by the flustered expression on each face was almost comical, from the three mature investors to the young fellow on his first mission for his family's wealth, and Mr Charles Chadwick, at thirty-six years old, somewhere in between. The callow youth flushed scarlet but Mr Chadwick at once contained his emotion at this unexpected ethereal vision of loveliness, and came forward to bow over her gloved hand.

'What a delightful surprise,' he said in his crisp London accent. 'I invested in Cherrybrook many years ago, but had I known Mr Maddiford possessed such a beautiful daughter, I should have paid a visit long before now.'

Rose's demurely lowered eyes flashed a vivid violet and she raised her chin stubbornly. 'My father does not possess me, Mr . . . er . . .?'

'Chadwick,' he answered, quite astonished.

'Well, Mr Chadwick, radical though it may seem to you, I believe my father sees me, if not as his equal, then as a complement to his own role. He protects and provides for me, and I ensure he has a comfortable home to return to at the end of each day. And should you have visited in earlier years, you would have found in me a mere cheel, not deserving of any attention.'

'Cheel?' Charles Chadwick raised a bemused eyebrow.

'Devonshire,' she replied somewhat curtly, 'for child. Usually female.'

She turned on him such a sweet, angelic, *stunning* smile, in contrast to the sharp sarcasm of her words, which were meant to remind him of the difference in their ages, that his heart turned over in his chest. That this graceful, sublime beauty possessed – and he was almost afraid even to *think* the word again – such intelligence and wit, was enchanting! Here he was, supposed to be questioning the finances of his investment, and instead finding himself bewitched by this spirited, quite glorious young woman.

'I did not intend to offend, Miss Maddiford.' He managed to draw the cloak of self-assurance around himself again. 'Quite the opposite, in fact. Please, I beg you, forgive me.'

Her eyes bore into his for a moment, trying to gauge whether his words of remorse were genuine, and then her long silken lashes swooped on to her flushed cheeks and she bent her head in an indication of a nod. She appeared calm and collected, and yet every pulse was vibrating inside her skull. What an idiot! She was supposed to be soothing troubled waters, and instead she was giving one of the major shareholders the length of her tongue! She felt so ashamed, and in an attempt to make amends, she looked up at Charles Chadwick with a beguiling smile.

''Tis I should be begging forgiveness, Mr Chadwick. I do

have this . . . this fierce independence that runs away with me at times.'

'Oh, don't apologize! I find vivacity in a lady quite splendid.'

His brown eyes danced somewhere between amusement and rapture, and Rose felt the relief sigh from her tense body. 'Will you take some Madeira, sir, or perhaps some dry sherry? 'Twill warm you after your inspection of the works. 'Tis quite chillsome today, though at least 'tis not raining. Gentlemen, which would you prefer?'

She moved away, the refined hostess once more, circulating amongst their guests with easy charm. Mr Frean, of course, she knew well. He was more like an adopted uncle, her father having no other living relatives, and so it was no difficulty to remain by his side, nodding politely when necessary, and waiting to recharge any glass that was in danger of becoming empty. She did her best to ignore it, but among the business discussions of the men she felt many a furtive glance in her direction, and most frequent of them all was Mr Charles Chadwick.

The knock on the door was hardly heard above the chatter, and when Florrie entered the parlour she glanced about nervously but Rose saw her agitation and came forward with a dazzling grin.

'Ah, Mrs Bennett!' She winked cheekily at the housekeeper, knowing that with her back to the room, no one else could see her face. 'I take it luncheon is served?'

'Yes, miss,' Florrie replied, adding a dip of her knees.

'Thank you, Mrs Bennett. Now then, gentlemen, would you care to come through?'

She gestured graciously towards the open doorway with her long slender hand and the company moved into the dining room. Henry, naturally, occupied the head of the table with Mr Frean on his right, while Rose sat at the far end facing her father in order to attend to the gentlemen at that end. To her utter dismay, Charles Chadwick seemed riveted to her side, and he it was who drew out the chair for her and then seated himself next to her.

'Thank you,' she smiled becomingly, though she could feel herself bubbling with animosity. Surely he could see that his attentions were not welcomed! He was supposed to be there to discuss business, not make advances towards the manager's daughter! If it had been young Mr Symons, it might have been understandable, but Mr Chadwick was old enough to be her father – at least, in Rose's eyes he was – and at his age, he really ought to know better!

'Well, Henry.' George Frean spoke between spoons of Florrie's mushroom and celery soup, laced with a generous measure of white wine. 'My word, this is good! You seem to have recovered quickly from the minor incident last week.'

'Thanks to the hard work of the men,' Henry replied guardedly. 'And their loyalty is very much due to the fact that we treat them with respect. Gunpowder manufacture requires skilled labour, skills acquired over years, so we do our best to avoid changes.'

'The repairs were not too costly, then?' one of the investors demanded over his rotund stomach.

'As you have seen, our machinery is made of wood to avoid explosions, and timber is not the most expensive commodity. 'Tis the carpenters' skills and dedication that had the corning mill up and running again in a few days. They know their jobs depend on it. And as for the practice that seems to have caused the incident, we are investigating.'

'You are following all the government directives?' the youthful Mr Symons put in, clearly to impress upon Miss Maddiford that he was not as wet behind the ears as he looked, for as he threw her a purposeful glance his cheeks suffused with crimson.

'Without question,' Henry assured him. 'I have the papers from the last inspection in my office if you should care to peruse them after luncheon. We never exceed the limits on storing powder at the various stages of its manufacture, and all the regulations are strictly abided by.'

'But it is still a dangerous and risky business,' Charles Chadwick considered, and then, turning to Rose with a half-patronizing, half-challenging smirk, he added, 'would you not agree, Miss Maddiford?'

Inside her breast, resentment fumed with livid force, but her face was a picture of composure, for the last thing she wanted was for the wealthy Mr Chadwick to withdraw his considerable investment in the mills.

'Indeed, I would not, Mr Chadwick,' she told him, her steady eyes meeting his. 'There has been no serious accident here since 1858, long before my father took over, whereas serious injury and even death occurs regularly in the quarries and mines hereabouts. Everything possible is done to reduce the risks to a minimum. As I'm sure you will have seen on your visit, all machinery is wooden, including shovels. All the men wear leather-soled shoes and leather aprons. The buildings are set well apart, especially those that require chimneys. The floors of the incorporating mills are covered in tanned hides, and the interior walls rendered to facilitate cleaning. And in the unlikely event of an explosion, the walls are thick and the roofs are made of flimsy wood and tarpaulins, so that the force of any blast is funnelled upwards, blowing off the roof rather than damaging the machinery or anyone inside. So I would say that over all, 'tis actually quite safe.'

Her mouth closed in a compressed line as she realized seven pairs of amazed eyes were trained upon her. If only her heart would stop bouncing in her chest, for she felt that Charles Chadwick had deliberately driven her into a corner from which she must fight like a tigress to escape. Was he playing with her, as a cat plays with a trapped mouse? It certainly seemed like it to her, and now the embarrassment flamed in her cheeks at her animated response that had drawn everyone's attention.

It was George Frean who rescued her. 'My dear Rose,' he chuckled good-naturedly, 'you speak so eloquently, I fear I will soon be out of a job! But everything our young hostess says, gentlemen, is quite true. And as for competition from dynamite, well, such change is often resisted. As you have seen from the accounts, trade is still lucrative and promises to be so for some time, although perhaps not quite at the same peak as in earlier years.'

'I fear you are being a little optimistic,' one of the older investors chimed in with a frown. 'I shall give it some thought on my return to London, but I may want to suggest some changes.'

'May I ask if you could give me an indication of what they might be?' Henry enquired cautiously.

Rose drew a calming breath through her nostrils and released it slowly as a lively discussion developed around the table. She rested her hands in her lap, bowing her head as etiquette demanded of a hostess in a man's world, but as she did so, her eye caught Charles Chadwick as he flashed her a sympathetic,

approving smile before he joined in the debate. Her face was
an impassive mask, but she listened intently to every word
exchanged. The conversation gradually drifted away from business, assisted by the arrival of Florrie's fish course of local
salmon followed by a magnificent crown roast of lamb. By the
time the sumptuous dessert arrived – Charlotte Russe made
with bananas she had travelled by train to Plymouth to purchase,
and topped with lashings of cream from Cherrybrook Farm –
the conversation had divided into several private dialogues of
little consequence, and Rose was vehemently wishing she could
escape the present company, saddle Gospel and head out across
the lonely moor to freedom.

'Tell me, Miss Maddiford, when you are not extolling the
virtues of the powder mills, what do you find to occupy your
time in this isolated location? Perhaps you are an expert in . . .
What is it ladies like to excel in? Ah, yes, needlepoint, or perhaps
some other virtue such as painting? Or perhaps music?'

Rose's heart had sunk like a stone as Charles Chadwick's
voice dragged her spirit back from its reverie, and she blinked
at him with disdain as she focused on him again. But his
expression was soft and inviting, warm flecks in his mahogany
eyes and the corners of his mouth lifting pleasantly. Perhaps
she was being a little hard on him, and it was her duty to
entertain her guests and instil in them feelings of goodwill at
the end of their visit.

'I have to admit to being quite skilled with a needle,' she
said with genuine shyness. 'Though I put it to practical use
rather than such things as tapestry. I make all my own clothes,
and shirts for my father and Joe. He's an ostler at the powder-
mills stable, but he helps look after Gospel and does the heavy
work around the house in exchange for a room over our
stables.'

'Gospel?' Charles gave an intrigued frown.

'My horse,' she replied flatly, but she could not prevent the
brilliant light that shone from her eyes at the thought of the
beloved animal.

'So, you *ride*, do you, Miss Maddiford?' he asked, his heart
almost tripping over itself in his enchantment. 'Or perhaps
you mean you drive a gig?'

'Oh, no,' she answered with a spark of indignation. 'I mean,
I can drive a gig, yes. Though 'tis a dog cart we have. But

'tis no good out on the moor. Gospel and I, we like to go for miles . . .' She stopped abruptly, her mouth clamped shut, as she realized she had let her tongue – and her passion – run away with her. Hardly the done thing for the lady of the house!

But Charles Chadwick was lost in some strange emotion that was beyond his usual comprehension. Had she been studying his face, she would have seen it tighten in some odd spasm that even he could not control, and he had to clear his throat before he could speak again.

'Splendid!' He surprised her with the strength of his exclamation. 'Then tomorrow I shall hire a horse and you can take me out and show me . . . well, wherever you would like on this beautiful moor of yours! We're all staying at the Duchy Hotel in Princetown. We were all to return to London tomorrow, but *I* shall stay on. I have thought what a wild and spectacular place Dartmoor appears to be, and I am sure, Miss Maddiford, you will prove a most knowledgeable guide.'

Did he see her flinch away, her jaw drop, the flints of ice in her eyes? Who did he think he was! But she had answered her own question before she had finished asking it. He was one of the major investors in the powder mills and it was her duty to humour him!

'Why, Mr Chadwick,' she almost croaked, her voice dry, 'I fear I cannot accept such an invitation. 'Tis hardly seemly, and my father would not allow—'

'Oh, I shall of course seek your father's permission,' he assured her with the enthusiastic smile of a young boy as he glanced along the table to where Henry was deep in conversation with Mr Frean. 'I am sure he will feel able to rely on my integrity as a gentleman, shall we call it?'

He watched as her lovely mouth tightened, her chin set stubbornly. She was magnificent, the most beautiful creature he had ever clapped eyes on, yet driven with such captivating spirit. His normal indifference to women had been wiped out in one fell swoop, and for the first time in his life, his heart was enslaved.

Charles Chadwick was deeply, hopelessly, irrevocably in love . . .

'Rose, will you please sit down!'

For once, Henry raised his voice to his daughter as she

angrily paced the parlour carpet, kicking at the full hem of her skirt each time she spun round. She halted then and glared at him, her lips in a petulant knot, before she swung into the chair opposite his and sat bolt upright, her head erect and obstinate as she stared sightlessly out of the window.

Henry sighed weightily, his shoulders slumped, as he lifted his weary eyes to her face. 'I do appreciate how you feel, but—'

'How could you, Father!' she rounded on him, her eyes glinting the colour of ripe mulberries. 'How could you give your consent to my riding out with a complete stranger?'

'A stranger to us, perhaps, but not to Mr Frean.' Henry pulled in his chin, knowing that was not the true reason for her objection. 'I didn't give my permission until I'd spoken to Mr Frean, who assured me Mr Chadwick is of a sound reputation and not known for frivolous dalliances. You don't think I'd allow you to go unless I knew you'd be quite safe, do you?'

Rose's mouth twisted, and then she lowered her eyes in submission. 'No. I suppose not,' she muttered under her breath. 'But—'

'Listen to me, Rose.' Henry leant forward and placed his hand over hers. 'This has nothing to do with the powder mills. This is to do with *you* and *your* future.' His voice was low, ragged with emotion as if it would break. 'I'm . . . Not to beat about the bush, I'm not getting any younger, and one never knows what lies around the corner. Some men are able to work into their seventies, but you can't rely on that. If there were to come a day when I couldn't work any more, well . . . To be honest, I've made little provision for my own future, let alone yours.'

Rose raised her liquid eyes to his beloved face, tears trembling on her lashes as she considered the unthinkable picture he was etching on her mind. 'Oh, Father, don't say such things,' she scarcely managed to whisper.

But Henry put up his hand. 'No, I'm sorry, Rose, but they *must* be said. I want to see you settled.'

The flame immediately reignited in her breast. 'Settled, perhaps. But not with that . . . that pompous, arrogant—'

She broke off, at a loss to describe the contempt she held for Mr Charles Chadwick, but Henry was not to be deterred.

'Well, perhaps not to Mr Chadwick,' he conceded gently, 'but think on it, Rose. Trapped out here in the middle of this wilderness—'

'But I love the moor—'

'I know you do. And so do I. But what opportunity do you have to meet suitable, eligible bachelors? A beautiful,' and his eyes softened, 'vivacious, intelligent girl like you should have the pick of society, and—'

'I don't want the pick of society! If I wanted anyone, which I don't, I love the people we live amongst, people like Joe—'

''T wouldn't work,' Henry stated flatly. 'I *know* you, Rose. Better than you know yourself. You deserve . . . No, you *need* more than that. You're twenty-one, and most girls of your age would be long married by now!'

'And Mr Chadwick must be at least forty, and I don't *want* to be married to anyone! I just want to stay here with you, Father!'

The tears were brimming over her lower eyelids now, and Henry came to put his arms around her. 'Oh, my dear child, you'll never know what comfort and joy you have always brought to me!' he murmured into her hair. 'But time must move on, and if you love me as much as you say, then you will listen to me in this. All I ask is that you at least try to get to know Mr Chadwick a little better. He is neither pompous nor arrogant as you said. He is simply accomplished and confident from the society into which he was born. The poor fellow is clearly quite bewildered by what he feels for you, and is determined not to lose you! And as for being forty, well, I should believe he is somewhat younger than that. I should have preferred someone more of your own age, I admit, but it means he can provide *security* for you. And . . . he's not exactly *ugly*, now, is he?'

He pulled back slightly in order to lift her chin to him. Her eyes met his, not seeing his face, but the image her mind was conjuring up of Charles Chadwick. He was reasonably tall and not the least overweight. Impeccably dressed, of course, closely shaven, and his chestnut-brown hair, which showed little sign of receding, was neatly cut. His eyes, too, were brown, not uniformly, but flecked with amber strands that made them gleam brightly. They were wide set and not unkind, and his shapely mouth was apt to turn upwards at the corners.

No, she had to admit, he was not unattractive, and perhaps she had been more than hasty in her judgement of him.

She focused on Henry's hopeful face again, and a faint smile tugged at her lips. 'All right,' she agreed with reluctance. 'I'll ride out with him tomorrow. And then after that, we'll see. I'll try and look out for his good points, but I can't promise you anything.'

'Well, neither of us can say fairer than that.' The lines on Henry's face moved into an expression of soft compassion. 'I wouldn't want you to miss out on such an opportunity without giving it your full consideration. But by the same token, I wouldn't allow you to enter into a loveless marriage just for the sake of money.'

'Well, then,' she replied, her eyes shining with crystal brilliance once more, 'we shall just have to see how Mr Charles Chadwick shapes up. Won't we?'

Four

A sharp wind had driven away the grey, overnight rain to leave a colourless sun glowing in a clear, azure-blue sky. Globules of water twinkled on the wild grasses, the bog cotton and the cobwebs that were slung across them. Rose had secretly hoped the lashing deluge would continue all morning and deter the cosseted Londoner from their expedition, but she supposed it would only have delayed the evil moment. And if she were honest, she was curious as to how Charles Chadwick would stand up to the gruelling terrain she had planned for him! Whether or not he was a good horseman, she didn't know. But she was about to find out!

Gospel was restless after a day without exercise and the damp weather of the past week had softened the ground, and so Rose allowed him to canter leisurely up and down the hills to the prison settlement of Princetown. Mr Chadwick had wanted to call for *her*, but she had insisted he might become lost on the moor, though that was something of an excuse as he could follow the road easily enough. The truth of it was that she wanted time to soothe her agitated spirit. She had never before considered the question of marriage, and was still not enamoured of the idea. She had brooded all night on what her father had said, tossing sleeplessly until she had spent an hour with her forehead pressed against the cool surface of the windowpane as the rain beat furiously on the other side of the glass. In her heart, all she wanted was to continue the pleasant life she led now, but though she fought against it like a demon, she knew that Henry was right. Perhaps Charles Chadwick would prove more acceptable today, and if it was going to make her father happy, she should at least give the fellow a chance.

As she came into Princetown, she slowed Gospel to a trot, rising and falling smoothly in the saddle to the rhythm of his pace. She could feel, with surprise, butterflies fluttering in her stomach. Charles Chadwick was only a man like any other, so why should she be feeling like this?

There he was now, waiting outside the attractive moorstone facade of the Duchy Hotel. He was seated upon a large chestnut horse, not an elegant, highly strung creature like Gospel, but a pretty animal nevertheless, a reliable mount that the hotel felt confident in hiring out to one of its clients. Gospel clearly liked the look of his companion for the morning also, for he could be quite amicable towards his fellow species – it was only humans he distrusted – and he whickered in welcome as he was brought to a halt just a few feet away.

'Good morning, Mr Chadwick.' Rose turned her vivid smile on the stunned businessman, the brilliant white of her perfect teeth and beautifully shaped mouth enslaving his heart even more deeply. His brown eyes stretched for a second before he gathered his composure and raised his bowler hat from his well-brushed hair.

'Good morning, Miss Maddiford,' he replied, grinning now with what seemed relaxed amusement. 'I see you ride *astride*. Most . . . unusual, shall we say, for a young lady.'

Rose's chin tilted obstinately. '*You* try riding Gospel side-saddle! Or on second thoughts, don't try riding him at all! He'll only throw you! The only other person he'll tolerate on his back is Joe.'

'Ah, yes, your stable boy,' Charles remembered, his eyes sparkling. 'And I meant no criticism, your riding astride. It simply . . . took me by surprise. But then, you are a very surprising person altogether.'

'And is that supposed to be a compliment?' she bristled haughtily.

'Absolutely!' He tossed his head with a short laugh, his face bright and expectant. 'Now then, where are you going to take me on this fine morning? I can't believe how lovely it is after that rainstorm overnight!'

'Oh, 'tis typical Dartmoor weather,' Rose shrugged. 'It can change in minutes. 'Tis one of its charms, and why one must always take care. A mist so thick you can hardly see the ground can come up that quickly!'

'Yes, I can imagine.' The chestnut had fallen into step beside Gospel as Rose turned him to retrace their way a few yards before taking a lane on the right which led almost immediately on to the moor. 'So, where *are* we going?'

'Well, I thought as I'd educate you in our local history. That is, if you're interested?' she added a little acidly.

'Why, I should be fascinated!' Charles turned to her with a smile so warm it reached his eyes. It made him quite attractive, Rose thought, then realizing she was studying his face too intently, abruptly averted her gaze as the heat flooded her cheeks.

'You know the gaol was originally a prisoner-of-war depot?' she went on briskly. 'During the wars against Napoleon Bonaparte? 'Twas all the idea of Sir Thomas Tyrwhitt,' she explained somewhat proudly. 'He were a wealthy gentleman towards the end of the last century, Member of Parliament and friend of the Prince of Wales. He built himself a country house called Tor Royal. You'll see it through the trees in a minute,' she told him, waving her arm vaguely ahead of them, 'where the road bends. 'Tis just a farm now, like any other. But he had great ideas about reclaiming the open moor and creating an agricultural community. Didn't work, of course, so they built the prisoner-of-war camp instead. There *are* parts of Dartmoor that are quite fertile, but up here, 'tis almost impossible. The prison farmlands, now parts of *that* are under cultivation, but of course, they've got all the free labour of the convicts to clear and drain the ground. Work them like donkeys, they do. 'Tis inhuman oft times.'

'Good heavens, do I detect some sympathy for the felons?' Charles asked, the surprise echoing in his voice.

'Oh, yes.' She glanced across at him with an adamant jerk of her head. 'Well, sometimes, certainly. Of course, some of them deserve it, I agree. For violent crimes, say. And I agree with the next man that crime of any sort merits punishment and imprisonment. But here, sometimes, 'tis downright cruel the way they're treated.'

'And do you never fear being attacked by an escaped convict, a lovely young woman like yourself?'

'What, when I'm out on Gospel? Goodness, no! 'Twould go badly with anyone who tried to accost me *then*! Besides, 'tis not often any prisoner gets away. They shoot them if they try running off, you see!'

She was looking at him now, her brow furrowed with the

force of what she was saying. Charles chuckled loudly, his mouth stretched with merriment.

'Well, I'm not quite sure I agree with your sentiments, but I'm pleased to be assured of your safety! Gospel is certainly a formidable animal! Oh, is that, what did you call it, something or other Royal?'

'Tor Royal? Yes, that's right. 'Tis fairly modest for the man who founded Princetown. Anyway, when the camp closed down after the war, he built a tramway from here down to Plymouth, mainly to serve the quarries on the moor and to keep the village alive. Only horse-drawn, mind. The part of it that came right into Princetown shut down about six years or so ago. I remember it. The village didn't flourish again until the prison re-opened for convicts in 1850. Transportation were coming to an end, and they needed something to take its place. Poor Sir Thomas never knew, though. He died long afore. But enough of the history lesson. We're heading out to the Whiteworks tin mine now. So what do you think of the open moor?'

Charles rose up in the saddle to obtain a better view, and scanned the horizon appreciatively. 'It's certainly breathtaking,' he nodded with enthusiasm. 'So vast and . . . I don't know . . . open.'

The muscles of his heart seemed to contract as a translucent aura glowed from Rose's face. 'Yes. 'Tis its endlessness, its . . . its enormity, I suppose. It makes you feel part of the earth, and yet part of the sky at the same time. As if you, too, can go on for ever. 'Tis very comforting, and yet so exciting. Do you not agree, Mr Chadwick?'

'I do indeed! But perhaps you might address me as Charles, at least when we're alone together?'

The resentment immediately prickled down Rose's spine. 'And how often do you believe that might be, Mr Chadwick?' she asked icily. 'I am merely obeying my father and showing a visitor some of the delights of Dartmoor! We're not actually going to the tin mine, by the way, but over to that stone cross over there,' she said flatly, the joy gone from her voice. 'There's lots of them on the moor, we're not sure exactly why. Possibly medieval waymarkers. And then I'll show you something even more mysterious.'

And with that, she dug her heels into Gospel's flanks and gave the animal his head. Gospel needed no more encouragement and catapulted into a headlong gallop, flying over the uneven ground with ease. The ancient cross disappeared past them in a blur, and then up and away they raced, skimming over the thick tussocks of tall coarse grass that peppered that part of the moor and forced Gospel to arch his neck as he lifted his fine legs to clear them. The sharp air whipped against Rose's flushed cheeks in their mad dash, cooling her indignation, so that by the time they finally gained the vantage point she was aiming for and they skidded to a stop, her piqued spirit had been calmed. She turned in the saddle to glance back at her companion. The chestnut mare was having difficulty picking her way over the rough terrain she was unaccustomed to, but Charles appeared quite comfortable and kept his seat perfectly. Rose's mouth twisted. Why didn't he fall off! That would have wiped the smugness from his face! Irritated, she turned her attention to the rugged vista before her while she waited for him to catch up, Gospel pawing impatiently at the ground and shaking his head so that the snaffle bit jangled in his mouth.

'Bloody lunatic.' Her sharp hearing caught Charles's muttering as he approached, and somehow it brought a satisfied smirk to her face. 'You really should take more care, Miss Maddiford!' he admonished, raising his voice as he drew level with her.

'Oh, Gospel's quite used to it! He'll slow down himself if he's unsure. I expect the mare only goes on the roads usually. She's very sweet, mind.'

Charles opened his mouth as if he would add some sharp riposte, but then his eyes focused on something strange in the distance and his brow puckered with curiosity. 'What on earth is that?' he asked instead.

''Tis what I was going to show you! 'Tis an ancient stone row. There's lots of them on the moor, but this is my favourite.'

'How fascinating!' His eyes shone with genuine interest, and Rose tipped her head in approval as she urged Gospel forward at a walk, in consideration of the chestnut's heavy breathing. 'And how unexpected! I had no idea there were such things on Dartmoor. I know of Stonehenge on the Salisbury Plain, but I thought it was unique.'

'You live and learn, Mr Chadwick. Not that these stones are anything like the size of those at Stonehenge. I've never been there, of course, but I have read about them.'

'You read quite a lot, then, Miss Maddiford?'

'Oh, yes. Especially about other places.'

'You'd like to travel, then?'

The radiant smile lit up her face again, pricking deeply somewhere about his heart. 'Oh, no, Mr Chadwick. Dartmoor is quite sufficient for me.'

'You wouldn't care to visit me in London? You and your father, of course,' he added hastily. 'You would be most welcome as my guests, and I could show you all the sites. We could go riding on Rotten Row!' he suggested with an enigmatic laugh.

'Rotten Row?' The puzzlement in Rose's expression was comical, and Charles's amusement deepened.

'It's a fashionable bridleway in Hyde Park,' he explained. 'You'd have to ride at a more moderate pace, though. If you cavorted about at your normal velocity, you'd upset all the sedate ladies who parade up and down on pretty little ponies a baby couldn't fall from!'

He chuckled easily at the picture it evoked in his mind, and Rose couldn't help but smile. Perhaps he wasn't so obnoxious after all. 'You ride quite well yourself, Mr Chadwick,' she admitted.

'Perhaps. But I've never seen anyone of the fairer sex ride like you do.'

Rose lowered her eyes. She knew she was a superb horse woman and she was proud of it, yet she found it an embarrassment to receive such a compliment from Charles Chadwick's lips. For once in her life, she felt unsure of herself, and it unsettled her. They rode on in silence, breathing in the fragrant freshness of the damp grass and peaty earth beneath their horses' hooves, both lost in tangled emotions until they reached the curious line of standing stones set in the ground. Rose eased on Gospel's reins and the animal came to a halt, standing quite still as even he became swamped by the uncanny atmosphere. Rose's eyes smouldered a smoky amethyst as she contemplated the mythical scene before her, its familiar power holding her in its hypnotizing spell.

'Oh, Mr Chadwick, no!' she called as she was shaken from her trance by the horse and rider moving slowly forward. 'You must dismount. To show respect.'

Charles stopped at once, and glancing back over his shoulder, landed lightly on the ground as she came towards him, leading Gospel by the reins. 'The stone circle at the other end,' she explained in a reverent whisper, "'tis an ancient burial site, or so we believe. For village chiefs. Or maybe priests.'

'And the stone row?' he replied in a low voice.

'We don't know. Perhaps graves of ordinary people, or marking the way to the sacred site.'

'Well, it's certainly impressive. It must be, what, nearly a quarter of a mile long at a guess.'

'There are some over a mile and a half, but they're much further away.'

'Good heavens.'

She looked at him askew as they ambled along the row of stones, the corners of her mouth lifted pleasurably. He clearly appreciated the mystic grandeur of the place, which elevated him considerably in her esteem. Her keen eyes scanned the horizon, the moor seemingly endless in that particular area, apparently stretching to infinity. It was easy to understand why it had been chosen as a ceremonial site.

'They must have been some sort of pagans. Druids, perhaps?' Charles mused softly.

'Possibly,' Rose agreed. 'But I don't suppose as we'll ever know for certain.'

They walked on, stopping a while by the stone circle before remounting. But there seemed little to say, and Rose set Gospel at a loping canter, leaving the ancient monument behind them and gradually heading more steeply downhill until they crossed over a small bridge and climbed the valley on the far side. Charles followed, not pausing until they reached the gushing, evidently man-made waterway that blocked their path.

'Dock Leat,' Rose answered his enquiring expression. 'There's lots of leats on the moor. Brilliant engineering, using the contours of the land to maintain the correct flow. For industrial use mainly. You must have seen them at the powder mills yesterday. This one's for drinking water and such at Devonport, mind. There's huge flat stones set across to form bridges. You may need to lead the mare across if she's not used to them.'

'You just lead the way, Miss Maddiford,' Charles enthused, following her advice, not sure which inspired him the more, Rose herself or her passion for the thrilling landscape of the moor. Which, when he thought about it, were really one and the same thing!

'Race you to the top!' she yelled unexpectedly as he sprang back into the saddle. 'Up there!' she nodded, waving at what to Charles seemed like an impossibly steep crag.

And she was off, laughing into the wind as Gospel charged forward along a narrow grassy pathway through the rock-strewn landscape. Charles shook his head. There was absolutely no way he could catch up with her. But he didn't care. He had never been one to long for women's company. The ladies of London society with whom he was acquainted held no pleasure for him. He had maintained a mistress once in his youth, a clean young girl who had been devoted to him, though he had always made it clear they could never be wed. She had been a virgin, as he had been, and though he had kept her purely for his carnal satisfaction, he had held a certain fondness for her. Foolishly, without telling him, she had fallen pregnant and sought help in a London back street, and the ensuing infection had killed her. Since then, Charles Chadwick had turned his back on the female race. Until now. His mind had been intoxicated, his heart quickened and enflamed. There was no one in the world like Rose Maddiford, and he would have her as his bride to honour and to worship.

Having dismounted somewhere near the bottom, she was now standing on the summit of the rocky tor, silhouetted against the skyline like some apparition from the realms of fantasy, her arms lifted and spread towards the heavens, as magnificent as the beast she had left to await her. Charles's heart was in his mouth as she appeared to be on the very edge of the sheer drop, and abandoning the chestnut mare next to the black gelding, he scrambled up the high outcrop of granite in a frenzy of anxiety. But to his relief, when he reached her, he realized she was in fact well back from the dangerous edge.

Rose was waiting patiently for him, a rapturous smile firing her face and tendrils of wild, curling hair escaping from the excuse of a hat on her head. He knew then that he loved her with a power beyond his comprehension. He *must* have her. And he was obliged to drag his gaze away from her to the direction to which she was gesticulating with a wide sweep of her arm.

'There! Have you ever seen a view like that?' she demanded.

Charles breathed in deeply, his eyes wide with delight. It was as if the world lay spread out at their feet, a gentler part of the moor with the river valley below them, and far in the distance, a shining tortuous ribbon of water.

'That's the River Tamar,' she told him, the exuberance quavering in her voice. 'On a clear day like this you can see all the way down to Plymouth, you see? And the sea all the way along!'

Charles squinted hard, but he knew his vision wasn't as sharp as it might be. But if Rose fancied she could see that far, it was good enough for him.

'And look! If you turn around, you can see right over the north of the moor! 'Tis like mountains from here. 'Tis an amazing view in all three hundred and sixty degrees, don't you agree, Mr Chadwick? In fact, when I'm up here,' she said solemnly, the sudden reverence in her words taking him by surprise, 'I feel as if I'm up in heaven. Looking down on the most beautiful landscape God ever invented. I feel so at peace, I'd have no regrets if I dropped dead just now, *here*, at the most wonderful place on earth.'

'Well, I sincerely hope you don't,' Charles murmured, 'drop dead, I mean, when I've only just met you.'

She blinked at him, her cheeks blushing a deep burgundy as she cleared her throat. 'This is Sharpitor,' she snapped hotly. 'That steep ridge in front of us is Leather Tor. And over there, that's Peek Hill, but the view's the same. And 'tis more than two miles to Princetown on the road, so I think as we'd better be heading back. The mare looks tired out.'

'Not surprising, chasing after you!'

Rose clamped her jaw, her eyes flashing a midnight blue, and with a disdainful flick of her head she scurried back down over the rocks and, leaping into the saddle, turned Gospel homeward. Charles sighed as he remounted and urged his horse forward. Damn it! It was meant to be a joke, and instead she had taken offence. He could see that if he wanted Rose as his wife, he would have to learn to treat her quick temper with kid gloves . . .

'Hello, Rose!'

A huge grin of relief split Rose's taut face as they trotted back into Princetown. The ride home along the Yelverton road had been tense, Rose being disinclined to respond to what she considered Charles's idle chatter with anything more than a monosyllabic grunt. He was a stranger, an outsider who had invaded her private world and somehow tricked her into disclosing some of her innermost thoughts. And she would never forgive him!

'Molly! How are you?' she responded with a brightness that was meant to slice at Charles Chadwick's arrogance.

'Oh, we'm fine!' Molly, a full shopping basket on her arm, screwed her head to look enquiringly up at Rose's companion. 'Been for a ride, have we?'

'Oh, this is Mr Chadwick,' Rose replied, flapping a casual hand in his direction. 'He's an investor in the powder mills on a short visit, and I were just showing him part of the moor.' And when Molly continued to gaze at Charles with her sweetest smile, Rose went on irritably, 'Mr Chadwick, this is my dear friend, Miss Cartwright. Her father's a prison warder.'

A stiff smile tightened Charles's lips as he raised his hat. 'Miss Cartwright,' he managed to grate with affected pleasure. 'You will forgive us, but I was just about to accompany Miss Maddiford to her home.'

But Rose rounded on him with barbs of rancour in her voice. 'I'm quite capable of seeing myself home, thank you, Mr Chadwick! Besides, Molly . . . Miss Cartwright and I have not seen each other this week, and I should like to converse with her. In private, if you please,' she added frostily as she swung her leg over Gospel's neck and alighted on the ground.

Charles merely bowed his head politely. 'Then I shall wish you both good day. But I should be obliged if you and your father would honour me with your company at dinner tonight at my hotel. I shall send a carriage for you both at, shall we say, seven thirty?'

And before Rose had the chance to force a word from her gaping mouth, he turned the chestnut mare and disappeared at a brisk trot towards the said hotel.

Rose's cheeks puffed out with indignation and she stamped her foot with an irate grunt as Molly giggled beside her.

'Oh, Rose, you do look quite funny!' she chortled.

'I don't know why *you're* laughing! That bumptious, impudent prig didn't like the idea of my having friends among the—'

She broke off, her lips twisted with shame, but Molly only shook her head. 'The working classes?' she suggested, linking her arm through her friend's. 'I don't mind you saying it, for 'tis true. We'm hardworking, honest people, and proud of it. We cas'n help it if we wasn't born with money. And I bet *he* works, only in a different way. And he looks as if he's took a shine to you, Rose!' she teased with an admiring twinkle in her merry green eyes.

'Well, he can take his shine somewhere else, the insufferable, boorish—'

'Handsome, polite, well-heeled gentleman!' Molly finished for her. 'You should be flattered, Rose! And thankful! I wish someone like that would show an interest in *me*,' she ended ruefully.

Rose bit her lip, the tang of remorse bitter in her mouth. Yes. To Molly, someone like Charles Chadwick would be manna from heaven. But no one of his ilk would ever look at her, pretty though she was, for anything more than a swift dalliance. Rose knew she should be grateful, for though her father made a decent living, they were still miles away from Mr Chadwick's league, and if his intentions truly were honourable, he would be considered by the circles he moved among to be marrying beneath him.

The thought clouded her brain, her forehead corrugated as she walked arm in arm with her friend, Gospel's reins trailing from her other hand. Perhaps she should give Charles Chadwick another chance, and this time do her utmost to be civil and draw on her better nature.

Five

'Rose?' Henry prompted gently over his plate of sausage, bacon and scrambled egg, for Florrie believed a man should go to work on a hearty breakfast.

Rose was staring blankly at the cup of tea she had been stirring for the past five minutes, her own plate untouched. Her father's voice startled her for they had been sitting in silence and she threw up her head with a jerk. 'Sorry, Father?'

'We were talking about Mr Chadwick, as I'm sure you remember. You must give the poor man an answer of *some* sort. You've kept him waiting long enough.'

His words were soft, compassionate, and the groan in Rose's heart deepened. Charles had returned to London after extending his visit to nearly a fortnight, almost every minute of which he had spent at Rose's side. But it seemed he could not concentrate on his affairs in the capital, and after a couple of weeks he had been back again, wooing her with flowers and other gifts, and trips to the seaside, culminating in his asking Henry for her hand the night before business matters required his urgent return home. It was now mid-November, dreary, wet and miserable up on the moor, and despite numerous letters from Charles, Rose still had not given him an answer.

Her eyes met Henry's across the table, wide and honest and bright with anguish. 'I don't know,' she moaned pitifully, her shoulders drooping. 'I've been over and over it in my mind, but I just don't know.'

'Have you discussed it with Molly, for instance?' Henry suggested mildly.

'Molly! She thinks just because he's handsome and has money, I should jump at the chance!'

'But . . .' Henry faltered, 'you're not Molly.'

'No,' Rose said stonily, her jaw set.

'Then you must tell *me* exactly how you feel. I know I'm

not your mother, God rest her soul, but I'll have to do. The whole honest truth, mind.'

He smiled encouragingly, and the frozen knot inside her chest melted a little. She sighed, a torn, painful exhalation of breath. 'I know you would like to see me settled and secure,' she began tentatively, and watched as Henry pressed the palms of his hands together and rested his joined fingers against his lips. 'But if I married Mr Chadwick, I'd have to live in London, so far away from you, and I couldn't bear that.'

'Not necessarily. I'm sure Mr Chadwick could afford to keep at least a modest house down here, and I should want proof of his financial security before I gave my consent anyway. But . . . there is far more to consider than that,' he said with an enigmatic lift of his eyebrows.

Rose licked her lips. There was something solid inside her, as if someone had rammed a fist into her stomach, and try as she may, she couldn't uncurl its iron fingers. 'Mr Chadwick is . . . polite. A true gentleman. Very attentive, of course.' She hesitated. Lowered her eyes. '*Too* attentive. I feel I'm being coerced into . . . into a relationship. He can be quite . . . forceful, I suppose, though in the most charming way. At least . . .' She bowed her head, not wanting to offend her father's feelings for the man he considered a suitable prospective spouse. 'At least, *he* thinks he's being charming. *I* just find him too . . . forthright. I'm sure he'd make an excellent husband, but I . . . I simply don't love him.'

Her mouth compressed into a harsh line and she swallowed before lifting her eyes to her father again. For several seconds, Henry sat motionless, then slowly he nodded his head. 'And . . . do you know what love is?'

Rose blinked hard and her pulse began to beat faster. 'No. Not for another man. I've never felt what that is. But . . . I know what my love for you is, Father. 'Tis good and warm. And trusting. And . . .' Her eyes suddenly sparked with a piercing sapphire light. 'I know what my love for Gospel is! He . . . he lifts something deep inside of me. We share so much together, as if . . . as if we share the same spirit. Surely . . . if you really love someone, you must feel something like that? Like a fire inside you!' And then her face closed down, as if someone had drawn the shutters over a window. 'And I *don't* feel like that about Mr Chadwick.'

Henry contemplated her a moment longer, her impassioned speech pricking at the pain he usually managed to bury deep in his soul. 'Then there's no more to be said. I shall write to Mr Chadwick this evening and inform him of your refusal. You know, Rose, you're so like your mother. And it makes me . . . so proud,' he finished, gesturing at her with his outstretched hand. 'Come here, my dearest child.'

In a trice, she came up to his chair and bent to wrap her arms around his beloved neck. He patted her shoulder, his cheek pressed against hers, and his eyes closed as he endeavoured to shut out his distress. For how could he break it to her that, without Charles Chadwick's money, Gospel would have to be sold . . .

Rose padded up and down her bedroom, unconsciously chewing on the nail of her little finger. She should feel relieved, but she didn't. She very definitely did not want to marry Mr Chadwick, but was it a wise decision? And was her father being his usual kind, understanding self, or was he really feeling deeply disappointed, despite his words?

She rubbed her hand hard over her forehead. If she didn't stop her restless tramping, she would wear a hole in the carpet, or so Florrie would have said. The shadow of a smile flickered on her pursed lips. Dear Florrie. At least she would always be there. And Joe, and Gospel and Amber, who at this moment was stretched out on the floor, nose on her paws but one ear cocked and her eyes dolefully following her mistress's movements.

Gospel. Well, of course, if anything could soothe her spirit it would be a crazed gallop across the moor. Perhaps over to Princetown to see Molly. Or to some lonely place, such as the twisted, stunted oaks of the eerie ancient Wistman's Wood. Somewhere she had *not* taken Charles Chadwick!

That was it. She pulled off her skirt and petticoats and wriggled into her tight riding breeches before donning the jacket and full skirt of her riding habit over the top. A small hat secured on the top of her springing curls with a long pin, a scarf wound around her neck for it was cold and penetratingly damp outside, gloves ready in her pocket, and her boots would be waiting by the back door after she had put her head around the kitchen door to tell Florrie where she would be going.

The icy dankness stung her nostrils as she strode across the yard, Amber bouncing excitedly about her heels. Joe had turned Gospel into the field behind the buildings early in the morning, for the animal needed to kick up his heels and expend some of his boundless energy. Rose went in search of his bridle before leaping over the gate in her customary unlady-like fashion, while Amber wormed her joyous way beneath the bottom-most bar.

Gospel whinnied with pleasure when he heard Rose call, performing a standing jump from all four legs before thundering across the wet grass and snorting great wreaths of hot breath into the already saturated air as he came to a slithering halt before her. He nuzzled into her shoulder bringing a full smile to her face as she stroked his strong, sleek neck. When she had first bought him, he had been the devil's own job to catch, fearing the worst from the martingale and strong bit. But now he knew that being caught usually meant a wild, exhilarating dash on the open moor with his gentle mistress on his back, and he was as eager for the adventure as she was.

She slid the bridle over his head, slipping the bit carefully into his mouth, and fastening the chin strap, led him towards the yard to remove his blanket and saddle him before they streaked off in whatever direction she decided upon.

Her fingers froze on the buckle of the girth strap . . .

Her sharp ears had somehow caught that hiatus of unearthly silence that precedes the boom of an explosion by a split second, and then the thunderous crash that shattered her eardrums, reverberating through the valley before slowly rolling away on an ever fainter rumble. For several moments, not a muscle in Rose's body moved, her breathing stilled and only her heart beating steadily while her brain absorbed what her heart did not want to believe. Her forehead pleated in an anguished frown and she slowly shook her head. But she *had* heard it, and as her pulse accelerated, pumping the frenzied life into her limbs, reality crept into her stunned mind, and with a hoarse cry, she abandoned Gospel and ran.

Fled along the footpath to her father's office. Flung open the door, expecting to see Henry pulling on his leather-soled shoes. He wasn't there. From years of habit, she changed her own footwear in an instant, and was flying down the hill, the breath dry and rasping in her lungs.

She stopped dead. Unlike the minor mishap a few months past, it was immediately apparent where the explosion had occurred. Away on the opposite hillside, number-one incorporating mill was engulfed in a curtain of black smoke ...

Rose was transfixed, her mind wrapped in fascinated, horrified curiosity. She wanted to run, but the leaden weight of her legs imprisoned her. And then she joined in the macabre, hushed convergence of leather-muted feet, speeding along the riverbank, past the various processing houses, across the bridge over the Cherrybrook and up the track on the far side. Those workers who could safely shut down their machinery had spilled out from their posts and were milling around breathlessly on the hillside, calling in restless agitation as they awaited instructions, or numbed into silence by the picture of destruction before them. The shroud of smoke was reluctantly drifting into the mist, revealing what little remained of the charred and broken roof timbers and the flapping remnants of the shredded tarpaulin that until a few minutes before had covered them. Splintered shards of the massive wooden machinery had been blown through the roof and window apertures in the blast, and lay scattered about the grass together with tatters of the heavy tanned hides that lined the floor of the mill.

Rose's heart caught in her throat and her limbs trembled. She turned her head in disbelief, yet her eyes still clung to the scene of devastation. She tore her gaze away, searching for her father among the crowd and expecting at any moment to hear his reassuring, authoritative voice as he calmly took control of the appalling situation.

It started as a tiny kernel deep in her breast, slowly unfurling until its fingers spread like strangling tentacles through her being, crushing the life, and the hope, from her very existence.

'Have you seen my father?' Her lips quavered as her eyes blindly quizzed every shaking head that swung before her. 'Have you seen my father?!?' she screamed now, frantically running from face to face, spinning, tripping, blundering over the rough grass, the sea of anxious expressions foaming into one blurred, surging wave. And as she turned to join her gaze to theirs as they stared at the smouldering building, her body drained and motionless, she knew ...

'*No!*' A savage wail echoed from her heaving lungs as her limbs found their strength again and she dashed forward, howling dementedly, only to be restrained in the iron circle of Fred Ashman's arms. He struggled to hold fast to her writhing, flailing body until the agony emptied out of her and she suddenly went as limp and lifeless as a rag doll . . .

The world gathered itself around her, cruel and tormenting. She wanted to slip back into the warmth and peace of unconsciousness, to snuggle beneath the safe and comforting blanket that had smothered her mind, but she knew even in her semiconscious state that she had to face the hostile cold of reality.

She forced open her eyes, but the effort made her forehead swoop in a fierce frown. She was in the kitchen, slumped in Florrie's chair by the range, carried there she imagined by some strong and compassionate arms. Florrie herself was seated at the table, her head bowed over an untouched mug of tea, her eyes red and swollen, and the usually merry lines on her face set into a grim, appalling mask.

It was the sight of her that made Rose remember.

Her spine stiffened and she sat bolt upright in the chair, her heart taking a huge leap and knocking against her ribcage. The last thing she remembered . . .

'Father!' she shrieked in her head, but her lips only mouthed the word, her eyes bright pinpoints of terror.

Florrie looked up, her plump cheeks wobbling. 'Upstairs, my lamb,' she murmured, her voice the croak of an old, old woman.

Rose's head swam as she sprang from the chair and raced up the stairs two at a time, her feet, still in their leather-soled shoes, making no sound on the carpeted treads. The cold brass of the doorknob was a shock in her hand, and her whole body froze. Was she ready? To see what was in the room? Her father, his arms crossed over his chest. Perhaps with Florrie's snowy sheet already laid over his head.

She trembled. Her hand hardly able to open the door. The blood pumping fearfully, angrily, through her veins. How dare they – whoever *they* were, God, perhaps? – take her dearest, beloved father from her like this . . .

There was a dark-suited man in the room, standing with his back to her as he sorted something on the bedside cabinet.

He turned when he heard her to smile gravely over his shoulder, nodding down at the bed before continuing with what he was doing. Dr Power, of course, from Princetown. Prison surgeon, but also physician to local people who sought his help, and so known to everyone.

The bud of hope blossomed, and then shrank, in Rose's breast as she drew her gaze to the bed. Only her father's face was visible above the neatly arranged bedclothes. It was still streaked with black grime, settling in lines in the folds of his skin, though someone, probably Florrie, had evidently tried to wipe away the worst without causing him too much distress. One side of his forehead, spreading down across the temple though thankfully missing his eye, was a raw mass of black and red seething bubbles that stretched into his matted, bloodied hair, but other than that, he lay perfectly still, like a corpse, but for the shallow, rasping breathing of his lungs.

Rose stood. And stared. As the horror washed over her in a pulsing torrent. But . . . somehow Henry must have been aware of her presence and his eyes half opened. 'Rose,' he choked, and his taut face relaxed.

The life drained out of her and she dropped on to her knees, fighting against the welling tears in her eyes. 'Father,' she whispered back, forcing a wan and deeply loving smile to her quivering lips. 'Oh, Father, you'll be all right now,' she told him fervently, her voice soft and gentle as an angel.

'Yes,' he breathed, and then coughed harshly so that she could smell the smoke from him. 'And Peter?'

Rose's heart squeezed. Even as he was, he was anxious, as ever, about others, his men. Rose turned her questioning eyes to the doctor, ashamed that she had not given a thought to anyone else who had been in the mill at the time. Dr Power gave a solemn, almost imperceptible shake of his head, his eyes shutting briefly as he did so, and Rose felt the ice run through her veins. Peter Russell, his wife, their five children.

Her loving, tender gaze moved back to Henry's blackened, damaged face. 'I . . . I don't know,' she lied, for how could she burden him with the knowledge? It could wait. For now.

'I were . . . giving him the length of my tongue.' Henry's voice chafed in his burning throat. 'There were grit on the floor. Some must have got into the trough.'

His words had become agitated, and as Rose stretched out

a calming hand, she was aware of the doctor leaning over her with concern.

'Hush now, Father,' she crooned through the sorrow that raked her gullet. 'You must rest. Have a little sleep, and I'll be here when you wake up.'

'Your daughter's right, Mr Maddiford,' Dr Power said firmly over her shoulder. 'The morphine will make you sleep. Don't fight it.'

Henry's bloodshot eyes lifted to the doctor's face, then rested back on his beloved child before drooping closed, the tense lines in his skin slackening. Rose bent forward. The reverent kiss she placed on his cheek leaving an acrid taste on her lips. She got to her feet, Dr Power ushering her politely out of the door, and as she glanced back, Henry was already asleep.

'A word, if you please, Miss Maddiford.'

Rose stood for a moment, his quiet tone taking some seconds to percolate through to her numbed brain. 'Of course,' she muttered, and led the way down to the parlour, floating down the stairs as if in some strange, unreal dream.

'Please, sit down,' he invited her, which seemed so odd in her own home.

She obeyed, perching uneasily on the edge of the armchair. The fire was out. One of their economies. She shivered, crossing her arms tightly across her chest. 'He . . . he will get better, won't he?' she stammered, not quite sure how she articulated the words.

Dr Power's forehead twitched as he attempted to detach himself from the situation. He was used to dealing with hardened criminals, treating ailments or injuries resulting from the harsh conditions inflicted upon them, or – the part of his job he hated – deciding if a convict was fit enough to endure some vicious corporal punishment. So how could his heart not be touched by this beautiful, distraught young woman whose grief already ravaged her lovely face?

'I'm afraid your father's condition is worse than it may appear,' he began compassionately. 'He has other deep burns to the front of his body. In time, they should heal, but burns are very much prone to infection. What I am most concerned about, however, is that somehow in the blast his spine has been damaged. It could well be no more than severe bruising which has compacted the nerves of the spinal column, in which case in . . . a few months, perhaps, things may return to normal. But . . . at the moment – ' he faltered, his gaze fixed on her bowed head – 'he feels nothing below the injury. He has already proved . . . incontinent. And . . . I fear I must warn you, Miss Maddiford, that if, as I suspect, the spine is permanently damaged, then . . . your father will never walk again.'

His voice had drifted about her, like a mist that would slowly dissipate as if it had never been. That would lift, and allow the sun to shine through and the world would be bright and happy again. But it wouldn't, would it? The cloud was there to stay. For ever.

She lifted her head, unaware of the tears that spangled in her eyes. 'Thank you, Doctor, for your honesty,' she managed to tear the words from her throat.

'I really am very sorry. I will do everything in my power to keep him comfortable, and God willing, he will make some recovery. Now, I do apologize, but I must return to my official duties. But I will be back again later. You know where I am if you need me in the meantime. Don't worry. I'll see myself out. And . . . well . . . Miss Maddiford . . .'

He squeezed her shoulder as he passed, for really they both knew there were no words. She listened to his footsteps in the hall, the front door closing softly. Silence then. Just the clock ticking steadily, incessantly, on the mantelpiece.

Just an hour or so ago, she had been deliberating the wisdom of her refusal of Charles Chadwick's proposal. That all seemed so . . . so unimportant now. So unimportant and of no significance whatsoever . . .

And she buried her head in her hands and wept till her aching soul could weep no more . . .

Six

R ose stood, staring blindly at the empty fireplace in the parlour, her mind hallucinating with visions of the flames which once upon a time would have crackled merrily in the grate. The moor lay frozen beneath the searingly cold blanket of February snow, and Rose subconsciously drew the shawl more tightly about her narrow shoulders, for exhaustion had clouded her brain to her own physical discomfort. Between them, she and Florrie had nursed her father, day and night, for three months. There was no time for long, carefree gallops on Gospel's lively back, or cosy chats with Molly by the Cartwrights' hearthside. What flesh had once adorned Rose's slender figure had fallen from her bones, and the skin was drawn taut across her cheeks.

She scarcely turned her head at the polite knock on the door.

'Come in,' she answered, her voice dull and lifeless.

Dr Power entered the room, his head bowed apologetically. He sighed, his heart heavy. 'No change, I'm afraid, Miss Maddiford.' He hesitated, the sight of the forlorn young woman tearing at his soul, but it must be said. 'I fear we must face up to the situation. Barring any unforeseen recovery, which, I may say, would constitute some sort of miracle, I believe your father will remain paralysed.'

Rose nodded her head without looking at him. Yes. She didn't need the physician to tell her. She knew already. The purple swelling on Henry's spine had long since disappeared, but he had still neither moved nor felt any sensation below the mid-point of his back, the only progress he had made being his regaining control of his bodily functions. His lungs remained weakened by smoke inhalation, and the thick scar tissue twisted the side of his forehead, but his upper body remained strong. He could feed and wash himself, and move

himself about in the bed, even issuing directives and to some
extent taking up his responsibilities once more as manager,
but never again would he stride amongst his men and the
various buildings of the factory they worked in.

'Thank you, Dr Power,' Rose murmured wearily. 'I know
you've done all you can. 'Tis much appreciated.'

The doctor drew an awkward breath through pursed lips as
he reached into the breast pocket of his coat. 'I only wish,'
he said gravely, 'that the outcome had been a better one. And
that I didn't have to present you with my bill. I have kept it
as low as possible.'

The memory of a smile strained at Rose's mouth as she
took the envelope from his hand. 'Mr Frean has kindly said
he'll pay for my father's treatment.'

'Ah.' Dr Power nodded, for there was nothing more to say
on the matter. 'And . . . to be honest, there is little reason for
me to visit again. You and Mrs Bennett are making an excellent job of caring for your father. As we've said before, the
most important thing is for you to exercise his legs several
times a day to keep the blood flowing and reduce the strain
on his heart. Of course, if you've any concerns, do send for
me at once.'

'Yes, I will. And . . . thank you again, Doctor.'

'Any time, Miss Maddiford. I'll see myself out.'

She was alone again, her gaze resting unseeing on the envelope in her hand as her eyes filled with unshed tears. So, that
was it. Her dearest, hardworking, active father cut down and
crippled for life. More than that. Condemned to his bed for
the rest of his days. Her face pulled into a determined grimace
as she squared her shoulders. There was nothing more the good
doctor could do. But *she* wouldn't give in! She would not sit
back and let Henry waste away! The fight began to creep back
into her veins. If her father's condition was never to improve,
then there must be ways and means by which his existence
could be returned to as near to normality as was humanly
possible. The tiny seed of hope had been planted at the back
of her mind. She would leave it there to germinate, to be
pondered upon so that the right decisions could be made. Right
now, there were other matters she needed to attend to. They
were running low on coal, and the pantry was nearly empty.
Time for a trip into Princetown. She wouldn't take Gospel, for

she could carry little on his back, but she would borrow Henry's dog cart and Polly, the gentle cob that pulled it. And even that put another burgeoning idea into her head . . .

Ellen Williams puffed up her flat chest, and her mouth worked into a partly livid, partly gloating sneer, for the young hussy was getting her comeuppance, though at Ellen's cost. Of course, she knew about the tragedy of the girl's father and she was sorry for that, but it was about time the flibberti-gibbet was taken down a peg or two.

'I'm afraid I can't serve you, Miss Maddiford,' she announced through tight lips.

Rose's neck stiffened and she blinked at the sharp-featured woman in astonishment. Had she heard right? She was aware of the chatter of the two other customers behind her coming to an abrupt halt, and her brow puckered into a frown. 'I'm sorry?' she questioned in bemusement.

'I'm afraid I can't serve you,' Ellen repeated with satisfaction, 'not until your account be settled. The cheque you gave me from your father has been returned by the bank.'

'What!' Rose's eyes narrowed with indignation, for she had always sensed that the shopkeeper resented her, but some-where deep inside, a cold fear began to slither into her blood.

'Here. Take it, if you doesn't believe me.' Ellen flicked effi-ciently through the wooden till, and waved the cheque, with its ugly red bank stamp, in front of Rose's nose.

A wave of disbelief, of horror, washed from Rose's throat down to her stomach and her shaking hand took the cheque that Ellen was dangling distastefully between her finger and thumb as if it was something evil she had picked up on the street. The writing, her father's signature, danced before Rose's eyes. She really couldn't believe . . .

'Thank you,' she mumbled incoherently, shame burning in her cheeks as she made for the door, the eyes of the other customers boring into her back. Outside, the biting cold stung into her body like a million piercing arrows. She was trem-bling as if her very core had been frozen, tears of humiliation turning to frost on her eyelashes. Surely there must be some sort of mistake? And yet the proof of it lay crumpled at the bottom of her pocket. She shook her head. An error. It must be! Some new clerk at the bank. Yes, that must be it.

So . . . what should she do? Well, if Miss Williams refused to serve her, there were two other grocers in the village. Her father didn't have accounts with them, but she had some coins in her purse, not many, but enough to buy some tea, flour and yeast, and a couple of pounds of potatoes. They could manage on that for a few days. Until the matter was resolved. With some chops and a joint from the butcher's, for she had settled that account with a cheque from her father on the same day as . . . Oh, good God! Would it be the same there?

She left Polly between the shafts of the dog cart tethered to the rail with the horse-blanket thrown over her back, for she could not leave the animal standing still without protection in these temperatures. Her feet crunched in the snow as she made her way to the other shops, the butcher's first, her hand quivering as she opened the door and a horrible sinking feeling in her stomach.

Mr Roebuck looked up with his usual kindly smile. 'Ah, Miss Rose, how be your father?'

His sympathetic tone restored her confidence. Oh, yes, definitely a mistake at the grocer's. 'No better, I'm afraid. But thank you for asking. Now, I'd like a hand and spring of pork, if you please,' she asked cautiously, for though it was an awkwardly shaped joint and therefore cheaper, there was usually plenty of meat to be found on it.

Mr Roebuck cleared his throat and glancing round the shop as if someone might be listening – though there were no other customers – leaned confidentially towards her. 'I'm sorry, Miss Rose,' he whispered, 'but the bank wouldn't accept your father's cheque. It puts me in a difficult position, you sees. I can maybies let you have a couple of strips of belly, and a pound of tripe for that dog o' yourn, but only if you pays me now. In cash. I cas'n let you have ort more than that till your account be settled.'

Rose gazed at him, slack-jawed, and she was sure her heart missed a beat. This could not be happening! But it most definitely was!

She forced her most winning smile to her lips. 'Oh, Mr Roebuck, I do apologize. I believe there's been some error at the bank. I'll have to go into Tavistock to sort it out. And I'm afraid I have little money with me, so I won't buy anything today. But I'll be back in a day or two.'

'As you wish, Miss Rose. And . . . I really am proper sorry.'

'Don't worry about it!' she beamed cheerfully in an effort to disguise the tremor in her voice. 'I do understand.'

'My regards to your father, then!' the poor man called as she left the shop.

She stood outside on the frozen ground, unaware of the gnawing cold that pinched at her toes and turned her flushed cheeks to ice. For some seconds, the shock numbed her brain, rendering her incapable of thought. She breathed in deeply through flared nostrils, and the pain of the glacial air in her lungs seemed to bring her to her senses. Flour and potatoes were all she could think of. She had enough in her purse for those. At least they wouldn't starve. But even they were useless without coal for the range to cook them on! She closed her eyes, forcing herself to think back. Henry hadn't given her a cheque for the coal merchants, had he? So perhaps they hadn't sent a bill yet. But it had been a long time, three months since the explosion. She took all the post up to her father unopened. He dealt with it, gave her back any papers to put away in his bureau in the dining room, which she did without question, and without looking at them, for they were her father's. But what if . . .?

She strode determinedly into Mr Richards's establishment. They must have coal! There was only enough to last a week in these arctic temperatures, two if they were blessed with a sudden thaw and were careful in their consumption. But they already were, the kitchen range and the grate in Henry's bedroom being the only fires that were lit, both she and Florrie shivering in their beds at night. It was warmer in Joe's room over the stables, she often thought ruefully.

The groceries first, for the shop served a dual purpose. With the weighty items safely stowed in her basket, she stepped up to the wooden kiosk that served as the coal-merchants' office, and tapped nervously on the window. Mr Richards glanced up at her over the horn-rimmed spectacles that were balanced on the end of his bulbous nose.

'Yes?' he asked gruffly, for he was not known for his friend-liness.

'Please could you deliver us some coal, Mr Richards?' Rose said politely.

She watched through the small square of glass as he thumbed

through a ledger and finally opened it at a particular page that seemed to warrant his scrutiny. He sniffed, wriggling his nose, before turning his small eyes on her. 'Your last bill's not been paid yet,' he growled with annoyance.

Rose's heart sank to her boots. 'Are you sure you've sent one?' she replied with feigned innocence. 'I've not seen one.'

He scowled and flicked through another smaller book. 'Definitely. But you can have this carbon copy.' And tearing out the page, he slid it through the narrow gap beneath the little window.

Rose took it between shaking fingers and pushed it, folded, into her purse, trying hard not to look at the faint blue figures at the bottom of the thin paper. 'I'm so sorry, Mr Richards. It must have been overlooked. You may imagine everything's been upside down since my father's accident. I'll see to it forthwith,' she smiled in what she hoped was an assured manner. 'Now, when can you deliver?'

'Hmm,' the man grunted as he pinched his moustache between his forefinger and thumb. 'You can have a couple of sacks the day after tomorrow. But 'tis all until that bill's paid.'

'Of course. I understand. Thank you.'

Her lips moved of their own accord, as did her feet which somehow took her outside and along the slippery ground back to where Polly was waiting patiently. Slowly, she pulled the blanket from the mare's back, and climbing up into the driving seat turned the cart for home. And once they were out on the Two Bridges road, she braced herself to take the folded sheet of flimsy paper from her purse . . .

'Your father's asleep now, Rose dear,' Florrie announced staunchly as she puffed into the kitchen late that evening and flopped into her chair by the side of the range. 'I'll just make myself a cup of tea, and then I'll be off to bed myself. Will you have one, my dear?'

Rose glanced up from folding the last of Henry's night-shirts that she had been ironing on the thick pad on the kitchen table. She knew she must have appeared inattentive ever since returning from Princetown, though she had endeavoured to hide her preoccupation. Florrie had been surprised at the lack of meat and other provisions in the shopping basket, but Rose had blamed the bitter weather for the delay in the delivery of supplies to the shops, and the older woman had accepted the lie unquestioningly. Rose had felt guilty at the deceit, but not for long. She had a far more serious matter to ponder at the moment.

'Oh, yes, please, Florrie,' she answered gratefully. 'I'm that weary.'

'And you'm not yersel today, neither,' the housekeeper commented shrewdly. 'Be summat amiss?'

Rose was aware of the flood of colour into her cheeks, but she disguised it with a heartfelt sigh. 'Oh, 'tis just Dr Power. He confirmed today what you and I have thought for some time. That Father's never going to get any better.'

Florrie pushed a mug of tea towards her, and then sat down heavily herself. 'Ah, well,' she muttered thoughtfully. 'I suppose us should be thankful for small mercies. We still has your father, which be more than can be said for poor Elisa Russell of her husband.'

Rose nodded solemnly. Yes, Florrie was right. But that wasn't all that was on her mind just now. They drank their tea in silence, easy in each other's company even though not another word was exchanged. Florrie finally bade her good-night and a distracted smile flickered over Rose's face. She listened for the weighty footfall on the stairs and then in the room above, and eventually all fell quiet.

She leaned forward to open the firebox door, then sat back, contemplating the dying embers that glowed an ever fainter orange among the grey ashes. The day had been a hard one, first the conversation with the doctor, and then her visit to Princetown. And it wasn't over yet. Surely there had been some sort of mistake? The cheques could both be the result of an error at the bank, but the unpaid bill at the coal merchants seemed too much of a coincidence. It was dated over a week before Henry's accident, so he must have received it before that horrific, fateful day, though it was possible that in his present condition it had totally slipped his mind. But it included not only the enormous delivery at the beginning of the winter, but also lesser amounts they had purchased in the spring and summer; all in all, a considerable sum. Did it really remain unpaid? If so, Mr Richards's attitude was hardly surprising, and he was being quite charitable in letting them have any more at all.

She rose to her feet, silent and floating as if in a dream, and taking up the oil lamp, quietly let herself into the dining room and opened her father's bureau, her fingers trembling as she reached for the growing stack of correspondence she had placed there at Henry's request. She glanced surreptitiously at the door as if she expected someone to enter and catch her red-handed like a thief in the night. But this was her responsibility now, and she had to know the truth.

Slowly, one by one, she unfolded the papers. Any private correspondence she put to one side. The rest . . . Each one made her heart thud harder until her whole body shook and she had to sit down abruptly as the strength emptied out of her in a flood of horror. Bills unpaid, final demands. Not just the two returned cheques for Miss Williams and the butcher's, both of which covered several months of purchases, but the wine merchant's in Tavistock, the shoemakers where she and Henry had each had two pairs of boots made the previous summer, a coat from Henry's tailor, animal feed – for Gospel, of course – and the fine new saddle and the necklace Henry had bought for her twenty-first birthday last June.

She really couldn't believe it. She knew they lived well, but she had always assumed they could afford to! Henry would always smile benevolently at her delight, but the appreciative kisses she bestowed on him were because she *loved* him, not because of what he gave her! How *could* he! How could he possibly get his own finances in such a state when he was such an excellent businessman, as Mr Frean had said on so many occasions? Her dear, *dear* father . . .

Tears of panic, frustration and utter despair pricked at her eyes as she shook her head in disbelief. In her fingers quivered an irate letter from the bank together with a copy of Henry's vastly overdrawn account. She hardly dared open the last document, for she was feeling physically sick and really didn't think she could take another shock. But it wasn't another demand, just a letter from Charles Chadwick.

The relief was so overwhelming that she began to read it without considering that she should never go through anyone's private mail. The neat, precise letters marched across the page like regimented soldiers, their regular form fascinating her eyes before their meaning began to filter into her brain. It had been written shortly before Christmas, commiserating Henry on his terrible accident which he had learnt of from Mr Frean, and saying that he fully understood how Rose's decision would have been put on hold for the time being. Though his heart yearned to be with her again, he would stay away until such time as Henry summoned him. That he felt he loved her more with each day they were apart, and he longed for her to do him the honour of accepting his proposal and allowing him to provide generously for her for the rest of her days.

Ha! The bitter laugh crowed in her aching gullet until her heaving lungs dissolved into racking sobs of misery. So upright, so correct! He'd hardly want her *now* if he knew the truth; that she was the daughter of a debtor; of a man whose crime not so many years ago could have seen him in prison. Oh, no! Not that she returned Mr Chadwick's affection in any way, and she had only entertained the idea of any relationship between them for her father's sake. But *now* . . .!

No. It was time to face facts. To face the stark reality of the cold and hostile world that lay outside the four walls of the solid house. And indeed within it, for three months ago, Henry had been a strong, vigorous man who had made her believe that life was bountiful, and the only problem she had to confront was whether or not to marry a man who was both considerate and rich, but whom she did not love.

Now everything was changed, her comfortable existence swept away from beneath her feet. And she had no idea which way to turn.

'Why didn't you tell me, Father?'

Her voice was soft, compassionate, afraid, hardly more than a whisper fluttering in her throat. She was sitting by Henry's bedside, holding his hand and stroking the skin which had always been brown from exposure to the elements, but was now pale after three months' confinement indoors. Henry lifted his misted eyes to his beloved daughter, his heart stung by the agony on her face.

'I were going to,' he said quietly, a frown of shame dragging on the ugly scarring on his forehead. 'But then . . . *this* happened,' and he waved his other hand towards his legs, 'and I really couldn't bear to. I knew 'twould put so much strain on you. That so much would fall on your shoulders. That you'd have so much to do, things . . . that no daughter should have to do for her father. How could I possibly make it so much worse by telling you the truth? To break it to you that we'd have to sell Gospel, and that were just to start? You love that horse, and because of me, you'd have to sell him.'

Rose had drawn back with a jerk. Sell Gospel! The thought had never crossed her mind! Of all the solutions that had tumbled in her brain, keeping her awake the entire night, selling Gospel was never amongst them. He was part of the family, like Florrie and Joe. And who would buy him anyway? He was a fine animal and worth a great deal if he'd had a temperament to match, but his distrust of the human race and consequent bad temper was immediately apparent to any stranger. It would either be back to the martingale for him, the harsh bit and the whip, or the knacker's yard. The shock pulsed down her body and then settled in the pit of her stomach with all the other horrors that were seething there, waiting to be accepted into her rebellious mind. She inwardly sighed. It was just another nail in the coffin.

'But . . . *why*, Father?' she moaned with a forlorn shake of her head. 'Why were you always giving me so many things if we couldn't afford them? I didn't *need* them. I'd have loved you just as much without.'

Henry's faded blue eyes glistened as a sad smile crinkled them at the corners. 'Yes, I know that, child. But I wanted you to have everything. Everything that I hadn't been able to give your mother. We were young, just starting out in life with little money to spare. Just enough to keep a roof over our heads and to employ Florrie. She were only meant to be temporary, to help your mother for a while when you were born. When Alice died,' his voice quavered, 'I thought I'd lost everything. That my life was over. And then I began to realize that I still had her. In you. You're so like her, you know. To look at, and in character. So I vowed that I would dedicate my life to making you happy. To making up for the fact that you never had a mother. And in doing so, I believed I were doing it for Alice, too.' He paused, and the devoted smile slid from his wan face. 'But it all went wrong. I never meant it to end like this. You've been a wonderful daughter to me, Rosie. No man could ever wish for more. And now I've got to break your heart. And I'm so, *so* sorry.'

Rose had listened, her head bowed, and now she raised her

eyes to him, deep crystal pools of anguish. Her wretched soul was torn by her love for this dear man who had been her life, and who had been cruelly reduced to a helpless cripple. She threw her arms around him, her tears dripping on to his greying hair as she rocked him back and forth.

''Twill be all right, Father, I promise you!' she spluttered between her sobs. 'I don't know *how* yet. But . . . I'll work something out. Just see if I don't!' And even as she spoke, her voice began to tremble, not with dejection, but with outright determination.

Seven

'Did you find Father a little better today, Mr Frean?' Rose smiled optimistically as the elderly gentleman entered the kitchen a few weeks later. She was certainly feeling more cheerful herself, as in that time she had set her plan of campaign in motion, and so far at least it seemed to be working. She had returned the saddle which, lavishly polished over the months she had used it, showed no sign of wear, and though the saddler could not cancel the debt entirely, he had reduced it by more than half. Likewise the jeweller, though she had been angered to see the necklace displayed in the window shortly afterwards at the full price, and no end of hard argument had persuaded him to come down on what he considered she still owed him for the 'loan' of the jewellery. The wine merchant was the only person to take back what remained of Henry's store of bottles at its full value, though she would still owe him a reasonable sum. There was nothing else that could be returned, but she had visited the bank manager, explaining all about Henry's accident and breaking down in wrenching sobs that had melted the poor fellow's heart. The sight of the beautiful, *helpless* young woman weeping wretchedly was really too much for him, since he was not a dispassionate man. For Rose's part, it hadn't been difficult, for though she had planned on play-acting, when it came to it, the appalling discovery of the dire straits of her father's financial affairs had once more grasped her by the throat, and the tears had come naturally. She had explained all the measures she had put in place, the manager suggesting she might also pay a visit to the pawnbroker's, and in the end he had agreed to allow her six months, interest free, to pay off her father's debts.

It wasn't going to be easy. She had deposited at the pawnbroker's everything she possibly could, down to their silver

cutlery and even all but one of her fine dresses and their petticoats and accessories, knowing she would never see them
again. They ate frugally, and no meat would grace their table
until all their debts were paid off. Most painfully, she had told
Florrie that if she wanted to stay on with them, she would no
longer receive any salary. Her cheeks wobbling dejectedly,
the loyal housekeeper had declared she would never leave
them. She only wished that instead of sending her wages over
the years to her widowed sister who had five children to bring
up, she had kept the money so that she could have helped
Rose now. Joe had been told he would have to pay for his
keep, but he was happy with that, knowing he had been on
the receiving end of Henry's generosity since he was a child.
Gospel, for the time being at least, could stay, his speed being
useful in conveying Rose quickly on the numerous errands
she had run in order to gain grace with their creditors. Besides,
she told herself, it would take time to find a buyer for him,
and time was a commodity of which she had very little at the
moment. The oil lamps were replaced with cheap candles, and
those were only lit when they could hardly see where they
were going. In the evenings, she and Florrie would sit, straining
their eyes, by the glow from the open firebox, and Henry,
warmed instead by hot-water bottles filled with water heated
on the range – which by necessity was alight all day – no
longer had a cheering fire in his room. Rose had lit one for
him this morning only because she knew Mr Frean was coming,
and she didn't want him to suspect their drastically impecunious state.

'Won't you take a cup of tea?' she invited him, deliberately
widening her smile when he seemed to hesitate. ''Tis so good
of you to come all this way just to see Father.'

'I don't come *just* to see him, you know, Rose,' he said
solemnly, drawing in his chin. 'I need to keep more of an eye
on the place now that your father is . . . incapacitated. And,'
his mouth twitched awkwardly, 'that's what I need to talk to
you about. So, yes, please. I should like some tea, and perhaps
we can have a little discussion.'

Rose winced as she spooned some fresh tea into the pot,
for they had got into the habit now of reusing the leaves until
they barely coloured the hot water before they were discarded.
She watched Mr Frean from the corner of her eye, her heart

sinking as she observed the sombre expression on his face. She passed him the cup of tea, hoping he didn't notice the tremor in her hand.

'So, how can I help you?' she asked, trying to sound casual as she sat down opposite him and took a sip of the steaming liquid.

George Frean raised a ponderous eyebrow. 'We need to discuss the future, Rose,' he said gravely.

'Oh, 'tis all taken care of. We're going to turn the parlour into a bedroom,' she told him, hoping he thought she sounded bubbling with enthusiasm. 'Some of the men are going to do it on Sunday, and carry Father down. 'Twill be so good for him to be out of the bedroom after all this time. And the dining room will become his office. We're going to bring everything up from his *old* office so that he can run the business from here,' she concluded with a satisfied smile.

Mr Frean sat back in his chair and drew the air through his flared nostrils. 'The manager of the powder mills needs to be on site, you know that, Rose.'

She felt her stomach contract as she nodded with fading confidence. 'Yes, I know, so I'm going to order an invalid carriage,' she announced, though she didn't add that she had no idea how she was going to pay for it. 'And if Polly – that's the mare that pulls the dog cart – is too big, we'll sell her and buy a smaller horse that can pull either. So Father will be able to get over the entire site, wherever he's needed.'

She stopped as Mr Frean lifted his hand in a gesture of reluctance and he slowly shook his head. 'I'm sorry, Rose. I have no doubt that you would make any measures you took work admirably. But I'm afraid it just wouldn't be enough.'

Rose blinked at him as a slick of cold, clammy sweat oozed down her back. 'B-but . . .' she stammered, her chin quivering.

'I really am sorry,' the older man sighed, the lines on his face deepening. 'I know you well enough, Rose. And I'm sure you'd make everything work superbly. As far as it went. But . . . you'd be relying too much on the other men, Mr Ashman for instance. While they were running back and forth here, they wouldn't be doing their own jobs. It is your father's responsibility to inspect the site *personally* all the time, and with the best will in the world, he could not do so from an invalid carriage. He would need a couple of men to lift him in and out of the thing all the time, and that would cost the company time and money it really can't afford. And I know we have an agent as well, but you know as well as I do that your father often has to visit the mines and quarries himself, and that would be impossible.'

Rose had listened, her heart beating tremulously. 'I'm sure Father could manage,' she protested in desperation. In disbelief. 'I could help him. All the time. I could—'

'Rose.' He reached out and squeezed her arm paternally. 'The practicalities of the situation are bad enough in themselves, and no answers you can come up with will ever provide a proper solution. But even if they could, I'm afraid I find . . .' His face twisted with embarrassment and his eyes searched deeply into hers. 'I don't quite know how to put this, but . . . Since his accident, Henry, well . . . he seems a different man. He's made some wrong decisions with regard to the business. Left other matters unresolved. Over all – and I really haven't come to this conclusion lightly – I'm going to have to ask your father to leave my employment.'

Rose lowered her eyes. She couldn't think of any words to say, and even if she could, they would have stuck in her throat. Leave Cherrybrook. She really couldn't believe it. Couldn't *comprehend* the notion of leaving what had been her home for as long as she could remember. She had seen the anguished expression on Mr Frean's face as he spoke, anticipated what he was going to say, and yet his words were too awful to contemplate. Held some dreadful, appalling meaning, and yet meant nothing at all. Her senses reeled away from her, and she managed to hold on to them by some tenuous thread. It wasn't real, and yet here she was, sitting in the kitchen, as familiar to her as her own hand. She remained motionless, silent in one of the grimmest moments of her life, and when she looked up, the violet brilliance had gone from her eyes.

Mr Frean coughed gently, for it broke his heart to be the cause of such misery in this vibrant child he looked upon as his own. 'I can offer you a month's notice,' he managed to say through the enormous lump that had suddenly swelled in his gullet. 'But I've had to stop your father's wages with immediate effect. However, I will be giving you a hundred pounds. Not company money. The repairs after the explosion stretched its finances too much and some of the shareholders aren't too happy. But out of my own pocket. As a token of my esteem for your father and his hard work and loyalty over the years.'

His face had somehow sagged, and Rose was sure she could detect moisture in his concerned eyes. Mr Frean was a good man, and always had been. A surrogate uncle, since she had no other relation but her father. She appreciated his integrity, his generosity in the circumstances. A hundred pounds. It might sound a handsome sum, but, her brain swiftly calculated as her natural determination to survive took over once more, it was roughly twenty weeks of Henry's pay. She had worked out that six months of living sparingly would clear their debts, and that was without any rent to pay, let alone . . . Gospel . . . and Amber . . .

She picked up the teaspoon and slowly stirred the contents of her cup for a second time. She must find it within herself to remain dignified. Not to allow George Frean to guess at their dire financial straits, even though she didn't know which way to turn and her head was exploding with bottomless despair.

'Thank you, Mr Frean,' she answered politely, though her voice was small. ''Tis most kind of you. I'll start looking for somewhere else to live straight away.'

'Have you no relations who might take you in?' he suggested, trying to be helpful, Rose realized.

'Unfortunately, no,' she replied, straightening her shoulders a little haughtily. 'But don't concern yourself. I'm sure we'll manage. 'Tis most kind you've been. But . . . have you told Father?' she asked in dismay, the apprehension taking hold of her again.

Mr Frean looked at her askew. 'I'm afraid I didn't have the courage. And I thought perhaps it would be better coming from you.'

Rose paused. Averted her eyes. Gave an almost imperceptible nod of her head. 'Yes. I'm sure you're right.'

'Well, I must be off.' He rose to his feet, clearly relieved the difficult interview was over. 'Other matters to attend to. But I really am so sorry, Rose. I'll miss you both. But perhaps we can keep in touch.'

'Yes, I'm sure. And I do understand 'tis not your fault.'

'Thank you.' He sniffed slightly as he wriggled into his overcoat. 'I'll see myself out.'

And he was gone, leaving Rose alone in the kitchen. She rested her elbows on the table and dropped her head into her hands. She realized with mild surprise that she was quite calm, not even shaking now. The shock was numbing her mind and her body to the harsh reality about her. She must make plans, decide on the most advantageous way to use the money which her pride would have refused under other circumstances. But first – and God alone knew how – she must break the bitter news to her father.

Rose's head was spinning with calculations as Gospel romped up the soaring hill from Tavistock on to the moor. She had secured the lease of one of the Westbridge Cottages in the town, not a palace but sound and adequate. One shilling and sixpence a week and, unbelievably in her opinion, two and threepence a week for a field and a stable for Gospel, though it was only a few minutes' walk out of the town, so she supposed she would be paying for the convenience of it. Food and fuel on top of that, candles and the occasional extra expense such as shoe repairs or medicines. Having paid off every single creditor with Mr Frean's generous gift, including the overdraft at the bank, scarcely thirty pounds remained, which wouldn't last long, and there was still an invalid chair to purchase, not the pony-drawn carriage she had originally planned, but, thankfully, a cheaper bath chair that she or Florrie could push on the more even surface of Tavistock's streets. The solution to the problem was, of course, quite simple. She would acquire a position, and the three of them – for Florrie was both indispensable and an integral member of the family – could live quite comfortably in the little cottage.

Feeling rather satisfied and even a little excited at the prospect of a new life, she gave Gospel his head. She would miss living in the centre of the moor, where she could lose herself in its boundless sense of infinity. But by keeping Gospel, she could reach its open vastness within minutes. She could still visit Molly and the workers and their families at the powder mills. And at the thought of the few people she would *not* need to see ever again, such as the strait-laced Miss Williams, her nose wrinkled with such distaste that she found herself smiling.

Molly. Her dear friend who at the moment knew nothing of

her enforced leaving of Cherrybrook. It was early March. The snow had melted in the returned prevailing wind, and though the moor was not cloaked in mist, it was a miserable yet mild afternoon. She could not stay long, but she did have time to visit Molly and still be home before darkness closed in.

She passed the recently opened quarry at Merrivale, stopping to make way for a farm wagon crossing the old stone bridge over the river. The quarry was experiencing some teething problems, but it was nevertheless a welcome addition to the powder mills' customer list. Rose's mouth thinned to a fine line. She would have to stop thinking like that, for it really didn't matter any more. Just one moment of . . . of what, they had never discovered – the tiniest granule of grit, perhaps – that had found its way into the circular incorporating trough, despite the stringent rules of cleanliness, and her father's still active life had been shattered, and her own world had come tumbling down about her ears. It would be so easy to give in, to let the tears that so often threatened to choke her, erupt in all their agony. But she gritted her teeth with determined resolve. She would *not* be beaten, and she dug her heels into Gospel's willing flanks as she turned him off the road at Rundlestone and headed towards Princetown. They arrived at a gallop, and as they raced over the tunnel that led beneath the road from the prison lands to the dreaded quarry the memory flashed through her brain of the ugly incident she had become embroiled in there at the end of the previous summer. It all seemed so long ago, so insignificant when she considered the fateful events that had overtaken her life since.

She deposited Gospel, as always, with Ned Cornish, who gave a churlish sneer when she pressed a penny into his greedy palm rather than the usual silver sixpence. It was months since last he had clapped eyes on her graceful figure that caused the crotch of his trousers to strain, though he had of course heard of her father's misfortune. Such an explosion at the powder mills had been the talk of Princetown for weeks. He watched her hurry down the road in the direction of the prison. If only matters would become *really* desperate for her, he mused malevolently, he could offer her some sort of solace, for his bed was always warm . . .

She found Molly, her mother and little Phillip proudly sitting by the glowing fire in the sitting room of their home in the new warders' block, one of the first families to move in, since the building wasn't entirely finished yet. A mug of weak black tea was at once thrust into Rose's hands. She had always hated the drink served like that, but now she hardly noticed, since she, too, had become accustomed to doing without milk and sugar. It was hot and wet, and she was thankful for that.

'How's your poor father?' Mrs Cartwright asked with genuine sympathy. She was a timid woman, but she always found it easy to speak with Rose Maddiford. There was something changed, though, in the girl's normal effervescence. Could you wonder at it, mind, after what had happened?

'He's quite well in himself, thank you,' she lied, as ever since she had broken the news to Henry that they would have to leave Cherrybrook, he had . . . *shrivelled* was the best way to describe it. 'But,' she hesitated, girding up the courage to sound quite cheerful, 'he's decided to retire from his work.' Her eyes caught Molly's quizzical gaze, and she knew at once that her friend could see straight through the deception. ''Tis not fair on his men,' she went on, looking down at the chipped mug in her hands. 'I've found a nice little cottage in Tavistock for us to live in. With Florrie, of course. 'Twill be good for Father to be in a town with lots of things going on.' She glanced up, smiling broadly, and got to her feet. 'I just thought as I'd let you know. I'll still be able to come and see you, mind. I've somewhere to keep Gospel, too, you see. Thank you for the tea, Mrs Cartwright. I'll . . . I'll see you soon.'

She bolted for the door. She hadn't meant her visit to be quite so short, but she found it so hard to keep the truth from these people who had been her friends for so long.

Her spirits dropped down inside her as Molly sprang to her side. 'I'll come with you, Rose,' she announced, grasping a worn coat from the peg by the door.

Molly followed Rose down the steps to the street, and Rose quickly changed the subject. 'You must be so happy to be in your new home at last,' she said.

'Oh, yes!' Molly enthused. 'With Father being a principal warder, 'tis why we were almost the first to move in.'

'I'm so pleased for you all,' Rose answered, but her words were flat and uninterested. 'And how's Annie getting on?'

But Molly glanced at her sideways as they walked up the street arm in arm. 'I knows when you'm not telling the truth, Rose.'

They stopped. Rose's mouth screwed into a pout, but it was no good. They had been friends for too long. Rose looked into Molly's shrewd green eyes, and her heart jerked.

''Tis the truth,' she muttered evasively. 'Except that . . .' She turned to Molly, her face working desperately. 'Please, Molly, I beg you not to tell anyone, but . . . Father never made any financial plans for his old age. He expected to go on working for years more . . .'

Her voice was ragged now with despondency, and Molly squeezed her arm tightly. 'Of course. No one expects . . . So, what you means is,' she said gently, 'you've no money.'

Rose threw up her head. 'Not quite. We do have *some* money.' Which wasn't a lie. Twenty-eight pounds eleven shillings and ninepence three farthings, to be precise. 'But if I want to keep Gospel, I shall need to find a position.'

The silence that followed cut into Rose's heart like a spear, and then Molly's incredulous face dissolved in laughter. '*You*, Rose!' she spluttered helplessly. 'A position!'

Rose's eyes snapped with offence. 'What's so funny about that? I'm not afraid of hard work, you know!'

'Oh, yes, I knows that,' Molly agreed, struggling to control her giggles. 'You'm my best friend and I loves you dearly, but I cas'n see you buttoning your lip like you has to if you has a *position*!'

'Oh, Molly, we *will* always be best friends, won't we?' Rose begged, her brow furrowed. 'No matter what happens?'

'Of course we will! And I'll keep you up to date with all the local gossip,' Molly promised earnestly. And then her expression changed, her eyes sparkling. 'I'll even tell you what's been happening with your convict!' she teased lightly.

'My *convict*?' Rose gawped at her in bewilderment, though even as she spoke, the vague recollection tugged once more at her memory. 'What do you mean?'

'Oh, 'twere back along, but you must remember! He saved Father from being attacked, and then *you* saved *him*, cuz the guards thought as 'twere him.'

'Yes, I do remember something,' Rose muttered with a frown, for as far as she was concerned, it was a nasty incident she would rather forget.

'Well,' Molly went on, lowering her voice as if they were entering into some great conspiracy, 'apparently, shortly afterwards, he were set upon by some of the inmates cuz of it. 'Tis not what you does, protect a warder. Father's in charge of him, see. Been giving him as many marks as he can towards his ticket of leave, so as he'll be released early, you knows. 'Tis cuz he's strong and works hard. Swears he's innocent, and that he can prove it. Can you imagine that, Rosie? Seems quite educated, Father says. Does as he's telt, and keeps to hissel. 'Tis why he's not popular with other prisoners. Beat up quite bad, he were.'

'Poor fellow,' Rose sighed, but there was an ironic twist to her lips. She supposed she should feel some sympathy at Molly's tale of injustice, but really she had far more pressing concerns to trouble her just now. Besides, the prisoner wouldn't be the first to claim he was innocent of whatever crime it was that had resulted in his being a guest at Dartmoor's largest hotel! Rose knew that if Molly's father had a penny for every time he'd heard such a thing, he'd be a very rich man indeed!

Eight

'We *will* be happy there, Father, I *promise* you,' she said tenderly, her voice torn with emotion as she stroked Henry's hand. His faded eyes had misted over as he stared blindly into the empty grate, something he had spent more and more time doing since she had told him of George Frean's decision a few days ago now. It worried her more than anything, for what did he see there? The flames that once would have burned, orange and red, against the black cast iron, or the life when he could walk and run, and keep up with men half his age?

He turned his head to her, his face radiant with some quiet serenity that belied the moisture in his eyes, and yet spoke of excruciating sadness. 'How could I be anything but happy with you, my dearest child?' he whispered, and Rose thought she would gag on the sorrow in her throat. This was her father, always so strong, so vibrant, reduced to a feeble wreck, and it was just so *unfair*.

'I won't be there all the time,' she frowned. 'I shall have to find myself a position. But Florrie will be there, so 'twill be just like living here really,' she added, her tone brighter now. 'Better, in fact, because you'll have your bed in the nice, warm front kitchen, and you won't be lonely like you are up here.'

She must have aroused his interest, for his expression sharpened. 'A job? Well, that would be a change for you. What sort of job?'

'Well,' she declared, his enthusiasm pleasing her immensely, as it seemed to have plucked him from his apathy, 'I've been looking in the *Tavistock Gazette*. There are two positions as governess advertised, both in the town, so either would be most convenient. I'm going to write to them tonight.'

Henry nodded his approval, his mouth smiling wistfully.

'Who'd have thought it, eh? My little princess going out to work?'

'I shall go into Princetown first thing in the morning to post them,' she told him emphatically as she stood up. 'And whilst I'm there, I'll have a word with the carrier. Arrange for him to take all our furniture to the cottage. And find out how much he'll charge,' she added with a rueful grimace.

'Furniture?' Henry's reply came with a swiftness that took her by surprise.

'Well, yes,' she answered, her brow knitted in confusion. 'We'll have to decide what to leave behind, mind. There won't be room for all of it at the cottage.'

'Rose, dear, the furniture isn't ours to take.'

'What?' She blinked at him, her neck stiffened with that horrible coldness she was becoming used to.

'Some of it is,' Henry went on, but the expression on his face told of his shame. 'Your pretty washstand, but I imagine you remember me buying that for you. My bureau, the rugs in each room. The octagonal table and the corner one in the parlour. The grandfather clock. Oh, and Florrie's rocking chair. I bought that for her on her fortieth birthday,' he mused. 'She was so delighted . . . But everything else came with the house. The carpets, the beds and wardrobes, the furniture in the parlour and dining room, the kitchen table . . . The linen, the cutlery and crockery, all that sort of thing is ours, mind,' he added more cheerily. 'The lamps, the pictures on the walls, the china figurines. You'll be able to make this cottage you've found look quite lovely.'

Rose had slowly lowered herself into the chair again, a chair that probably wasn't theirs either. Henry didn't know, but the handsome pictures, the china, had already gone to the pawnbroker's, and now she had learnt they didn't own most of what they *really* needed either. The essentials. Beds, for instance. She could manage on a home-made straw mattress on the floor, but Florrie could hardly be expected . . . And Henry himself . . . Oh, it was just one more agony to cope with! Her tense lungs collapsed in a bitter sigh, and she shook her head. The money they had left would have to cover at least two beds and the bath chair, and anything else that they really could not do without. She had hoped to put aside most of the small sum for a rainy day, in an interest-bearing account, perhaps, to supplement her wages. And as yet, she didn't even *have* a position!

'Now you put your feet in that, young lady!' Florrie ordered, stirring a great spoonful of mustard into the bowl of hot water that she had placed on the floor by Rose's chair. ''Tis a miracle you found your way home in that blizzard, and it coming on dark and all. We had visions of finding you froze dead in the morning, like that schoolmaster back in sixty-five. Your poor father's been frit witless, as if he hasn't got enough to contend with!'

'Oh, Florrie, I'm so sorry you were so worried,' Rose croaked. Her throat was raw from breathing in the icy wind that had ripped across Dartmoor as she had battled her way home from Tavistock. 'But I know the moor like the back of my hand. Even in the snow, there are landmarks along the way, but I must say, if it had been coming down much harder, I wouldn't have been able to see where I was going.'

'And you've only been in five minutes, and 'tis already total darkness, Rose Maddiford! You shouldn't have been so tardy!'

'Really, Florrie, I was perfectly safe, honestly I was!'

Nevertheless, she lowered her cold, wet feet gratefully into the water. Perfectly safe, indeed! It had been an absolute nightmare and she had been petrified, but she didn't want to alarm poor Florrie any more than she already had. She had only reached halfway up Pork Hill when winter had returned with a vengeance. The snow had begun to fall thick and fast, the sky an all-encompassing white dome that was hell-bent on smothering the earth beneath. The further out on to the moor she went, the wilder the driving wind that whipped the snow into deep drifts and lashed mercilessly into Rose's face. The flakes collected on her eyelashes, blinding her, and she had to keep dashing them away as she peered into the growing gloom. She had taken Polly and the dog cart rather than riding Gospel as she could hardly arrive for an interview as a governess dressed in her riding habit. The wheels of the cart kept getting stuck in the deepening snow, and Rose ended up walking by Polly's side to help the poor animal. She would have been better off on foot, she had thought ruefully, though Polly was company on the deserted road, which was becoming increasingly difficult to follow in the blanketing whiteness.

Three attempts it had taken her to light the hurricane lamp, the gale extinguishing the flame each time she struck a match. Once lit, she had stumbled on, holding it in one hand whilst the other held Polly's reins, sometimes stopping to lift it high and get her bearings.

At last, way across to the right, the unmistakable sight of the tiny gas lights glowing from the massive new prison block, row upon row of small cell windows, pinpricks, like stars in the gathering shadows. Downhill and over the river at Two Bridges and the Saracen's Head. Not so far now, but she hadn't seen a soul for what must have been an hour, and she really was beginning to panic. Desperate, soaked to the skin with icy damp, snow on her shoulders, in her eyes and in her mouth, every taut muscle screaming, tears of fear and despair turning to frost on her cheeks. Somehow, she had struggled on, and when the lights of Cherrybrook had come into view, she had shouted aloud with relief.

'Hmm!' Florrie snorted as she bustled round the kitchen, adding extra coal to the firebox, and wrapping Rose in layers of warm blankets as she still shivered in the chair. 'Well, I hope 'twas worthwhile, and you got yoursel a *position*!' she added with a strange emphasis on the last word as if to say it was hardly worth risking one's life for in a blizzard!

Rose's eyes darted upwards, her still blue lips puckering into a knot. She said nothing, but Florrie tilted her double chin, and Rose knew she had understood. She couldn't bear to tell Florrie that the first interview had been a total disaster. The second had resulted in her being offered the post, but it was live-in with a salary that wouldn't cover the rent for the cottage and the field, let alone anything else. The lady of the house had been most sympathetic to Rose's situation, but was not in the position to offer anything more. Rose had then made other enquiries as to employment in the town, but had drawn a blank in every direction.

'Oh, well, never mind, my pet,' Florrie said gently. 'Summat will turn up. Now then, you get this inside you.' And she thrust a mug of steaming tea into Rose's shaking hands. 'I'll go upstairs and get you some dry clothes. Oh, this came for you this morning after you left.'

She dropped an envelope into Rose's lap and waddled out through the door. Rose slumped back in the chair, trying to relax and stop the painful tremors that rattled her teeth in her head. Her muscles, her arms, her legs, her back and especially her neck ached viciously. If only she could calm them into submission, but beneath it lay the bitter gall of defeat. She sipped at the hot black tea, feeling its warmth seeping into her flesh. Oh, that was good, but . . . what *was* she to do?

She idly turned over the envelope. She prayed to God it wasn't another bill, something else her father had bought and never paid for. Her heart was soothed when she realized it was a private letter, and then tripped over itself when she saw it was from none other than Mr Charles Chadwick. Good Lord, she hadn't even given him a thought in weeks – months even – for it had been . . . when? About Christmas he had written last, and she had never had the time or the inclination to reply. Indeed, it hadn't even crossed her mind, and even now her eyes moved uninterestedly along the lines of writing, scarcely taking in their meaning. And then . . . something stirred within her and as she read the words a second time, a sudden light shone its way into her brain.

When Florrie came back into the kitchen, she was surprised to see her young charge deep in concentration over the sheets of paper – for there were several of them – in her hand. And when Rose finally lifted her head, there was a strange expression on her face Florrie could not quite fathom.

Nine

'**M**r Chadwick!'

Rose's startled eyes stretched as she answered the polite knock on the front door. Her surprise was followed by an unfurling kernel of apprehension and then of excitement that tingled down to her fingertips. It was less than a week since she had staggered home in the blizzard, dragging herself miles through the deepening snow, numbed with the piercing cold and wondering if she would survive. The following morning had dawned crisp and clear, the sun shining down in glittering ripples on the newly fallen snow and turning the landscape into a magical wonderland. The nightmare of the previous evening had seemed just that, a hideous, unreal nightmare, and Rose's head had filled with a clarity as sharp as the new day. She had read Charles Chadwick's letter with a fresh heart. It was kind, concerned and caring, and full of his tender love for her. Had she misjudged him, dismissed his affections simply because he did not share all her views on life? Surely the most loving of spouses must disagree on something! And so, with the deepest reflection, she had taken up her pen.

She must word the letter carefully. Their impecunious state must not be immediately apparent. After all, she didn't want him to think she was marrying him for his money. Besides which, it would not altogether be true. She had agonized long and hard over his original proposal. He was polite, respectable, most attentive, not unattractive and appreciated her love of Dartmoor, to whose charms he was not insensitive himself. Most important of all, he liked to ride. Surely, considered in that light, the passion she had spoken of to her father would come in time? And even if it didn't, they should be able to live peaceably enough. And if she closed her eyes and imagined her father wasting away in the workhouse, well, she was positive she would make Mr Chadwick a good wife!

And now here he was, standing on the doorstep at ten o'clock in the morning, his eyes brilliant with delight and his face positively glowing. 'Oh, my dearest Rose!' His voice sang out like a bird's. He took her hands in his gloved ones, his gaze boring deep into her astonishment. Stepping inside so that she was obliged to take a pace backwards, he removed his hat and placed it on the hall stand, still holding tightly on to her other hand and his eyes scarcely leaving her face. His left hand instantly returned to her right, and then he lifted both of hers to his lips, kissing each in turn, not in a sensuous manner, but in a boyish gesture of pure joy. It was in such contrast to the utterly proper and restrained conduct she had known from him during his courtship the previous autumn that it chased away all Rose's doubts, and her mouth opened in an amused laugh.

'Oh, my dear, I could not keep away for a moment!' Charles told her, his words falling over themselves in his haste to say them as quickly as he possibly could. 'I received your letter the day before yesterday – was it only then? It seems such a long time ago! And I thought, surely I could get here as quickly as a letter, and my poor heart could not wait to be with you again! So I caught the morning train from Paddington yesterday and arrived in Tavistock at six o'clock last night. But I could find no cab willing to venture so far on to the moor in the dark, so here I am now! I telegraphed ahead to the Duchy Hotel, and the fellow is to take my baggage there now,' he explained, waving his hand back towards the open door and the carriage that was turning round outside. 'But I trust my presence would not inconvenience you today?'

His forehead had ruched with consternation, his eyebrows drawn together in such earnest that Rose chuckled aloud. His unexpected arrival was like a whirlwind whipping away the fetid air of misery that had stagnated in the wretched household all winter, and it had left Rose breathless. Oh, surely, *surely* she had made the right decision!

'Oh, Mr Chadwick, I am *truly* delighted to see you!' she smiled, the strength of her own feelings confounding her. 'Do come in! To the kitchen, if you don't mind. Florrie – Mrs Bennett – and I have such a lot to do caring for Father that we don't bother with the other rooms any more.'

The false excuse cast but a fleeting shadow in her conscience as she found herself almost skipping around her visitor. She led him – since he had not relinquished her hand – down the hallway, and his expression shone with that almost foolish state of a man enraptured by love. Kitchen? Just now, he would have followed her to a hole in the ground!

'Oh, Rose, seeing as we are to be married,' he breathed excitedly, 'could we not hang propriety, at least when we are alone? Could you not call me by my given name?'

The word 'married' made her heart flip over. Charles was lingering indecisively in the doorway, his usual confidence seeming to forsake him, unaware that his conduct was endearing him to Rose's soul. He really did seem a different person from the suitor she had deliberated over for so long, and she began to curse herself for putting off her decision, for it would have saved her so much heartache.

She turned to face him, her eyes smiling their warm, lavender blue. 'Charles,' she said, her lips savouring the sound. And before her brain gave her time to consider, she raised herself on tiptoe, and Charles, so naturally, brought his mouth softly down to meet hers. She caught the faint aroma of cigar smoke on his breath, more distinct to her now since her father had not smoked since the accident, but she found it not unpleasant, since it must be a good-quality, sweet tobacco he favoured. The unfamiliar sensation of someone else's lips on hers rippled down to her stomach, and when they finally parted and she sank her weight back on to her heels, she gazed up at him, wide-eyed. He was smiling back at her, his eyes crinkled at the corners and skittering about her face as if trying to imprint indelibly in his mind every detail of their first kiss.

'Er . . . will you have some tea?' she stuttered, her eyes sweeping about the kitchen. 'Or coffee, if we have any. We've had heavy snow. 'Tis almost melted now, as you see, but I haven't been able to go into Princetown to shop.' Not the real reason, of course, but a valid enough excuse.

'No, thank you. Tea would be fine.'

Charles was standing awkwardly, and Rose flapped a hand towards the table. 'Won't you sit down? Charles?' she added with a merry lift of her eyebrows. 'Florrie's upstairs,' she went on as he obediently settled himself in a chair, 'seeing to Father, so we can have a moment or two to ourselves.'

Charles's face at once sobered. 'Your poor father,' he stated gravely. 'I really can't imagine how he must feel.'

Rose bowed her head, biting her lip at the sudden, over-whelming desire to cry. Perhaps, after all these months of having to be so strong, the relief of having someone to turn to at last was letting the strain flow out of her in one furious torrent. And Charles was being so kind that she was begin-ning to curse herself for hesitating so long.

She gulped down her tears. 'Yes, it has affected him greatly. But I'm sure 'twill help him tremendously when he can get out and about again.'

'And to know that his beautiful daughter is to be married to a man who adores her!' Charles's shining eyes met hers across the table.

Rose averted her gaze. 'I . . . I haven't told him yet,' she faltered. 'I mean, I thought as 'twas best to await your defi-nite reply first. But . . . here you are in person.'

'Well, shall we go up? If you don't think he'll mind my presence in his bed chamber? When Mrs Bennett has finished, of course. But in the meantime . . .'

He stood up, and coming around to Rose, drew a small package from his pocket. She knew what was coming, and her heart reared away. For this was the moment. There would be no going back, and she was inwardly bracing her daunted spirit.

Charles took her trembling left hand, and slid the exquisite ring on to her slender third finger. She felt the breath leave her body. Not so much at the beauty of the piece, but at what it meant.

'A diamond for my eternal love, and two sapphires to match your eyes. Though yours have a hint of violet in them no jewel could ever rival.'

He was indeed studying her eyes with an unsettling inten-sity that forced her to look away and turn her attention back to the ring. 'Oh, Charles, 'tis beautiful. Thank you so much.'

'It is but a token of my love. And in return, I wish us to be married as soon as possible.' Rose glanced up at the change in his voice. It was somehow less passionate, effi-cient, and it sent the misgivings wavering through her breast. But surely he was right. There were many plans to be made. 'I stayed last night at the Bedford Hotel,' Charles went on, 'and got talking to some gentlemen at dinner. They have told

me of a property near Princetown called Fencott Place which
is up for sale. Originally built as a somewhat grand farmhouse, apparently. By a wealthy friend of your Sir Thomas
Tyrwhitt, inspired by him to try and reclaim some moorland.
But as you told me, all that failed and it's just a residence
now. From what these gentlemen said, I think it would suit
our needs adequately. It has several bedrooms, servants' attic,
and enough space for your father to have a bedroom and a
dayroom on the ground floor. I imagine it will be your wish
that he lives with us? What say we go and have a look at it
later on? There is some land available with it to be leased
from the Duchy, so there'll be plenty of room for that
monstrous horse of yours, and a stable block. So, what do
you say?'

Rose was gawping at him quite rudely, she realized, and
had to snap her mouth closed before it broadened into a joyous
grin. Oh, it seemed the answer to her prayers!

'Oh, Charles! Are you sure?' she barely had the breath to
whisper.

'Well, I knew you'd want to remain living on the moor,'
he attempted to shrug, but couldn't stop his lips curving
upwards. 'But I would ask that you accompany me to London
on occasion. I realize that we must be apart for certain periods,
as my business concerns are mainly in London, but it will
make our time together even more precious. I wish that we
could live together in London, but I appreciate it would not
suit you, and that you will want to be near to your father in
his . . . condition. But you will allow me to show off my
lovely young wife to my colleagues in London just occasionally,
I trust?'

His eyes were dancing roguishly, and the colour blushed
into Rose's cheeks. 'We . . . you can afford all this?' she
managed to croak before blurting out shamefully, 'I . . . I have
no dowry, no money to bring into our marriage, you know.'

But Charles merely shook his head. 'What you will bring
into our marriage is priceless. And, dear Rose, I am a rich
man. I have plenty of money. And I've never had a better
reason to spend some of it. And I want you to have the most
beautiful dress for your wedding. *Our* wedding.' He had taken
her hands again, kissing them reverently, and was clearly about
to take her in his arms when Florrie pushed her way into the

room, carrying a heavy bowl of dirty water, so that when Charles swiftly turned and took her arm, it nearly slopped over the brim.

'Oh, Mr Chadwick, what on earth do you be doing yere?' she mumbled in surprise.

'Rose has agreed to marry me!' Charles crowed ecstatically. 'Isn't that wonderful, Mrs Bennett?'

Rose felt the doubt sear into her heart at the shuttered look that came across Florrie's face.

'Charles, I should be grateful if you would allow my daughter and me a few moments alone,' Henry said five minutes later, his voice perfectly polite though perhaps a little dry, Rose considered, but at least her news had lifted him from the apathy he had been wallowing in of late. 'I'm sure Mrs Bennett will make you comfortable downstairs.'

'Of course. I understand.' Charles tipped his head in an almost military style bow, but he could not conceal the happiness that radiated from his face and he smiled broadly across at Rose, a smile that she returned with enthusiasm, before he left the room. Rose listened as he tripped lightly down the stairs, and then she sat down on the edge of the bed, her mouth still stretched in a grin.

'Well, Father?'

Henry drew in his breath. 'Rose, I'm not happy about this.'

The jubilation slid from her face. 'Father?' she frowned.

Henry pursed his lips. 'Why this sudden change of heart? No, don't answer that. 'Tis because of our changed circumstances, isn't it? Without Mr Chadwick's money, we will be penniless, or at best, living hand to mouth. I won't have it, Rose. I won't have you marrying someone you don't love because of me. You must do what is right for *you*. Forget about me! Take the position with that nice family in Tavistock that you found.'

Rose met his gaze for a moment and then lowered her eyes, chewing on her fingernail. 'Yes, 'tis true,' she answered hoarsely. ''Tis our changed circumstances as you put it that made me reconsider. And you know, Father, I'm *glad*!' She turned to him again, her eyes lit with a curious brilliance. 'You know how hard I found it to turn Charles down before. How I just couldn't make up my mind. Well, this has all just made me realize my true feelings. I can't tell you how happy it made me to find Charles on the doorstep just now! I really am doing the right thing, I'm sure of it!'

But Henry was looking at her from under fiercely swooped eyebrows. 'The right thing? What happened to that passion you spoke about so eloquently not so long ago? What happened to *love*?'

'Oh, I do believe I love Charles,' she assured him, vigorously nodding her head. 'Especially now I can see things in their proper perspective. I shall make him a good wife, and you can see how he is devoted to me. Fencott Place will be a wonderful home for us, just you wait and see!'

'There's more to marriage than a wonderful home,' Henry persisted, his tone more solemn than Rose had ever known. 'Friendship, trust. And have you . . . have you thought about children?'

His voice had become oddly husky, but Rose turned his wariness aside. 'Oh, yes!' she cried with elation. 'I should love to have Charles's children! And you'll be their beloved grandfather!'

Henry studied her exultant expression, and then he puffed out his cheeks with a reluctant sigh. 'Well, you're twenty-one, so I can't stop you. But I do hope you know what you're doing! I only want what's best for you, my child, you know that.'

'Yes, I know you do!' She flung her arms about his neck, hugging him tightly. 'We'll all be so happy, I'm sure we will!'

Henry patted her back, his pale eyes misted. He prayed to God she was right!

'Oh, Rosie, 'tis . . .'tis proper lovely!' Molly breathed, twisting this way and that on the seat of the wagon in order to take in every detail, every angle, of the building that was Fencott Place. 'I mean, I've seen it many times afore from a distance, but you cas'n see it properly cuz of the wall and the trees. And 'tis so big!'

'Well, 'tis grander than Tor Royal,' Rose conceded modestly, but she could not contain her buoyant grin for more than an instant. 'But you shall see every inch of it in a minute!' she laughed, dangling the keys tantalizingly in front of her friend's nose.

She swivelled round to climb down from the wagon, but Joe Tyler had already jumped down from the other side and come round to offer her his hand. She took it with a lively chuckle, thanking him with a jaunty flick of her head as they played the game, for hadn't all three of them been friends for years! Rose waited patiently, straightening her skirts, since she had retrieved her good dresses from the pawnbroker's. Charles would expect her to dress like a lady at all times, so she thought she might as well start now! She turned, just in time to catch the blush in Molly's cheeks as Joe helped her down from the high seat.

For some strange reason she could not herself fathom, Rose whipped about and stood with her back to them, feasting her eyes instead on the house that was to be her marital home. It was a mild spring day, a sea of daffodils in the borders against the dressed-stone walls bobbing their heads in the light breeze, and grape hyacinths coming into bud amongst them. Her heart gave a jerk as Molly appeared at her shoulder, and driving her qualms to the deepest recess of her mind, she linked her arm through Molly's as they waltzed up to the double front door.

'This hallway's bigger than the whole of our flat!' Molly gasped, craning her neck in every direction as they stepped inside. 'And 'tis so light and airy! Oh, Rose, you'm so lucky! Mr Chadwick must be so rich! A real gentleman! But then, only a gentleman'd be right for you! I told you you should marry 'en, didn't I? Oh, I be that pleased for you!'

She enfolded Rose in her arms, jumping up and down and dancing her round in circles until Rose was helpless with laughter. Oh, *of course* Molly was right! As they spun around the spacious hallway, the uncertain figure of Joe standing in the doorway flashed past her eyes, and when they came to a giddy halt, she waved playfully at him.

'Oh, do come on in, Joe! There's only us three here, so make yourself at home! Wander round wherever you please! Go and have a look at the stables if you like. I'm going to open some windows and let some air in whilst we're here.'

Joe's crystal blue eyes shone with admiration. 'Yes, thanks, Rose, I will. But first, where would you like me to put the things you've brought over?'

'Upstairs, if you wouldn't mind, Joe. Turn right along the landing, and 'tis the door facing you at the far end. You can't miss it! 'Tis the biggest room up there, with a dressing room *and* a bathroom going off. There's another door to the bathroom directly on to the landing,' she explained to Molly as Joe went back out to the wagon. ''Tis so as when you've finished bathing and gone back into the bedroom, the servants can empty the dirty water without going through the bedroom.'

Molly shook her head with a fit of giggling. 'Oh, my! And how many servants does ma'am have exactly?'

Rose pulled a mocking face. 'I don't know yet. There's several servants' rooms in the attic. I'll show you in a minute. Now this is the morning room, but we've builders coming tomorrow and they're going to divide it into two for Father, so as he can have a bedroom and a dayroom. He'll have a lovely view out over the moor. Then there's the kitchen and scullery through there, the library – Charles will use that as a study for his business affairs – and the dining room and a drawing room.'

Molly put her lips together and whistled. 'I think I'd lose myself in a place like this! You'll need so much to fill it!'

'Well, once we have some beds, Father and Florrie and I can move in! Charles has told me to buy everything we need, so I wondered if you'd come with me, Molly, to visit some furniture makers in Tavistock and help me choose?'

'I'd be honoured!' Molly's face stretched incredulously. 'But won't Mr Chadwick want to choose hissel?'

''Tisn't really practical. He's trying to arrange his affairs in London so as he can have a complete fortnight down here for the wedding.'

'And when is the big day?' Molly marvelled.

'First week in June.'

'And doesn't you miss him, with him being so far away?'

Rose felt her heart tear harshly. She did miss Charles. But did she miss him as much as she should?

'Yes, of course,' she told Molly, but as much to answer herself as her dear friend. 'But there's so many exciting things to do in such a short time that I really don't get a chance to miss him too much. And he will be coming down for a few days soon. Staying at the Duchy Hotel, of course,' she added as an afterthought.

''Twould be bad luck otherwise!' Molly observed with a grin that Rose couldn't quite comprehend.

'Well, come on, Molly. There's still so much for you to see!'

She led the way, proudly, but sharing her joy in the house with Molly and watching the wonderment on the younger girl's face. There was something she would ask Molly, but not yet. She wanted Molly to get used to being at Fencott Place first, for she mustn't frighten her away, and besides, she must ask Charles's approval, though she was sure he would agree.

They spent more than an hour exploring every nook and cranny, making plans and mental lists, suggesting colours and designs, basking in a new-found fantasy world neither of them had ever dreamed of. Joe waited patiently for them, sitting up on the wagon, long legs dangling casually as he enjoyed his free Sunday afternoon. After all, he had nothing better to do, and just now he was finding it increasingly pleasant to be in the company of one young lady in particular, even if they had known each other since childhood.

At last, the two girls' heads were so brimming with ideas that they were feeling dizzy, and they agreed they should leave before they exploded! Molly scampered down the sweeping staircase, leaving Rose to shut all the upstairs windows. Rose cast one final glance around the massive empty bedroom she would share with Charles Chadwick, and a shudder of uneasiness shot down her spine.

She descended the stairs slowly. Regally. And stopped in the hallway. Molly had left the double front door wide open, and out on the driveway, Joe had hopped down from the wagon and was holding both of Molly's hands in his. They were standing so close, Joe's fair curls clinging about his head in the sunshine, and Molly's face lifted eagerly to his as if they would kiss.

A spasm of pain twitched at Rose's lips. The couple outside appeared so natural, the fondness between them so fitting. And wasn't that what Rose had once felt, that she wanted to marry someone she felt so at ease with? Someone more like Joe, for example?

And now she was to marry Charles Chadwick.

Ten

Rose stood, and trembled, on the threshold of Princetown chapel, her face so pale that her skin had taken on the patina of ivory to match the glorious silk gown that clung about her slender figure and cascaded down over the small bustle in a frothy effusion of ribbons and lace. The organist deftly slipped from the subdued background medley into the rousing wedding march that boomed within the echoing walls and resounded like thunder in Rose's head. Her heart was crashing painfully in her chest and all she wanted was to pick up the hem of the splendid dress and flee. But a multitude of awestruck eyes had turned upon her, the entire community from the powder mills and many people from Princetown filling both sides of the church.

Charles had invited a mere handful of acquaintances from London to witness his marriage to this country bumpkin. Moreover, the church had been seriously damaged by fire several years previously, and being just a chapel-at-ease, lack of funds meant that it had only been partly restored. Signs of the fire were clearly visible, and Charles had protested that they should be married in Tavistock's lovely parish church instead. But Rose was adamant that her friends would find it difficult to travel so far, and Charles had not been able to refuse her pleas, even if he was reluctant to allow his own guests to see him married in a burnt-out shell, as he put it. But if they had questioned his sanity over his choice of bride, the instant they gazed on her ethereal beauty, they too fell under her spell. Her shape beneath the closely fitting garment was magnificent, and as she lifted her chin, her eyes spangled sapphire with determination. She was resplendent, and there was no man present who could honestly claim he was not a little envious of Charles Chadwick that day.

Rose squared her shoulders and glanced up at the bursting

pride on George Frean's face. She smiled faintly, her cheeks
frosted, as he walked her majestically down the aisle. He must
have sensed her nervousness, as he patted her hand as it rested
in the crook of his arm. Every nerve in her body quivered,
but surely every bride had cold feet at the last moment? The
question tore at her brain for one final time, and was then
answered as her father, elegant and distinguished in a new
suit, was wheeled forward in his spanking-new invalid chair
to be at her side at the altar to give her away to her waiting
bridegroom. Her father would want for nothing. He would
live out his life, crippled but in luxury, and that was all Rose
needed.

The thought set strength flowing through her veins. Henry
was looking up at his beautiful daughter, smiling though she
could see tears welling in his tired eyes. Rose shot him her
most confident, reassuring smile, and then as her gaze fell
upon the groom, the tense knot in her chest uncurled. Charles's
adoring eyes were riveted on her, his face not so much smiling
as stunned, enraptured by her loveliness, his mouth slightly
open and totally stilled as if she had taken the breath from
him. He looked so handsome, his deep chestnut hair brushed
until it shone, his figure trim in its grey morning suit, every
inch of him overflowing with obvious devotion to his radiant
bride. Rose dipped her head demurely, her long lashes resting
for a moment on her pearly cheeks. Charles Chadwick loved
her passionately, and if she did not return his feelings with
quite such intensity, there was still enough love between them
to make a happy marriage.

Her voice lodged in her throat as she made her vows. Beside
her, Charles's words were low and pronounced with reverence, and as he placed the ring on her finger, she noted with
some sort of comforting content that his hands, too, were
shaking. They moved to the vestry, Rose floating as if in a
dream. Some light banter with the vicar as she signed her
single name for the last time. The organ struck up once again
as they walked back down the aisle arm in arm, the clam-
orous tones swelling the air with deafening sound, and when
they stepped outside, the bells were pealing vigorously from
their smoke-blackened tower. A sea of beaming faces then,
guests shaking the groom's hand, and who could not resist
kissing the cheek of the heavenly bride? She could not help

but smile broadly at so many well-wishers, her countenance a picture of elation. As they climbed into the ornate open carriage pulled by two superb dapple-grey horses, she turned to the crowd. Her violet-blue eyes searched out her father, but he was lost to her in the milling throng. Instead her gaze landed upon Molly's grinning face, Joe beside her, waving his hat merrily at the bride, his other arm around the pretty girl at his side. And Rose felt the thorn prick her heart at their happiness.

The wedding breakfast was held at the marital home. A string quartet played softly in the corner of the drawing room, and a sumptuous meal was set out in the dining room. Rose sat at the table, glowing modestly between her husband and her father. On Henry's other side, Mrs Frean was warm elegance personified, with Mr Frean on her right. Rose was acquainted with no one else, as they were all friends of Charles's from London, and she struggled to remember their names. All of them polite, and most of them not unfriendly, the meal passed quite pleasantly and Rose felt her uneasiness melt away. She could hold her own in the conversation, aware of Charles's approval beside her, and she felt proud that she had pleased him. She only wished that Florrie and Molly and Joe had been present. She had invited them, but they had declined, preferring to enjoy the festivities in the vast hired marquee in the garden. Food was laid out on three trestle tables, cider on tap from enormous barrels at one end, and after the feast, a little band of two fiddlers, a piper and a drummer played their lively tunes, and soon the marquee was bursting with merriment. Raucous voices were raised in enjoyment as dancers cavorted up and down, weaved in hopping, jigging circles, or swung round in partners until cheeks were flushed in giddy delight.

The sedate meal in the house was over, and Charles stood up, offering Rose his arm. She linked her hand through the crook of his elbow, her fingers tingling with excitement as her shining eyes met his. Yes, she was very happy. She began to relax as they led Charles's guests out into the grounds which had been hastily knocked into shape by the elderly part-time gardener and his boy, who, along with a live-in housekeeper-cum-cook and a housemaid, Charles had instructed Rose to employ, since Florrie was now to devote her entire time to Henry. To Rose's amusement, Charles was playing lord of the manor to the workers who doffed their caps at him, for he was clearly unused to mixing with the working classes on a social basis.

'Congratulations, Miss Rose!' Noah Roach waved gaily as he went back inside the marquee, evidently taking full advantage of the free alcohol.

Rose shook her head with a light chuckle, and lifted her jubilant face to her husband. 'Oh, Charles, would you mind very much if I spent a little time with all the people in the marquee? I've known them all so long . . .'

Charles's eyes softened as he gazed at her. 'How can I refuse you anything, my darling?' he breathed. 'But don't be too long.'

'Please excuse me,' she said aloud, turning to the ladies and gentlemen who accompanied them. 'I must just thank our other guests for coming.' And with a quick, affectionate kiss on Charles's cheek, the naturalness of which surprised even herself, she skipped off towards the marquee.

The distinctive odour of canvas wreathed inside her nostrils, and all at once she was hailed by the people she had lived among for so many years. A cry went up, toasting her name and wishing her well before the music started up again with a jolly reel. The merrymakers at once returned to prancing up and down to the jocund rhythms, and Rose's head spun with the jovial faces that flashed across her vision.

'Oh, Rose!' Molly's eyes were as brilliant as stars as she tugged on Rose's sleeve. 'This is such fun! And you look wonderful!'

'And would your husband mind if I asked you to dance?'

Joe's face was split in a carefree grin, and Rose responded with a whoop of glee. In an instant, she was swirling dizzily amongst the revellers, her head thrown back with the joy of the dance, holding on to Joe's bony shoulder while he supported her round the waist. He whisked her all the way round the circle before the music came to a noisy halt, and she scampered breathlessly to Charles's side as he came in through the flapping canvas entrance.

'Shall we join in?' she panted playfully.

'I don't think so,' Charles smiled down at her like an indulgent father.

Rose looked up at him, her eyes still sparkling, as he led her from the marquee and she waved back over her shoulder.

'Really, Rose,' he bent to whisper in her ear, 'could you not show a little more decorum? Thank goodness my visitors couldn't see you.'

Rose's eyes snapped. 'Just because I'm married to you, doesn't mean I'm going to turn into some upper-class prig and turn my back on my friends, you know!'

Charles tossed his head with a short laugh. 'I should hope not! But do remember that acquaintances can be most useful in business, and we ought not to offend. You've had your jig, so could you possibly behave now? At least until *my* guests have departed, which won't be long. *Please*, Rose!' he begged, fingering a curling ebony tendril that had loosened from the pearl combs and flower blossoms that were intricately worked into her hair.

She pulled a mocking grimace. 'All right. But only if you promise to dance with me afterwards until your feet hurt!'

'I promise!' He grinned like a schoolboy. 'And woe betide any man who tries to take you from me!'

He kept to his word, though his constrained stance was not suited to the chaotic mayhem of the country dances. By the time the last workers and their families had left for their little cottages on the moor, and the hired caterers had packed everything into the carts that had trundled away down the drive, the bride and groom were quite exhausted. Darkness was falling, the quiet of the moorland dusk a welcome relief after the hectic revelries of the day.

'I think as I should like to retire now,' Henry announced as they all sat out on the terrace, enjoying the evening air.

'Of course, Mr Henry.' Florrie at once jumped to attention, relishing in her promotion to nurse and companion.

'Oh, goodnight, Father!' Rose leapt to her feet and bent to hug Henry tightly. 'Hasn't it been a wonderful day?'

'It certainly has, my dearest child.' In her own exhilaration, Rose did not notice the catch in his voice, nor see the moisture collecting in his eyes. And when he drew away, he shook hands with Charles, who seemed glued to her side. 'Congratulations,' Henry said stiffly. 'You will ... take *care* of my daughter, won't you?'

'Naturally.'

Rose frowned. Was there some tension between the two men? But then Florrie had clamped her arms about her, rotund cheeks wobbling as she openly wept. Rose pulled back, laughing lightly.

'Oh, Florrie, I'm so happy!' she told her, and the older woman sniffed.

'Goodnight, then, Rosie.'

'Yes, goodnight! Sleep well!' Rose watched as Florrie pushed her father up the specially built ramp into the house, followed by Amber contentedly waving her tail, and then she put her hand in Charles's. 'Shall we take a turn about the garden afore we go to bed? 'Tis such a beautiful night! And I must see Gospel! He'll think I'm neglecting him.'

'You and that horse!' Charles chuckled, dropping a kiss on to her hair, which had become somewhat awry during the dancing. They threaded their arms about each other's waists, Rose leaning her head on Charles's shoulder as they picked their way across the silvery, moonlit grass, Rose enjoying the sense of protection, of closeness, that was so new to her. Gospel came trotting up in the adjacent field as soon as he smelled her familiar scent. As she stroked his soft, velvety muzzle, crooning into his ear, Charles's lips on the back of her neck sent a shiver of emotion down her spine. She finally gave Gospel one last kiss on his hairy nose, and ambled back with Charles towards the warmly lit house, pausing for a moment to gaze up at the satin indigo sky, peppered with pinprick stars. The Dartmoor weather had been kind for their special day, and now offered them a still, romantic night. The balmy air entwined itself about them, and as Charles held her closely to him, his mouth came down on hers, not kind and caressing as it had always been before, but harsh and urgent. Rose tightened. It sent a strange sensation shooting down to her stomach, and she wasn't sure she liked it.

'Time for bed, I think, my love,' Charles said, releasing her. 'You go up. I'll just have a cigar out here, and then I'll lock up.'

Rose nodded with a faint smile, grateful to escape the uncomfortable moment. Charles had instantly returned to his normal self, and she felt at ease again. Perhaps she had imagined, or misinterpreted, his forceful ardour, for after all, they had all consumed a great deal of alcohol during the day and weren't quite themselves. She went in through the half-glazed double doors to the drawing room, then through the spacious hallway and up the elegant stairway to the master bedroom. Her light footsteps echoed through the silent house, for there was not a sound from her father's quarters, and Florrie and the two female servants had been given leave to retire to their spartan but adequate rooms in the attic.

In the little dressing room, Rose contemplated her reflection in the looking-glass one last time before stepping out of the beautiful gown. Would she ever wear it again? So many brides could only be married in their Sunday best, or if they could afford it, a new outfit of a style that could be utilized again afterwards. But Rose's gown was so exquisite it would only be suitable for a society ball, or some such event. Charles wanted her to go to London with him sometimes, and perhaps she would have an opportunity to use the lovely garment again then. She sighed as she reluctantly placed it on a hanger. She was so lucky! And though nowhere else could possibly hold the same place in her heart as her beloved Dartmoor, she was looking forward to visiting the capital with Charles, and playing the perfect wife as a thank you for all his generosity.

She climbed between the sheets, leaving the lamp turned low so that Charles could see his way when he came up. She had been sleeping in the big bed for the past two months, and shook her head with a musing smile. It would be strange to have someone, a man, lying beside her. But that was what you did when you were married, wasn't it, share a bed? And she had to stifle a giggle as she wondered if Charles snored!

She snuggled down and was almost asleep, images of the magical day swirling in her head, when Charles padded into the room. She was vaguely aware of his shadow passing from the bathroom to the dressing room, emerging again in a pristine nightshirt. Rose was curled on her side, but turned on to her back and stretched like a kitten as Charles came and sat on the bed next to her. She smiled languidly at him, her dark curls flowing about her in a curtain of silk, as she waited for his goodnight kiss. She watched his eyes moving about her face, two cinnamon-flecked orbs alight with wonderment.

'Well now, Rose,' he whispered, his voice thick. 'Take off your nightdress and let me see what I've married.'

Rose blinked at him as some sickening horror lacerated her heart. Had she heard right, her confounded brain demanded, as a vile, disgusted realization began to dawn. She reared away, pressing herself into the pillows.

Charles's eyes opened wide, and he threw up his head with a snort. 'Good God!' he groaned in disbelief. 'Do you *really* not know? Has no one ever told you what happens between a man and his wife?' He stared at her ashen, rigid face, and then his lips curved into a wry smile. 'Well, I suppose it will be even more pleasurable to *show* you, my darling. Now, if you won't take off your nightdress,' he said as he saw her fists tightening about the top of the blankets, 'I'll have to do it for you. Now don't look so disapproving, Rose. This is what you get married *for*! Millions of couples all over the world will be doing it as we speak.'

Rose could not move. Every muscle in her body was paralysed, apart from her heart that hammered frantically in her frozen chest. Her eyes stared sightlessly at his lecherous smile, her pupils so wide with fear that the cobalt of the irises had all but disappeared. Her small hands were powerless as Charles wrenched the bedclothes from their grasp and flung them aside, and as his fingers tore hungrily at the buttons of her nightgown, a petrified whimper did no more than flutter in her throat. She wanted to fight back, but was weighed down like a block of granite and could only lie there motionless as he took her exposed breasts, kneading their fullness and moaning her name against their milky whiteness.

It was only when he started to fumble with the hem of her nightgown, drawing it up to her waist and forcing her knees apart, that her instinct to protect herself was galvanized into action. She lashed out, pummelling his shoulders and writhing beneath him like some madwoman from an asylum. But above her, Charles's face hardened, his eyes narrowed with anger, for if she would not give it to him freely, he would take her by force. He was not particularly muscled, but he was tall and stronger than her, and in the lamplight, she caught one stunned glimpse of the hideous thing that stuck out from between his legs before he plunged it into that innermost part of her she had hitherto hardly known existed. The chilling shock made her hold her breath until the pain seared into her, slicing at her tender flesh, and she screamed aloud. Charles's sweating hand clamped over her mouth, choking her, stopping her from breathing. Her senses reeled away and she struggled viciously, hysterically, her muscles straining crazedly as he rammed himself ever more forcefully into her in a grunting frenzy. And then suddenly he stopped for just one split second before his body gave one mighty shudder and he cried out her name before he fell down on top of her, panting heavily and pinning her to the bed.

'Oh, Rose, oh, my darling,' Charles murmured hotly into her ear. 'I love you so much. You'll never know how I've yearned for this. You were wonderful, moving like that. Oh, my little Rose.'

His words came at her through a fog. He moved away, blew out the small flame in the lamp, then came back to kiss her once more before he settled himself on his side of the bed, sighing contentedly. Rose lay, as rigid as a stone, staring into the blackness until her eyes adjusted to the slither of moonlight that filtered through the curtains. Charles, her husband, had taken himself from her, but her insides still burned, scorched, as if the red-hot poker were still being thrust into her. For ten minutes, perhaps more, she didn't dare to move for fear it would increase the pain. Charles's heavy, steady breathing beside her at last began to seep into her numbed mind, convincing her he was asleep, and slowly, gingerly, she rolled on to her side with her back to her new husband, and drew up her knees, oblivious to the silent tears that were dripping down her cheeks. She felt dirty. Abused. *Ashamed*. And yet she had done nothing wrong. It was all falling into place now. That was why her father had not been happy about the marriage. Why he had spoken about love and passion, although quite why *love* should make anyone *want* to do what she had just been subjected to was beyond her. But Charles had just done that appalling thing to her *because he loved her*. She could not blame him. But . . . if only she'd known! Why hadn't her father told her! But then . . . how could he have done? The accident had weakened him not only in body but in spirit also. And it wasn't the sort of thing a man could tell his daughter about, was it? Sons, perhaps, and surely it would have been a mother's role to . . .

She bit down on her thumb, something she had never done even as a child. And for the first time in her life, she missed the mother she had never known. Florrie had been her mother, a devoted servant, but perhaps it hadn't been her place to speak of such . . . delicate matters. And perhaps Florrie herself didn't know. There had been no Mr Bennett. Like so many in her position, she had assumed the title of 'Mrs' because cooks and housekeepers were expected to be married women or widows. It gave the household respectability. What a ridiculous convention . . .

And what a ridiculous farce life was, if everything was supposed to be so upright, and yet *that* was what went on at night between married couples. And all that jolly celebration of a wedding ceremony, just so as *that* could take place! She had thought marriage consisted of romantic walks, friendship . . . What a fool she had been.

Her heart closed in a bitter fist. All those dreams she'd had, and now she was imprisoned just as surely as the convicts just a few miles across the moor. Except that in five, ten years' time, they could look forward to being released, whereas she was trapped for life. Till death us do part. With my body I thee worship. Worship! It was hardly how she would put it.

The acrimonious, livid thoughts tumbled in her head, firing her own anger, her own wretchedness until the morning light began to creep into the luxurious bedroom, and outside the moorland birds were twittering their chorus to the new day. Finally, when her soul was saturated with misery, it could take no more, and her exhausted mind took refuge in sleep . . .

Charles's warm, moist kisses on the creamy skin at her throat brought her from her fitful slumber. Her eyes sprang open, and there was his face, so full of love, hanging over her. He smiled, stroking a hank of her long, lustrous tresses.

'Oh, my lovely girl,' he muttered. 'I hope you slept well.'

He didn't wait for an answer, but was running his hand up and down her arm, and then the inside of her thigh, his fingers seeking out the place his body had possessed the previous night. Rose's shattered soul had no time to blink away the sleep before the hideous memory slashed at her in all its foul clarity. She could not go through that again, and a spark of flashing rage whipped her tongue to a cutting sharpness.

'No, Charles! Get off me!' And she pushed hard against his shoulders.

But he only grinned back. 'Oh, come, my lovely girl! This is what we got married for!'

His words were like shards of glass in her heart, bleeding

the fight from her soul. It was useless. But she couldn't . . .
'Oh, *please*, Charles,' she begged him, tears of desperation,
of hopelessness, glittering in her terrified eyes. 'It *hurts!*' she
moaned, just praying . . .

'Only at first,' he said gently. 'You'll get used to it. Now
just try and relax, and it won't hurt so much.'

A groan of resentment drowned somewhere inside her. She
was beaten. And it wasn't Charles's fault. She turned her head
away, lying as still as a corpse as he did what he had to do
to her frail, aching body. When he entered her, the agony
ripped through her again, and she rammed her fist into her
mouth to stifle her screams, biting down through her knuckles.
No one must hear. Her *father* must not know. He must not
know that this diabolical thing that was being done to her was
pure torture. She had married Charles because she thought
she loved him. Now she knew that she didn't. But it was too
late. Charles had always been kind and generous, but now she
realized she had bought security for herself and her father
with her body, and there was nothing she could do about it.

Charles had finished, and he rolled on to his back with a
satiated sigh before propping himself on one elbow and gazing
down at her, his eyes crinkled softly at the corners. 'You are
so beautiful,' he whispered, his voice quavering with passion.
'You'll come to enjoy it soon, I promise. Oh, I must be the
luckiest man alive!' He jumped up in the bed, spreading his
arms wide above his head in a gesture of sheer jubilation that
under other circumstances would have made her laugh. 'Now,
what would my beautiful wife like for breakfast? No, don't
tell me! I'll make it a surprise! I'll go down and speak to
Cook, and you shall have breakfast in bed. And think what
you'd like to do on the first day of our married life. It's such
a lovely day, how about a walk over the moor?'

He had slipped into his dressing gown and slippers, and with
a grand flourish, plucked one of the red roses from the vase on
the dressing table, placing it reverently on her chest before
taking her limp hand and kissing it, first her wrist and then
working his way up her arm. One final kiss on the tip of her
nose, and he was gone, singing tunelessly on the top of his
voice as he waltzed along the landing and down the stairs.

Rose realized she had been holding her breath, and now
she released it in a broken sigh. Charles was as ecstatic in his

love as she was devastated by it. Oh, God in heaven, what had she done? She rolled dejectedly out of bed and on to her feet, for she could not stay there, between the sheets where it had happened, a moment longer. But as she dragged herself across the floor, the pain cut into her and she could hardly walk. She staggered into the bathroom, blindly, only her instincts functioning. She used the chamber pot, hoping it would bring some relief, but it only stung her bruised flesh more deeply, and when she looked down, there was blood on her thighs.

A whimper of despair uttered from her lips. This was to be her life from now on, with no escape, and she must keep the agony of it to herself. Her heart was empty, beyond tears, and all she wanted just now was to free herself from the physical suffering that bore into the very core of her. There was water in one of the huge jugs on the washstand. Cold water that had stood there all night. She tore off her nightdress and setting the matching china bowl on the floor, crouched down over it and poured the cooling water over that intimate part of her, soothing the soreness and washing away the filth and degradation. The morning air brushed against her naked skin and made her want to weep. Could she ever *feel* as she should, ever truly love a man so deeply that she could give herself willingly to him? Even take pleasure from it herself?

Now she would never know.

Eleven

'Would you like another cup, Rose?' Florrie asked, dropping the 'Miss' Charles had instructed her to use, seeing as the master was in his study attending to the pile of business correspondence that had arrived that morning.

Rose looked up from the book she was reading. The three of them – Henry in his invalid chair, Rose and Florrie – were taking morning coffee on the terrace of Fencott Place, for the fine summer weather, amazingly, was holding. It was ten days since the grand celebration of Miss Rose Maddiford's marriage to Mr Charles Chadwick, ten days in which she had realized she had made the greatest mistake of her life – except when she studied her father, who was being so well fed and cared for, and appeared healthier now than at any time since the accident. It was worth the terrible ordeal she was subjected to every night and most mornings, at least it seemed so at moments like this when peace and harmony comforted her bruised heart. And yesterday, her 'monthly' had started, and she had welcomed the few hours of painful cramps because it seemed it would provide her with several days' respite from Charles's onslaughts. It still hurt her dreadfully, although possibly a little less than at first, but she felt so degraded, so filthy and ashamed afterwards, and perhaps she always would. But those minutes of vile obscenity – for thank goodness that was as long as it lasted – were locked away in a nightmare of bitter shadows during the bright sunny days in between, when Charles was everything a loving, attentive husband should be. More so, for he was clearly reluctant to leave her side for more than a minute.

Indeed, he came hurriedly out on to the terrace now before Rose even had time to reply to Florrie's question. His face was set in a deep scowl that, Rose considered, robbed him of his handsome looks, and he came to stand behind her, laying his hands on her shoulders with an irritated sigh.

'I'm afraid I must go into Princetown to send a telegram,' he announced. 'The telegraph office will be open, I take it?'

'Oh, yes.' Rose deliberately patted one of his hands in a show of affection she did not feel, for at that moment, Henry had glanced across at them. But her sharp mind was busy inventing an excuse not to accompany Charles if he invited her to do so. 'For such a small and isolated place, we're lucky to have one, but I suppose 'tis because of the prison.'

'Having dangerous convicts on one's doorstep can have its advantages, then,' Charles muttered grimly.

'They're not all dangerous,' Rose corrected, leaping at the opportunity to disagree with him. 'Some are forgers . . . or thieves. Not necessarily violent.'

'Well, my dear, I don't have time to argue about that now.' Charles cut her short with uncharacteristic crispness. 'I must get to Princetown as soon as possible, and I'll have to wait for a reply, so I'll be some time. You could come with me if you don't mind the waiting. We could have lunch at the Duchy Hotel.'

Rose felt her heart thump in her chest as she whipped up the courage to defy her husband for the first time. 'Well, if you don't mind, darling,' she said, lifting her vivid smile to him, 'I think I'll go out on poor Gospel. We haven't been out for a ride since before our marriage, and the poor animal will be champing at the bit. Literally,' she added with a forced grin.

'All right, sweetheart, but take care on that monster.' Charles dropped a swift kiss on the top of her head, and then, pulling on his coat which he had left on the back of one of the garden chairs, strode back into the house and, they assumed, away down the front driveway.

Relief swamped Rose's limbs and for a few seconds, she slumped in her chair before stretching with delight. She was free. Free! For a few hours, she could be her old self again, carefree, reckless Rose Maddiford, and her spirit soared.

She leapt to her feet. 'I'd better go and change, then!' she declared brightly, and as she sprang forward, Henry caught her hand.

'You are happy, then, my child?' he asked mildly.

Rose looked down on him, and her chest squeezed painfully. 'Oh, yes!' she cried, the lie burning her lips as she forced them into a broad smile. It wasn't as difficult as she had imagined, for she was becoming used to the deception. Henry must never *know*. And besides, the thought of racing hell-for-leather across the moors, alone, on Gospel's back, filled her with joy.

The gelding kicked up his heels when he saw the saddle, and as Rose slipped on his bridle and fastened the chin strap he shook his head vigorously in eager anticipation. The warm weather meant he had remained out in the field overnight for the past few weeks, as having something of the thoroughbred in him, this was not sensible for much of the year. But even so, he was as desperate as his mistress for a long, mad, unrestrained gallop.

They paid a visit to the gunpowder mills first, avoiding the old house where the new manager was now installed, since it held too many memories of a life when Rose had been truly happy. But she chatted with many of the workers, catching up on all the news and taking tea in Mrs Roach's cottage surrounded by her growing brood. And then she and Gospel took a vast circular route across to the East Dart and down the riverbank to the stone bridge and ancient clapper bridge at Postbridge. They continued along to the swirling waters at Dartmeet before charging westward back across the open moor towards home, Rose's wild hair streaming out behind her as she crouched down over Gospel's flowing mane. As his strong legs ate up the miles, the wind rushed through Rose's head, blasting away the anger and resentment from her soul.

Charles was waiting for her as she crossed the stable yard with the heavy saddle, humming to herself with relaxed pleasure. She stopped, her heart immediately gripped with defiance.

'Where the hell have you been?' Charles demanded.

Rose lifted her chin, squaring her shoulders so that, unwittingly, her breasts jutted out pertly, causing the saliva to run in Charles's mouth. 'Out for a ride,' she frowned at him in exasperation. 'Just like I told you.'

'But you've been hours! It's half-past three, for God's sake!'

'So?' she shrugged as she tried to push past him. Yes, she thought. Five hours of sheer bliss. Away from you.

But he caught her by the arm so that she was swung round to face him. 'So?' he repeated angrily. 'I've been worried sick! Anything could have happened to you!'

'I've told you afore, I'm perfectly safe when I'm out on Gospel. Now, if you don't mind, this saddle's heavy.'

'Oh, of course,' Charles murmured, and shaking his head as if coming to his senses, he relieved her of the said item and followed her into the tack room.

'And now I'm really thirsty,' she told him tersely as she hung Gospel's bridle on its hook.

'Well, it's lucky Cook has just brought out some lemonade, then, isn't it?' he answered with equal acidity.

Rose flicked her head and, neatly sidestepping him, strode out of the yard and across to the terrace. But for the changed position of the sun, the scene was almost as she had left it earlier that morning. Henry glanced up with an unconcerned smile as he sipped at a glass of freshly made lemonade.

'Did you have a good ride, Rose, my dear?'

'Yes, wonderful, thank you, Father,' she answered, flinging herself into a chair.

'You see, Charles, I told you there was nothing to worry about. You'll just have to get used to Rose dashing about on Gospel.'

'Well, I just don't think I could ever get used to having my precious wife gallivanting all over the moor on her own, and putting herself in all sorts of danger. And now I won't have to,' Charles beamed, his attitude changing to one of complacency. 'I have a surprise for you, Rose, my darling. Whilst I was waiting for the reply to my telegram, I had my lunch at the Duchy. And remember the chestnut mare I hired out from them last autumn? Well, they still have her, and she was such a suitable mount for me that I bought her. They were reluctant to part with her so I had to pay twice what she's really worth, but no matter. So now I can always accompany you on your excursions, and she'll be good company for Gospel. They got on well together, as I remember. So, what do you think of that, my love?' he grinned triumphantly.

Rose blinked at him. And her heart sank like a leaden weight. The long ride had refreshed her spirit, and she had begun to think that, if she could escape on Gospel's back two or three times a week, she might be able to tolerate Charles's nightly attentions with some degree of stoicism. But this! Dear God, she would suffocate!

'Oh,' she muttered as she felt the blood flush into her cheeks.

'Oh, er . . . I don't know what to say. You've left me quite speechless.'

'And 'tis not often that happens!' Henry chuckled beside her.

'And I've been thinking,' Charles went on, his face split in two by a satisfied smile. 'It was a pity that the dog cart and, er, Polly, was it? belonged to the powder mills. I'm going to have to go to London, but when I get back, we must look for some sort of carriage for you, Henry. Perhaps a wagonette, and employ a carpenter to adapt it so that we can push you up a ramp into it, or some such arrangement. Then you can get out and about more easily.'

'Oh, my dear boy, that would be so kind!'

'Yes, thank you,' Rose mumbled almost to herself. It *was* good of Charles, she could not deny it. And she supposed she couldn't blame him for buying the chestnut. He would *need* a horse here, anyway. But to be with her on her liberating escapades, well, they would hardly be liberating if *he* was there! 'London, you say?' she asked, for that might at least bring her some respite.

'Yes. I'm afraid I must leave you for a few days, my dear.'

Rose's lips compressed into a thin line in order to conceal her pleasure. You couldn't make that a few weeks, could you? her vexed mind rejoindered.

'Nothing wrong, is there?' her father enquired.

'No, Henry, not at all. Just the opposite, in fact.' Charles raised a speculative eyebrow as he sat down. 'My broker has had word of a new mine opening in South Africa, and it could prove a good investment. They're expecting to find gold.'

'Gold?'

'Yes. It may just be wishful thinking, which is why I need to go to London to attend some meetings. Investigate their claims before I put any money into it. I have fingers in many pies, but one of the best things I ever did was to speculate in diamonds some years ago now.' Charles smiled proudly at the impressed expression on Henry's face. 'I sponsored an acquaintance to go out to the diamond fields at Colesberg Kopje before it became known just how rich the area really was, and the licences were still cheap. You may have heard of it now as the Kimberley mine. There was a slight problem last year, but that's all sorted now, and as a shareholder, I've done very well out of it. So I'm quite inclined to take a risk with a speculation in gold. Nothing we can't afford to lose if it were to go wrong,' he added reassuringly. 'But I will only go ahead if my enquiries are satisfactory. However, it does grieve me that I must leave you, my dearest.'

He took Rose's hand and brought it lovingly to his lips. Rose shuddered with revulsion as the warm moistness on her skin reminded her of what went on in their bed at night, but she managed to say quite calmly, ''Twon't be for too long, though, will it, Charles?'

His eyes softened as he gazed at her. 'I sincerely hope not. And when I return, we shall go in search of some suitable transport for your father. And for ourselves, of course, when necessary. The mare will be arriving tomorrow afternoon, by the way. Her name's Tansy, if you remember. Now, I shall be leaving after dinner this evening. A cab is coming for me at eight o'clock, so I have already instructed Cook to have our meal served early. I'll be staying at the Bedford Hotel in Tavistock tonight, ready to catch the train to Plymouth first thing in the morning so that I should be in London by six o'clock tomorrow evening.'

'You're certainly well organized,' Henry nodded in approval.

'Years of having to be one step ahead, my dear fellow. That's how the Chadwicks have made their money into a moderate fortune. And why I have yet another surprise for you. I thought, with the mare coming tomorrow, and another animal needed to pull whatever conveyance we acquire, we'll need someone to look after them all. That beast of yours has been out in the field, but it will need to come in when the summer's over, and I can hardly expect my wife to muck out not just one but three loose boxes, now, can I?' He laughed as he patted Rose's hand with the enthusiasm of a young boy. 'So while I was waiting for the reply from my broker, I asked around and I've taken on a stable lad. I've told the maid to clean out the loft over the tack room. There's an old iron bedstead up there already, and the boy can have a mattress from the servants' quarters when he arrives with the mare tomorrow. Cornish, I think he said his name was. He can help with the heavy work in the house, too—'

'Ned!' Rose's eyes were wide with astonishment.

'Do you know him, then?'

'I've known Ned Cornish for years! Stable boy at the Albert Inn.'

'That's the chap. I thought I'd feel happier if there was a strong male about the place while I'm away. Which is why I wanted him to start at once. And I wondered if you'd like to think about furnishing the guest rooms to give you something to occupy your time?'

'Well, I must say you've had a busy and fruitful day,' Henry observed. 'You've made me feel quite weary just listening to you, and I feel I could do with a lie down before our early dinner. Would you mind, Florrie?'

Florrie, who was apt to keep her lip firmly buttoned in the master's presence, got to her feet with a devoted smile and pushed Henry up the ramp with a noisy heave. Charles turned his head sharply and went to go to her assistance, but they were already disappearing into the house, so he sat down again.

'Cornish can help Florrie with your father, too. I really feel it's too much for her.'

'What on earth do you think you're doing, employing Ned Cornish?' Rose rounded on him. 'Why didn't you tell me we were to have a groom? We could have asked Joe! He's the only person who can handle Gospel. Ned positively dislikes—'

'Joe Tyler!' Charles's brown eyes bulged from their sockets. 'After the way you were dancing with him at our wedding!'

'What?'

'Yes, I saw you!' Charles spat at her with vitriolic anger. 'Arms around each other, laughing! Making a spectacle of yourself with that vermin!'

Rose's jaw fell open as she stared at him in horrified disbelief. 'But . . . Joe is like a younger brother to me!' she cried defensively as tears of humiliation, though for Joe and not herself, welled in her eyes. 'He's a respectable person. And besides, he and Molly—'

'Oh, don't give me that! I'm not a fool, Rose! And I'm glad I've taken on this Cornish fellow if you're not too keen on him. At least there won't be anything going on between you behind my back!'

Rose's mouth snapped shut at the sour taste that stung her tongue. 'How dare you!' she almost choked on her disgust. 'How dare you even *imagine* that I'd do anything like that! I'm married to *you*, Charles, for better or for worse, remember?'

As Charles glowered at her, the muscles òf his face began to twist, and before she knew it, she was encircled in his embrace and she could hear him all but sobbing into her tousled hair.

'I'm so sorry, my sweetest, dearest love.' His words were scarcely audible, and Rose's forehead set into a deep frown. 'But I've employed Cornish now, and unless he proves unsatisfactory, there will be no reason to dismiss him. I *am* sorry, Rose, my darling. It's just that I love you so much, I just can't bear the thought of you being with another man. Please, I beg you, forgive me.'

Rose swallowed as she gazed over his shoulder into the house. She prayed to God that neither her father nor Florrie had heard their bitter exchange. 'Of course I do,' she muttered in reply. But in her heart, she wasn't at all sure that she did.

'Oh, Rose!' Molly's eyes shone like emeralds in her amazement. 'Do you really mean to tell me you had no idea? You'm living with animals all over the moor all your life, and you didn't *know*?'

Rose rocked her bowed head from side to side, and when she looked up, her eyebrows were arched in excruciating anguish. '*Animals*, yes! And that's just it! With animals, 'tis so . . . so *bestial*! With no feelings or emotion. I thought human beings were supposed to be above animals. I thought 'twould be different. Animals don't kiss, so I thought—'

She broke off as her throat closed and she gazed up at the sky with a tearing sigh. Beside her, Molly sucked in her cheeks and gave her friend's arm a squeeze, the only thing she could think of to offer her comfort.

'Oh, Rose,' she groaned. 'With all they books you read, did you never read one on . . . on—'

'Oh, yes! But in flowers and butterflies,' Rose answered scornfully. 'But never in *people*. I mean, I've never seen one in the public library. If they exist. And if they do, they're probably considered too disgusting to put on the shelf of a public place.'

Molly nodded in agreement, and for a few minutes, the girls sat in silence staring out across the moor. On the prison farmland, parties of convicts were tending to the hardy crops, clearing the ground of massive boulders or, most hated of all, digging drainage ditches up to the waist in what was cold water even on a perfect summer's day such as this. There would be no dry clothing to change into on their return to the prison; indeed, they would be lucky if their ugly uniforms dried out overnight ready for the following day. But neither girl took any notice, each lost in her own thoughts, though they had not enjoyed one of their private meetings since before the wedding.

'It must have been quite a shock, then, the wedding night,' Molly ventured at last. 'But . . . once you've gotten used to it . . . 'tis nice, isn't it?'

'What!' Rose's eyes opened wide as she whipped her head round to gaze at her friend. 'You don't mean . . . you and Joe—'

'Good heavens, no! We'm close, but nort's ever . . . Not like that.'

'Oh, so you don't know what 'tis like, then. I mean, 'twouldn't be so bad if Charles were as polite and caring as he is in everything else. But when it comes to *that*, 'tis as if he's a different man. And I just don't think I can . . . But 'tis not your problem.' Rose suddenly jumped down from the rock they were sitting on. 'I ought to be getting back. Ned's bringing the mare over later, so I suppose I should be there. I really don't fancy having him as our groom, but there you are. 'Tis too late now. I'd far sooner have had Joe.'

''Twouldn't have been enough work for Joe. He likes to keep busy. Not like that sloth Ned Cornish. No wonder he jumped at the chance, the great lummox!'

Rose couldn't help but laugh, and as she waved goodbye, she felt her heart eased by Molly's compassion.

'Rose, my darling!'

'Charles!' The shock rippled through her body, his sudden appearance in the bedroom as she brushed out her hair taking her completely by surprise, and she fought to disguise her displeasure. 'Your telegram said you wouldn't be home for another few days,' she said, praying he didn't see her flinch as he bent to kiss her long, graceful neck. They held each other's gaze in the mirror, and she saw his eyes dip to the swelling of her breasts beneath her fine cotton nightdress.

'Well, I just couldn't stay away from my beautiful wife a moment longer!' he declared with a suggestive smile. 'And I have been away nearly a week longer than expected. A very profitable week, I might add – at least, I believe it will prove to be in the future – but now I want to make up for it. Here, let me do that,' he crooned in an oily voice as he wrested the brush from her hand.

She shuddered, the pulse suddenly beating hard and fast at her temples. He drew the brush through her shining curls, his other hand gripping her slender shoulder. She tried to brace herself against his closeness since she was his wife, after all, and her conversation with Molly had made her think that perhaps she was being unreasonable. But her resolution failed her.

'You must be hungry after your journey,' she suggested, turning to him with a loving smile on her lips. 'I'm certain Cook will have something cold she can—'

But Charles shook his head. 'No. I had something to eat while I was waiting for the connecting train. I want something else just now.'

He replaced the brush on the dressing table in a slow, sensual gesture, his eyes burning bright with desire as he brought his mouth down on to hers, soft and caressing. Rose closed her eyes, trying to respond to his gentleness, which did not seem so repellent. But then his kiss became more demanding, more urgent, his tongue flicking into her mouth and his hands moving frenetically over her breasts and down between her thighs. She whimpered deep in her throat, suffocated, *crushed*, and suddenly she could not breathe.

'Charles, no, please,' she gasped, spluttered, as she managed to pull her head away and push hard against his shoulders.

But he merely moved his kisses down to her throat, forcing her tiny waist against his hardening manhood as he held her in an iron grip. 'Oh, struggle away, my precious one!' he murmured into her cleavage. 'I love it when you pretend to be a little tigress.'

He growled, baring his teeth, and then with a bawdy laugh, picked her up bodily, despite her kicking legs, and padding across the luxurious carpet, dropped her on to the soft, well-sprung bed. And before she had time to scramble away, he leapt astride her, pinning her down, and catching both her small, flailing hands in one of his, held them firmly on the pillow behind her head. For a brief instant, they faced one another, panting heavily, Charles's eyes gleaming with lust while Rose glared at him in contempt.

'Now then,' he leered, his free hand wiping the saliva that dribbled from the corner of his mouth before he ripped open the front of her nightgown. 'Hmm! Let me see what I've been missing!'

Rose could have screamed with revulsion. She dug her heels desperately into the bed and pushed upwards in an effort to lever him from her, but he was too heavy. He sniggered again, taking her retaliation as play-acting as his eyes devoured her nakedness. She stared up at him, every taut muscle ready to fight, but it was futile. She was trapped. He was her husband, who not so long ago she had thought she loved, and he was doing nothing wrong.

But at that moment, Rose wished that she could die.

Twelve

'Rose, dear, 'tis your turn.'

She turned her head from gazing absently out of the drawing-room window and smiled at Henry before forcing her attention on her hand of cards. It was mid-September, but chilly enough to have a welcoming blaze in the fireplace. The glorious fortnight in June had rapidly deteriorated to a poor summer, and now the rain was coming down in stair rods and streaming against the windowpanes. It was only half-past three in the afternoon, but the lamps had already been lit against the gloom.

'Oh, is that the best you can do, sweetheart?' Charles asked fondly, and clamping the smouldering cigar between his teeth, laid his winning flush on the table.

'You lucky devil, Charles!' Henry chuckled.

'And my poor Rose has lost every game! Never mind, my love. Perhaps you'll win the next one.'

'No, I don't think I'll play any more, if you don't mind.' She smiled wanly at her husband as she stood up. 'I think I'd rather get back to my book.'

'Well, if you're sure, my darling.'

Rose settled herself in the window seat, wedging a plush cushion behind her back. *Pride and Prejudice*. One of her favourite books, but just now, even the exploits of Mr Darcy and Miss Elizabeth Bennet held no interest for her. Within five minutes, she had let the book slip on to her lap, and she leaned her forehead against the cold glass of the window. Her heart was heavy, leaden, her mind wandering and preoccupied. Her stifled spirit was out there, flying across the wild moorland, the wind in her head and driving the misery from her soul. She could feel Gospel's muscles rippling beneath her, sharing the infinite freedom of the open skies and the endless miles of the savage beauty of Dartmoor. A veil of mist dimmed the lavender clarity of her eyes, and her shoulders sagged with emptiness. The irrevocable chasm in her life was deepening by the day, and there was nothing she could do about it. Beyond tears. Beyond hope.

'I'm going for a ride.'

It was as if someone else had spoken the words, had leapt determinedly from the window seat and stood in defiant pose in the centre of the vast rug that covered much of the polished oak floorboards. Three pairs of eyes were riveted on her, Florrie's plump face white and aghast.

'You'm not going out in this, Rose!' she cried, forgetting the 'Miss' she was supposed to employ in Charles's presence. But even as she spoke, she knew her protest would fall on deaf ears.

Rose was already out of the door and halfway across the hall to the stairs before Charles caught up with her. He was still holding his cigar in one hand, and with the other, he grasped her by the arm.

'You can't possibly go out in this weather, my love. You'd be soaked to the skin in no time, and catch your death. If you don't want to play cards, is there anything else you'd rather do?' he asked earnestly. 'Shall I order Cook to make us a pot of tea?'

Rose blinked at him, and the absurdity of it drew a bitter laugh from her throat. She was perfectly capable of making some tea herself, of cooking the meal, black-leading the range. But since the day she had married Charles, she hadn't been allowed to *do* anything. Charles saw to it that Cook and Patsy, the housemaid, attended her every need, wanting her to live the pampered life of a lady, but it just wasn't *her*. And though he treated her like a princess during the day, in their bed she was no more than a human marionette to satisfy his carnal lust.

'If I don't go out, I think I shall go mad!' she told him, flames of crimson burning in her cheeks. 'And if you're not man enough to brave a spot of rain, then I shall go alone, just like I always used to!'

They glared at each other, eyes locked in raging conflict, Charles looking as if he might explode and Rose's chin lifted high with audacity.

'But you're a married woman now,' Charles hissed, glancing over his shoulder as if he were afraid they would be overheard.

'And I won't have my wife gallivanting all over the place looking like some rain-drenched witch for everyone to see.'

'Huh!' she snorted, her eyes glinting a livid indigo. 'And who's going to stop me, tell me that? How many of your London dignitaries am I likely to meet, anyway?'

Charles inflated his chest. 'Rose, I forbid you to go!'

'Forbid me?'

'Yes! And it'll hardly do Gospel any good.'

Rose stared at him, her lips knotted as anger pumped through her veins. But the mention of Gospel's welfare pulled her up short. She hated to admit it, but perhaps Charles was right.

She lowered her eyes. 'All right. But I *am* going out to the stables for a while. You won't object to *that*, I take it?'

'No, of course not.' His face slackened with relief as he turned away, drawing deeply on the cigar as he went.

'And Charles, please don't smoke in the same room as my father. I've asked you before. You know his lungs were weakened in the accident.'

'I'm so sorry, my dear. I'd forgotten. I'll finish my cigar in the study. I've some business matters to catch up on anyway.' And so saying, he disappeared into the study, closing the door quietly behind him.

Rose sank down on the bottom stair with a weary sigh. She didn't like arguing. But lately she seemed to be doing just that more and more. It was just that Charles didn't want her to do anything without him, and it was driving her insane. The carefree independence Henry had always allowed her had been taken from her overnight, but if she had to obey her husband, she wasn't going to give in without a fight!

She went out through the back door, shrugging into her voluminous waterproof that hung in the small boot room and changing into her riding boots, as she could hardly go out to the stables in the soft kid shoes she was wearing. Fortunately she was dressed in a modest outfit with a russet skirt that would not spoil, though she picked up the hem as she ran across the stable yard, dodging the puddles and bending her head so that the driving rain simply ran down the back of the waterproof hood. Gospel occupied the loose box at the far end in the corner because, with the dog-leg, it was by far the largest. Inside, it was warm and dry, the fragrance of clean straw fresh and welcoming, for it had to be said that Ned

Cornish cared well for the three horses in his charge, Charles having acquired, as promised, a wagonette converted for Henry's use and a pretty roan called Merlin to pull it. The work was hardly onerous, but Ned was diligent enough. He would hardly want to lose his comfortable position, now, would he? The only task he was apt to skimp on was grooming Gospel, since the highly strung animal retained the habit of sinking his teeth into anyone he disliked, Ned in particular. So Rose picked up the brush and began to attend to Gospel's tail, as Ned had been on the receiving end of a well-aimed hoof twice in the last week. Gospel whinnied softly, turning his long, sleek neck to nudge her shoulder. She laughed, her heart soothed as she kissed his soft muzzle, and by the time she had untangled the long, coarse hair and the rest of his coat was gleaming, she felt at peace once more and ready to face the fray.

She wreathed her arms about his neck, her cheek pressed against his strong muscled shoulder and whispering into his warm flesh before she braved the weather again, but not without first slipping into the adjacent box where Tansy, the chestnut mare, was lying contentedly on the thick carpet of straw. Rose knelt down, stroking the docile creature's pretty head and alert ears.

'Happy as a lark, that one, not like that brute o' yourn.'

Rose looked up. Ned was leaning indolently over the lower half of the stable door, supposedly oblivious to the continuing downpour and chewing on a blade of straw.

''Tis not my fault Gospel doesn't like you,' Rose answered, and went back to running her fingers through Tansy's mane.

'And what about you, Rose? Do *you* like me?'

Rose shrugged as Ned came in and crouched down beside her. They remained shoulder to shoulder in silent admiration of Tansy's smooth, bright coat for some moments before Rose glanced at him askance. ''Tis a strange question when I've known you for years,' she finally answered.

'I like *you*, Rose. Very much.' Ned's voice was suddenly very close to her ear and his hand closed over hers as she stroked Tansy's hairy neck. ''Tis why I wanted this job. To be near you. Even if it means being bitten by that nag next door. You wouldn't mind now, would you? Just one little kiss? I mean, now that you know what 'tis like to be bedded?'

Rose was so shocked, she didn't have time to regain her senses and come back with a scathing retort before Ned turned to her, grasping the back of her head and kissing her so fiercely he lost his balance and fell on top of her.

'Get off me, you great lummox!'

To her surprise, she found she wasn't particularly vexed or afraid, but rather she was irritated by his behaviour, for she knew how to handle a numbskull such as Ned Cornish, especially now she knew what it was men were after! She managed to free one hand, and before Ned could dodge it, she slapped her palm across his face with a resounding wallop. He pulled back sharply, his eyes flashing with anger.

'That weren't fair, Rose!' he protested. 'I've given up a lot for you! All they maids I used to bring back to the stables at the Albert Inn. I cas'n bring no one back yere! Just one little favour?'

His gaze dipped meaningfully towards her breasts, and with a cry of indignation, she pushed him aside and scrambled to her feet. 'How dare you, Ned Cornish!' she snarled, glowering down at him with intense loathing. 'I've a good mind to tell my husband, and you'll be out on your ear!'

'Oh, yes?' Ned sneered, unconsciously nursing the reddening fingermarks on his cheek. 'And what if I tells him that *you* were making up to *us*? He might just believe us, seeing as he seems to be the jealous type, and *you* might be the one to come off worse, like!'

Rose's head jerked backwards, her eyes blazing and her chest heaving with resentment. Ned Cornish, towards whom she had never felt anything but indifference, was shrewder than she had given him credit for. Fury bubbled inside her now and it cost her dearly to swallow it down. For he could have a point.

'All right,' she conceded, though it tore at her heart to do so. 'But I'll remember this!'

And so shall I! Ned thought venomously to himself.

Rose spun on her heel and charged out of the loose box in a maddened temper. She cursed herself, for the torrential rain at once lashed into her face, trickling down her neck, and, too late, she pulled the hood of her waterproof over her head as she scurried across the stable yard.

It was then that she saw him, a bedraggled, sodden vision

of dripping grey fur, short black snout and huge doleful eyes that gazed beggingly at her as he limped through the puddles. Rose peered at him through the rain, mesmerized as he came and sat at her feet, his tail sweeping the wet cobbles as he whined at her beseechingly.

'Oh, you poor thing! Where on earth did you come from?' And she scooped the pathetic mongrel into her arms and carried him inside.

'You don't expect us to keep that mangy creature, do you?' Charles asked with mild amusement as he climbed into bed that night.

'I assume you mean Scraggles?' Rose replied indignantly. She was sitting up, hugging her knees beneath the blankets, and for once the nightly ritual was far from her thoughts. 'And he isn't mangy. He was cold and wet and hungry, and one of his paw pads was badly cut, but if we can't find his owners, what else can we do but keep him? Oh, *please*, Charles? He and Amber really seem to like each other.'

Charles shook his head with a chuckle. 'Well, if we really can't find who he belongs to—'

'Oh, thank you, Charles!'

For the first time since their marriage, she snuggled up beside him as he settled into bed, her head resting on his shoulder. The disruption caused by the unexpected arrival of the endearing stray dog had thrown the entire household into turmoil, and Rose's aching soul had been distracted. It had started her thinking. Perhaps if she had other matters to keep her occupied, she might be able to be a better wife. Might deplore Charles's physical attentions a little less. Which for once he didn't seem in too much of a hurry to begin, his arm around her simply drawing her closely against him.

'Charles?' she began cautiously, though her heart had suddenly begun to beat like a battering ram as she considered how to broach the subject that had been at the back of her mind for some time. 'Charles, I've been thinking. When you have to go to London . . . even when you're here . . . what would you think of the idea of my having a lady's maid?'

She had said the last words quickly, before she lost the courage, but Charles merely raised his eyebrows in surprise.

'A lady's maid, eh? Hmm,' he appeared to reflect slowly.

'Well, it mightn't be a bad idea. Certainly when you accompany me to London – which I hope you will soon – it would be good to have someone to make sure you're correctly attired. And to keep you company when I have to attend to business matters. Accompany you to art galleries, that sort of thing. Mrs Bennett is hardly suitable, and besides, she needs to stay here to look after your father. All in all, I think it's an excellent idea,' he nodded approvingly. 'We must put an advertisement in the *Western Morning News*, or perhaps one of the London papers would be better.'

'Oh, I don't think we need to advertise. Molly would be ideal.'

'Molly Cartwright!' Charles jerked so violently that Rose's head slipped from his shoulder. 'Don't be ridiculous!'

'But Molly would be perfect! We're such good friends and—'

'Rose, you need a trained lady's maid to see you are suitably dressed in the latest fashion, that your hair is properly done, and, especially when we go to London, that you are versed in all the ways of society etiquette. I hate to say it, but you have a great deal to learn in that direction! If you were to employ Miss Cartwright, *you* would have to be teaching *her* the little you know yourself, and she would bring nothing but ignominy upon us! Besides which, I cannot have my wife associating so closely with some little trollop whose father is no more than a turnkey at our most infamous prison!'

Rose sat up abruptly and she turned on him eyes that glinted like the flash of the sun on polished silver. 'How dare you speak of Molly like that? She's bright and intelligent, and just because she comes from a working-class background, doesn't make her any worse than you or I! They're a good, honest, hardworking family, and I defy anyone to—'

'Oh, you are so beautiful when you're angry!' Charles almost laughed at her, but then his eyes hardened icily. 'But you will not have Molly Cartwright as your lady's maid!'

'I shall have Molly or no one!' Rose grated between fiercely clenched teeth.

'Then no one it shall be, and there's an end to it.' Charles's mouth closed in a firm line as he jabbed his head towards her, but then his face softened and he smiled suggestively at her as he fingered a thick lock of her cascading curls. 'Now then,

before this conversation, I believe we were enjoying an intimate moment together, so if you don't mind, I'd like you to
lie down again so that we can get back to where we were and
begin afresh. Now, my lovely girl, have you forgotten that we
need to do something before we go to sleep?'

For several seconds, Rose continued to glare at him,
convinced that she was about to explode with resentment. He
was mocking her. Humiliating her. And yet if she demon-
strated her anger, fought him, it would be as if he had won.
As if she really was the ignorant child he was making her out
to be. Inside, she was seething, but she lay down like the
submissive wife, keeping perfectly still while Charles satisfied his need. And each thrust of his body seemed to drive
another nail into her fading affection for him. She had tried.
Had wanted to love him. But she couldn't. Just now, she hated
him for what he had said about Molly and her family. But
she hadn't lost yet.

The battle was far from over.

Rose squeezed her heels into Gospel's flanks and he careered
forward with a surge of bursting energy. She hadn't told
anyone, least of all her husband, but had simply taken the
animal's tack before anyone had realized, saddled him and
ridden quietly out of the yard. And now they were flying
across the moor towards Princetown. Rose was still furious
with Charles. But if he thought he could dominate her like
that, well, she'd jolly well make him think again!

She eased on the reins, slowing Gospel to a trot as they
came into the prison settlement. She would leave him at the
Albert Inn, as always, though the new stable boy was even
more wary of Gospel's temper than Ned had been. She would
leave him saddled as it wouldn't hurt and she didn't intend
to be long. She wanted to return, triumphant, to her husband
as soon as possible to announce that she had employed Molly
whether he liked it or not!

'Good morning, Mrs Chadwick!' Ellen Williams smiled up
at her obsequiously as she swept the front step to her shop.
'I've some lovely autumn materials just come in if you'd care
to take a look.'

Rose scowled as her determined reverie was interrupted by
the woman's servile flannel. Two-faced cow! she thought bitterly.

Didn't want to know when she was in trouble, but now Rose had money in her pocket . . . 'I'm sorry, Miss Williams,' she smiled with deliberate sweetness. 'But I'm afraid my husband only allows me to order material from Harrods in London. And Crebers in Tavistock supply our groceries now.'

She flicked up her head, relishing the snub as she continued down the street. If her marriage to Charles was growing more irksome by the day, she might as well enjoy the advantages it did hold to the full! She even gave the startled stable lad a florin, as in her heart she was hitting back at Charles, and in the mood she was in, it filled her with immense satisfaction that she was giving away his money in a way he would not approve of!

She didn't even have to walk as far as the new warders' block, as Molly was coming towards her, battered shopping basket on her arm. The instant she spied Rose, her pretty face broke into a delighted grin.

'Hello! What you'm doing yere so early?'

Rose grimaced in reply. 'I wanted to get out before anyone realized I was gone.'

'Oh, dear, that don't sound too good.'

Rose flashed her a warm smile. 'Oh, no, 'tis not that bad really. 'Tis just that I couldn't wait to see you.'

'See *me*?'

'Yes. You see . . .' She glanced sideways at Molly as they walked on up the street, Rose's pulse accelerating at the lie she was about to tell her dear friend. 'Charles and I have decided that I really need a lady's maid, and we thought, well, that it should be you.'

Her cheeks were aglow with guilt, but also with excitement at the prospect of Molly's constant companionship. But why should she feel so guilty? Damn Charles! She paid heavily every night for her father's security, so why shouldn't she have her way in this small matter that meant so much to her?

Molly barely faltered in her step, not even turning to look at her. Rose held her breath, convinced that the unexpected surprise had left Molly speechless, and it was indeed several seconds before she spoke.

'Oh, Rose, 'tis terribly kind of you. I should love to be your maid. To live in that there grand house. Only . . . only I cas'n.'

Rose stopped dead, her frozen heart plummeting to her feet

as she caught Molly's arm. 'You . . . you can't?' she stuttered feebly. 'Why . . . why ever not?'

'Cuz . . . Oh, Rose, I'm that sorry. A year ago, 'twould have been wonderful, but . . .' The remorse on her face faded, and in its place a suppressed joy shone in her eyes. 'Can you keep a secret?'

'Of course,' Rose gulped, her voice no more than a faint whisper.

'I *did* want you to be the first to know. I haven't even told my parents yet, so you will keep it to yourself? For now, anyways. Until Joe's asked my father. You see, Joe and I are to be married. We'm just waiting for one of the cottages at the powder mills to become empty.'

Rose's heart contracted in strange pain as Molly's sparkling eyes danced in front of her, and deep inside, she felt something die. Molly and Joe to wed. She was stunned, though why, she didn't know. She should have guessed. A vile sensation she recognized as jealousy gripped her soul. Not jealousy that Molly was to marry *Joe*, for he was like a brother to her. But a choking envy because they were to marry for *love*. A true, free love that fate had put beyond her reach for ever. And because it meant that the one thing that might make her life bearable was now out of the question. But the other part of her, the *real* Rose, was so happy for her friend, and she swallowed down the bitter gall of her own anguish.

'Oh, Molly, congratulations!' She forced the jubilation into her voice. 'And I promise I won't tell a soul!'

'Thank you, Rose!' the younger girl beamed. 'And thank you so much for asking me to be your maid. But 'twould not be worth it for just a few months. I be so sorry. 'Twould have been such fun.'

'Yes. Never mind. 'Tis not the same as getting married.'

'Well, you should know that!' Molly chuckled jauntily.

The knife sliced into Rose's heart. 'Yes,' she murmured. 'Well, I'll leave you to do your shopping.'

'Goodbye, then, Rose.' And Molly sauntered off towards Princetown's shops.

Rose watched her, sadness raking her throat. She should not feel like this! And yet she was shaking, as if she was cut off from reality as she fetched Gospel from the inn and set off back over the moor, this time at a sedate walk, much to the gelding's annoyance. The previous day's torrential rain had released the heady aroma of the long grass and peaty earth beneath Gospel's hooves, and Rose filled her lungs with its calming sweetness. She really should count her blessings. She had Gospel and Amber, and now the scruffy mongrel, Scraggles. She had a lovely house on her beloved Dartmoor, a financially secure future. Above all, she had provided a happy home for her father who remained, she was sure, ignorant of her own wretchedness, when he had been so close to entering the workhouse. She had a husband who was devoted to her . . . but who loved her so much he wanted to possess her body and soul, to crush the spirit from her. She brushed away the tears that misted her eyes, for she would not let him win! Rose Maddiford, the carefree, wilful girl who roamed the wilds of Dartmoor on the massive black horse would never give in, though at this moment she would as soon ride over to Vixen Tor, climb to the top and throw herself over the edge . . .

'Where have you been?' Charles's stiff tone reached her as she stole up the stairs to change out of her riding habit.

She took a breath, then turned to face him, her shoulders squared. 'Out,' she said flatly.

'I can see that. But why creep out in such secrecy?'

'So that I could go alone, if you must know.'

'You don't go out alone without my permission.'

Rose pursed her lips and her eyes snapped dangerously. 'You may remember I told you on the day we met that no one owns me. If I choose to ride out alone, then I shall.'

'Oh, no, you don't, my lady. Your father may have allowed you such inappropriate behaviour, but I would remind you that you are now a married woman, and as such, you will do as you're told.'

'And who's going to make me?'

'I am, if I have to. But perhaps, madam, you'd take more care of yourself if you had a child to think of! So the quicker you become pregnant, the better!'

Rose stared at him, horrified at the brutal cruelty that darkened his face. He grasped her arm, dragging her up the stairs, his fingers digging painfully into her flesh. She did not resist. For her father and Florrie were probably taking breakfast and would hear any altercation on the stairway.

He flung her across the bedroom. She broke her fall on the

edge of the bed, unhurt but shaken, the bile rising in her gullet. She wasn't afraid of him, oh, no! And she certainly wasn't going to let him think he had won! So when he turned back from locking the door, instead of cowering from him, she was leisurely discarding her riding clothes, but didn't stop when she was down to her shirt. She threw the fine garment on to the floor, followed by her chemise so that her bare breasts bobbed tantalizingly as she spun round to face him, clad in nothing more than her drawers.

Charles's face was like thunder. 'Stop behaving like a whore,' he grated savagely.

'Well, 'tis what I am to you, so if the cap fits . . .' Her eyebrows arched sardonically, but then she turned her vivid smile on him. 'Besides, I happen to agree with you that a child would be wonderful.'

Under different circumstances, she would have found the change in his expression quite laughable. Total astonishment had dashed away his rage, and his hand, poised and ready to strike her, fell aimlessly to his side.

'Do you?' he quizzed her as if in disbelief.

'Yes, I do.' Although to be honest, she wasn't really sure.

Charles's mouth spread into a slow smile. 'Well, I'd better see if I can oblige,' he muttered. 'A son. Oh, yes, you've no idea how I've longed for a son.'

His soft, genuine tone took Rose by surprise. She didn't know, of course, of the child his young mistress had robbed him of all those years ago, taking her own life along with the back-street abortion. But just now, his gentler attitude had given her some hope. She had been ignorant of what marriage meant, and she had married Charles for an affection she knew now fell far short of love, and to provide a safe home for Henry. None of which was Charles's fault. And to have a child was something that might unite them.

Not that the thoughts were quite so clear in her head, just part of a jumble of emotions that churned inside her as Charles ran his finger from the well of her throat down to the gathered waist of her drawers, and then slowly untied the drawstring.

Thirteen

Rose missed Dartmoor dreadfully. She missed Molly and Joe and Florrie, the dogs, and most of all, her father and Gospel. London, however, was not without its attractions, a real adventure, and she wrote everything down in a notebook to help her relate her experiences in detail to everyone at home on her return.

Charles's house in the smart, fashionable square was a delight. Rose was particularly fascinated with the bathroom where, to her astonishment, running water poured forth from the taps. The house had its own small, well-tended garden to the rear, but across the road was a private park to which only residents were entitled to hold a key.

It was Rose's refuge. Though the autumn leaves had turned to a glorious display of orange and russet, copper and bronze, and were gradually drifting down from the trees, still enough of them clothed the branches to screen the tall terraces on three sides of the square. The communal garden was hardly Dartmoor, but it provided a haven of peace for her saddened heart when she yearned for the days to pass before she could return home.

Charles had taken her to the principal sites, the immense gothic-style Houses of Parliament, St Paul's Cathedral and the Tower of London. The 'new' London Bridge, though it was more than forty years old now, was built from Dartmoor granite. Likewise, the more recent Trafalgar Square with its astounding Nelson's Column was constructed from moorland stone from the quarries near Princetown. Rose's spirit was filled with pride that the Cherrybrook powder mills had supplied the gunpowder for the quarries.

It went without saying that her going to London with Charles on his next visit had been his idea, though she had not been averse to it. She had been curious to see his house and experience the hustle and bustle of the capital and what it had to offer. But they had been there for nearly the whole of October, and she was longing to return home.

There was an endless round of social engagements, dinner parties and trips to the theatre. Charles seemed pleased with the way Rose conducted herself among his acquaintances, but the disapproval on his face if anyone paid her *too* much attention was alarming. They were returning one drizzly evening from a particularly enjoyable concert, the beautiful music still whirling in Rose's head and filling her with elation so that she had put to the back of her mind the carnal ritual Charles would demand of her despite the late hour.

As they climbed the steps to the front door, it was already being opened from the inside.

'Oh, ma'am,' Dolly, the young parlourmaid announced, dipping her knee. 'A telegram came for you, not five minutes since.'

Alarm ran through Rose's veins. A telegram. It could only be bad news. She picked up the envelope from the silver tray with shaking fingers and struggled to tear open the thin paper. The faint letters danced a jig before her wavering vision. Their meaning sank almost unheeded into her brain as her heart refused to believe it, and she handed the note to Charles for confirmation, praying desperately that her eyes had deceived her.

'ROSE COME HOME STOP,' he read gravely. 'HENRY VERY ILL STOP LOVE FLORRIE STOP.'

Charles looked up, and as Rose's legs seemed to give way beneath her, he caught her in his arms and she slumped against his shoulder. She was swamped by a nauseating dizziness and found herself pressed down into the chair that stood beside the hall table. When the hazy mist cleared from her eyes, Charles was crouched down before her, holding her hands and gazing anxiously into her face.

'Oh, Rose, my dearest, I—'

'I must go to him at once.'

She sprang to her feet, but swayed perilously and had to sit down again abruptly. Charles rubbed his hand over his jaw, his forehead creased in a deep frown.

'There's no point setting out now, my love,' he told her gently. 'I can't imagine there'll be any trains going all the way to Plymouth until the morning.'

'Perhaps to Exeter—'

'And find some lunatic mad enough to drive for miles across the moor in the middle of the night? No, Rose. It isn't practical. Especially as . . . oh, dammit, I can't come with you.'

'What!' Rose's eyes opened wide with pained disbelief, but Charles's face lengthened in an anguished grimace.

'If it was any other day, but tomorrow is the first board meeting of the South African mining company, and I *have* to be there. God knows if it was anything else . . . But you get packed. Dolly will help you. In fact, Dolly can travel with you. But just pack a small valise for yourself. I'll bring everything else the next day. So you do that, and I'll take a cab to the station and book all our tickets and find out the times of the trains so that I can telegraph Florrie and have Ned meet you from Tavistock. It's the best I can do.'

Rose looked up at him, her eyes liquid with moisture as she nodded. Whatever else Charles was, he could be relied upon to think rationally in a crisis, and it gave her strength.

'All right. But I don't need Dolly to come with me,' she added as she smiled at the maid, who had turned a strange colour at the idea of travelling to what seemed to her the opposite end of the earth. 'I can manage perfectly well, and to be honest – and no offence to you, Dolly – but I think I'd rather be on my own.'

For an instant, Charles looked horrified, but he recognized the stubborn determination on his wife's face, and with the telegram containing such bad news, he wasn't going to argue with her.

'As you wish,' he agreed. 'I'll book first class, of course, so you should be safe enough. And Rose, I really am sorry I can't come with you straight away.'

And that night, for the first time in their married life – apart from when they were apart or her monthlies prevented it – he did not force himself upon her.

The nine-hour train journey from Paddington to Tavistock seemed to last an eternity. As the railway skirted the southern edge of Dartmoor, Rose's eyes were drawn in the direction of the distant uplands, knowing that somewhere out there her beloved father lay seriously ill. But what was wrong with him? Had Florrie panicked and it was really only something quite trivial? Rose's tortured mind clung to that comforting thought, though her heart beat tremulously in time to the rhythmical clatter of the train. Each main station had been a busy cacophony of hissing steam, slowly chugging engines, scurrying feet, raised voices and piercing whistle-blowing, after which the line up to Tavistock seemed almost peaceful. The grey autumn day disappeared into the gathering dusk, and the breathtaking views over the moor were lost in the gloom. Rose was nearing home, but the expected elation was buried deep in her constricted chest. She felt cut off from the rest of the world, every nerve on edge. She hadn't eaten all day, the delicacies Charles's cook had packed in a little tin box for her quite untouched.

It was almost dark when she alighted at Tavistock station, and she was grateful even for Ned's company as she sat beside him on the driving seat of the wagonette. Her father *was* very sick, Ned told Rose, though he knew no more than that, and from his solemn expression and unusual silence, Rose knew it was true. Ned had lit the carriage lamps but they did little to illuminate their way, and as they ascended the steep hill up on to the moor, Rose was reminded of another time, less than a year before, when she had struggled along the very same road in a snowstorm. So much had happened since then. She had thought she had found the solution to their problems, and to some extent she had. But the happiness she had expected was proving as elusive as a moonbeam.

She didn't stop to remove her coat and hat, but flew straight into her father's room, her heart hammering with dread. Florrie had been dozing in the chair, and she did not have time to blink the startled confusion from her eyes before Rose threw herself on her knees beside the bed and took Henry's hand in hers. He appeared to be asleep, but when he heard her soft, quavering voice, his glazed eyes half opened in his grey face.

'Ah, Rose, my darling girl,' he mumbled, his words so frail she could hardly hear him. 'What a picture you are. Quite the lady. And happy. You are happy, aren't you, Rose?'

A mist dimmed the crystal violet of her eyes. 'Yes, Father,' she managed to say as she swallowed down the strangling constriction in her throat.

'Then I can die in peace,' he whispered, and his eyelids drooped closed again.

Something jerked, and then settled irrevocably in Rose's chest. 'Don't say that, Father.'

But all she received in response was a serene smile.

Dr Power spread his hands. 'I believe your father has suffered a pulmonary embolism,' he said grimly.

Rose lifted her eyes to him from the opposite side of the drawing-room fireplace where she shivered with cold, despite the roaring blaze. 'Pulmonary . . . his lungs, you mean?' she asked quietly.

'Yes. A clot on his left lung. You know his lungs were weakened by the smoke inhalation last year. And the clot may be the result of his inactivity, or he may have had a predisposition to it anyway.'

'And . . . and his chances?' Her voice sounded strange to her own ears, disconnected. She had not slept for more than forty-eight hours, neither her last night in London nor the night she had spent in Florrie's chair by Henry's bedside. She was exhausted, her mind ready to shut down and accept the inevitable.

'Not good, I'm afraid.' Dr Power's mouth twisted sadly. 'The clot may disperse, but if it does, the fragments could lodge elsewhere, in the heart or the brain perhaps. In the meantime, your father's in a lot of pain from the clot. That's why I'm giving him morphine injections night and morning, and Mrs Bennett has laudanum to supplement it if necessary. But, if we can't reduce them, the drugs in themselves will be very dangerous.'

'So, what you're saying is, one way or another, my father is dying.'

The doctor released his breath through pursed lips. 'Almost certainly.'

Rose nodded, staring down at her tightly intertwined fingers. 'Your frankness is appreciated, Dr Power. And . . . and how long does he have?'

He faltered, shaking his head slightly. 'If we have to keep up with this high dose of morphine, a week, possibly less. But better to let him go without pain, don't you think? And when the time comes, he will drift asleep in peace and calm.'

'And if he does improve?' Rose asked with a spark of hope.

'I am a mere mortal, Mrs Chadwick, and cannot predict

what miracles God may produce. I am so sorry, but in my opinion, you should prepare yourself for the worst.'

Rose felt her heart drag with sadness. 'It hasn't been much of a life for him,' she croaked wearily, 'not since the accident.'

'You've done the best for him that anyone could. Take comfort from that. And I suggest you try and get some sleep. Mrs Bennett will sit with him, and there are servants to relieve her.'

'But 'tis my place to—'

'Not to the detriment of your own health. Now I believe your husband will be arriving this evening?'

Rose realized she had hardly given Charles a thought. 'Yes,' she answered absently. 'He had a business meeting of the utmost importance yesterday, and so could not accompany me, and I was not prepared to wait.'

'Of course. And he will be of great strength to you.'

'Yes,' she replied, though something inside her died.

'Rose, my darling, you must eat.'

Charles was gazing at her with pleading eyes, but she turned her head from the tray with her hand over her mouth. 'Please, Charles, take it away. Just the thought of food makes me feel sick.'

'All right.' He released a heartfelt sigh. 'But you will drink the tea. Or would you prefer something cold and refreshing? Cook's lemonade, or some ginger beer? I'll ride into Princetown to buy some if there's none in the pantry.'

But Rose looked up at him with a wan smile. 'The tea will be fine, thank you. But maybe some lemonade later on. Perhaps I can rouse Father enough to drink some, too.'

'Yes, my dear. Perhaps.'

He patted her shoulder, and her hand closed over his. The last few days, he had been the man she had believed she had married, kind, considerate, affectionate but without demanding his conjugal rights. Not that she had been to bed since she had returned home, a fact that worried both the doctor and Charles. And now he padded silently out of the room with the tray, sensing that she would prefer to be alone in her vigil.

The tea was hot and sweet, soothing her agitated mind. The autumn sunlight penetrating the room in hesitant shafts gradually faded into noiseless twilight, and she was aware of Florrie coming in to draw the curtains. Amber trotted in behind her and came to rest her golden muzzle on Rose's knee, staring up at her with doleful brown eyes. Rose blinked awake and fondled the soft fur at the dog's ears, and not to be outdone, Scraggles scampered across with his head on one side in that amusing way he had, so that one pointed ear flopped over comically, and Rose stroked his scruffy head with a faint smile. She hardly dared to look at Henry, and when she did, his chest was rising and falling regularly but in shallow, slightly wheezy breaths.

Florrie straightened up from poking the moribund fire into life and adding more coal. 'He seems peaceful enough, poor lamb,' she whispered.

Rose nodded her head, but a painful lump squeezed her gullet. 'What shall I do without him, Florrie?' she could hardly mouth.

'What shall we all do without him?' Florrie's fat, wet cheeks wobbled.

She drew up the other chair and sat by Rose's side. They exchanged not another word. They had no need of it, both lost in a private world of sadness that admitted no intruders. The fire hissed in the grate, the clock ticked on the mantelpiece, echoing in the hushed room, and the dogs slept together on the hearth rug, Scraggles making tiny squeaking sounds as he dreamt of chasing some fleet rabbit.

Charles came in with the promised lemonade. They all stirred, including the dogs. Even Henry groaned in the bed, his eyes opening in a confused daze. Rose sprang to his side, her eyes spangled with unshed tears.

'Father?'

'Ah, my dearest Rose.' The agitation flowed from his face as his vision focused on his beloved daughter, and in its place a supreme calm seemed to smooth out the lines in his skin.

'We were just having some of Cook's lemonade. Would you like some?'

For a moment, she thought she would break at the normality of the question, but Henry managed a weak smile. ''Twon't be as good as Florrie's, but yes, I should like some. If you can sit me up . . .'

Florrie, leaning over Rose's shoulder, went to assist him as Rose already had the heavy glass jug in her hands, and as Florrie's strong arms went about him, there was a look passed between them that Rose had never noticed before, and it filled her with a cruel joy. Had there been more between her father and their housekeeper than she had ever realized? Some sort of understanding that had brought them happiness all those years? It tore at Rose's heart, for she hoped so, but it would mean parting would be so much the worse.

Charles had gone to the other side of the bed to help, and Henry turned his tired eyes on his son-in-law. 'You will look after them, won't you?'

Charles nodded gravely. 'Of course.' There was no more said, and Rose poured some of the refreshing liquid into the feeding jug and held the spout to Henry's lips. But he had only taken a sip before he indicated he wanted no more, and Rose replaced the little jug on the bedside table.

'Would you like me to stay?' Charles whispered in her ear.

Rose could hardly bear to turn to him. At this appalling time, she should want to lean on her husband, on the man she was supposed to love, but she couldn't. She didn't love him, and that was what she needed, and so it was better to face this alone. With Florrie, who knew her better than she knew herself.

'No. 'Tis all right,' she smiled sweetly, cutting his heart for he knew hers was breaking.

'I'll just be in the drawing room,' he breathed back.

The ache that clawed at Rose's throat prevented her from replying, and Charles slipped quietly out of the room. The dogs followed him, their claws clicking softly on the wooden floorboards as they passed the edge of the luxurious carpet. They had had enough of the tense atmosphere and the smell of death.

Henry took a deep breath and winced. Rose leapt to her feet. 'Do you want some laudanum?'

Henry's eyes misted with love. 'No. Not yet. 'Tis not so bad if I don't move. I should like to spend some time with my daughter. And my dear Florrie.'

He gave the older woman that special smile again, and this time it brought a certain peace to Rose's soul. They had been so happy together, the three of them. For more than twenty-two years. Without Florrie, it just wouldn't have been the same.

They spoke of the past. Of distant memories. Tears and laughter, ending in wistful smiles. A good life. But one that was to be curtailed by possibly twenty years, though no one said so, because of a granule of grit that had somehow found its way into the mixing trough. The room was quiet, stilled, their voices low and bitter-sweet. Trembling with a lifetime of deepest love. Henry was tiring, and though he tried to conceal it, Rose knew that the morphine had worn off, and the pain in his chest was agonizing, but still he refused the laudanum. She knew why.

Dr Power arrived at seven o'clock, picking his way in the darkness along the now familiar route on his trusty mare, but it was a clear moonlit evening, and the first heavy frost of the waning year pinched the night air. His greeting when he entered the bedroom was that of a friend, rubbing his cold hands as he held them out to the warmth of the fire. He spoke in his usual calm and reassuring manner, telling them of the bitter weather and apologizing for his delayed arrival due to some problem at the prison. Kind and warm-hearted, but what did Rose care of what was happening beyond the four walls of the house?

He took Henry's pulse, extricated the stethoscope from his bag to listen to his patient's chest. Henry's eyes were clouded with pain, and the doctor frowned. 'I think you're ready for the morphine,' he said gently.

'Just give me . . . five more minutes.' Henry's voice was no more than a thin trail, feeble, almost inarticulate, and Dr Power nodded slowly, closing his eyes in understanding as he patted Henry's shoulder and withdrew to the far side of the room.

Rose held Henry's limp hand, stroking it, not able to speak, not able to think of any words, drowning in the tidal wave of sorrow that gripped her heart, relieved almost, and yet ashamed of it, as Henry turned his head to Florrie who held his other hand from the opposite side of the bed.

'Florrie, what a comfort you have always been to me,' he mumbled.

Florrie's double chin quivered. 'And you, Henry,' she answered in a faltering whisper, 'you gave me a home like no other.'

Her tear-filled eyes met Rose's across the bed, and when Henry rested his wandering gaze on his daughter, a look of such compassion, of tenderness and love came over him that his face appeared lit with a transcendent glow. 'And you, my darling, darling child, you will never know . . . what joy you have given me.'

His eyes seemed to spark with life, the deep blueness of

his youth flooding into them as he stared deep into her grieving soul. She was lost in the choking misery that closed her throat and made the glittering tears spill down her cheeks. 'I love you, Father.' She dragged the words from her lungs, struggling against her wrenching sobs.

But Henry smiled back. 'I know,' he rasped. 'But you must . . . let me go now. Just promise me one thing, Rose. Whatever happens in your life . . . always be . . . yourself. Be the headstrong, feckless Rose . . . I have known . . . and loved.'

'Yes, I promise.' But this time the words were merely mouthed as the agony overwhelmed her, strangled her. Crucified her.

Dr Power, silently, was beside her, syringe at the ready. Rose could not watch, blinded, and when the doctor moved away, Henry was watching her again. Peacefully.

'No life for me now, Rose.'

His eyes closed, and he slept. Dr Power checked his pulse and breathed in deeply.

'He's very weak,' he said with quiet compassion. 'I think it might be best if I stayed a while.'

Rose's heart thumped hard in her chest. 'You mean . . .?' She could not say it, but the doctor nodded soberly, and Rose's mouth contorted into an ugly grimace as she fought against her tears. 'Thank you,' she murmured. 'At least I know . . . and can be with him.'

Dr Power nodded again. 'And, I'm sorry to have to mention such a thing, but perhaps your groom could stable my horse? On such a sharp night . . .'

'Of course.' An understanding smile slipped across Rose's lips. 'Florrie, would you mind?'

'I'll see to it at once.'

'And I'll . . . wait in your drawing room with your husband, unless you'd rather I were here?'

'No, no. That's . . . But Florrie, you'll come back?' she added, desperately seizing her plump arm.

'Yes, of course, my lamb.'

And so they sat, one on either side of Henry's bed, in virtual silence, each respecting the other's need for innermost contemplation, and yet welcoming any exchange. The room was darkened, the heavy curtains drawn against the cold night, just the incandescent orange and gold brilliance of the fire, and the lamps turned low. Breathless. Unreal. Midnight ticked on into the new day. The doctor glided in on soundless feet to observe his dying patient, and disappeared like a shadow. At two o'clock, Florrie went to make a pot of tea, leaving Rose trembling and alone, and while she was gone, Henry took a few sudden, rattling gasps, opened his eyes to look at his daughter, and remained staring at her, unseeing, for ever.

Rose felt the life force drain from her limbs. For several minutes, she sat without moving, numbed, in a strange way glad, because the waiting was over and the dreadful time had come, and she would be forced to admit to reality instead of refusing to believe it. She floated to her feet then, bent to lay her lips on Henry's motionless forehead, and sat back down in the chair, for there was no need for her to do anything for her father ever again. When Florrie came back in with the small tray, Rose's head was resting on the hand that would never clasp hers again, and when she slowly, reluctantly looked up, she was dry-eyed with grief and an invisible vice around her neck was throttling her.

Florrie silently put down the tray and seconds later, Charles and Dr Power were in the room. Rose still sat like a granite statue, her eyes in a stunned, sightless stare. Ten, twenty minutes, and she could not be stirred except to push Charles aside when he tried to take her away.

The doctor squatted down before her and took her icy hands. 'Mrs Chadwick . . . Rose . . . Death is an inevitable part of life. The only certain thing that comes to us all. I watch men die, prisoners, who have endured a living hell. Who have been pushed beyond what their bodies can take, albeit part of their punishment. Their last days are full of misery, and they die unloved. Probably haven't seen their families for years. And they are buried in Princetown churchyard, as you know, with not even a stone to mark their graves. But your father died peacefully and with dignity, with his loving family all about him. Please, I beg you, take comfort from that, and think of your own health now, as you know your father would have wished.'

A faint light seemed to come into Rose's eyes, and she blinked, a painful swoop and lift of her silken lashes, before she nodded, and rising to her feet, floated out of the room.

Charles followed her, but instead of climbing the stairs, she made for the back door. Before Charles could stop her, she was out across the stable yard and into Gospel's loose box where her howls of misery lacerated the still, frosty night as she clung about the surprised animal's neck.

The funeral took place three days later. Rose Maddiford – for no one could ever think of her by her married name – walked behind her father's coffin, refusing to take the hired carriage as her husband requested. So he walked at her side, supporting her, since it was clear that if he had not she would have collapsed. She resembled a little ghost, dark smudges under her sunken eyes in her gaunt white face, her springing curls swaying down her back like the wings of a raven from beneath the small black hat on her head. For she was keeping her promise. Being herself as she laid her father to rest.

The hearse with its decorative engraved glass and gold and black coachwork was drawn by a pair of shining ebony horses with matching plumes standing up from their heads, and a rainbow of flowers adorned the mahogany coffin. Behind Mr and Mrs Chadwick shambled Mrs Florrie Bennett on the arm of Mr George Frean, the humble housekeeper leaning on the wealthy businessman, proprietor of the Cherrybrook gunpowder mills. And behind them, Joe Tyler, who had virtually been a son to the dead man, and his betrothed, best friend of the deceased's grief-stricken daughter. At a respectful distance followed the entire workforce of the powder mills, plus all the wives who did not have small children to care for. There were local quarrymen and miners, too, shopkeepers, the carrier and the telegraph officer, all wanting to offer their support to Rose of Cherrybrook as she buried her revered father.

And after the interment, when she staggered, half carried by her husband, through the churchyard, she remembered Dr Power's words and stopped for just a moment to glance back at the plot reserved for the unmarked graves of the prisoners. And her heart overflowed with sorrow.

Fourteen

'Really, Rose, you cannot keep galloping over the moor like some deranged creature from an asylum!'

Rose glowered at him from the dressing-room door as she tucked the tails of her fine cotton shirt into the waist of her riding breeches and strode across to the bed where her riding overskirt lay at the ready.

'I'm not behaving like a madwoman, I'm simply going for a ride,' she said coldly, her eyes narrowed in her haggard face.

'And that's all you ever do, charge about on that wretched nag! I might as well not exist! I've stayed here for weeks on end to talk to you, comfort you, when I should be in London seeing to our business affairs. But you're never *here*!'

'And why should I be?' The expression of contempt, of loathing, on her face was so ghastly, so removed from the lovely beauty he had fallen in love with just over a year previously – was it so little time ago? – that Charles took a dismayed step backwards. But she came towards him, her eyes livid with anger. 'My father has been dead for little more than a month, and you expect me to be over it! I feel trapped inside this house, lovely as 'tis. But when I'm out on the moor, I feel some sort of peace. So if I want to escape for a few hours, neither you nor anyone else will stop me! And if you need to go back to London, then go. I shan't be the one to miss you.'

Charles lifted his chin, his jaw set. 'No, I don't suppose you would,' he murmured bitterly. 'And I really do need to go to London, just for a few days, anyway. And I suppose,' he paused to sigh, 'you wouldn't come with me? The change might do you good. Take your mind off of everything. After all, Mrs Bennett saw the wisdom of going away when she went to stay with her sister. And it must be doing her some good, seeing as she's decided not to come back yet. If you come to London with me, I know I should be out most of the day, but we could go to a concert or the opera every night. You enjoyed that, didn't you, the music?'

Rose's spine bristled. It was like a thorn in her side, that Florrie had gone, abandoning her when she needed her most. But Rose understood. They each had to deal with their grief in their own way, and if Florrie's was to stay with her sister, Rose's was to fly across the wild openness of Dartmoor on Gospel's back.

'You honestly believe that would stop me thinking about my father? No! You go to London. I have my friends here, even if you disapprove of them.'

'If you are referring to the Cartwrights or Joe Tyler, then yes, I do disapprove,' Charles answered tightly. 'You would hardly associate like that with Ned, and they are no better than he is.'

'How dare you say that? Ned is—' She bit her lip, and her cheeks flamed hot and red. She didn't want Charles to know what had happened in the stable that day. Ned was right. Charles *was* the jealous type, and though he could dismiss Ned – or worse – God alone knew what he might do to her! 'Ned is just Ned,' she continued less vehemently. 'But Joe and Molly and her family are my friends, and just now I really need them.'

'More than you need me, apparently.'

'You said it.'

Charles stiffened and his face hardened to stone. 'All right. I'll go to London alone. But I'll give you something to remember while I'm gone. And it may help you to remember that you are *my* wife and no one else's.'

Before his words had a chance to sink into Rose's brain, he pushed her backwards on to the bed and leapt astride her, pinning her down.

'You know, you really do look very fetching in a shirt and breeches.' He smiled down on her, but there was an unsettling look on his face. 'I can see those lovely breasts, and the way the breeches fit tightly about your hips—'

'You know perfectly well I'd be wearing the jacket and skirt over the top,' she retorted, for she knew only too well that excited gleam in his eyes.

'Just as well, my lovely girl. We wouldn't want every man jack to desire you as I do, would we now?'

His fingers were at the buttons of her shirt, and she tried to pull them away as the blood seemed to circle about her heart.

'For God's sake, Charles, can't you leave me alone for five minutes? You've already had me this morning, and—'

'And I shall have you as many times as I please, my little tigress. You seem to forget you are my wife, and I get precious little else in return for the luxury I provide for you!'

His face had set into rigid lines, and Rose felt the rush of fear cramp her stomach. 'And can you wonder at it! You're like an animal!'

'Oh, animal, is it? Well, we'll see about that!'

She glared at him, exploding with fury, as he ripped open the carefully sewn buttons, and in her outrage, her lashing fists pummelled at his chest. He laughed. And her fingers opened like claws, missing the target of his face, but catching his neck and drawing blood. His expression turned to a mask of iron, and he trapped her flailing hands in his, transferring both her fragile wrists into the forceful grip of one of his own strong hands while with the other he pushed the camisole beneath her open shirt up to her armpits. She scowled up at him, baring her teeth, incensed that she did not have the physical strength to fight him off, no matter how she struggled. He merely grinned back as he fumbled with the buttons of her breeches and she knew there would be no stopping him. She turned her head away with a tearing sigh of infuriated resignation, biting hard on her lip and waiting for the moment when it was over. Charles writhed and jerked on top of her, and finally rolled away, his face flushed and damp with sweat. Rose lay for several seconds, her teeth gnawing at the knuckles of one of her released hands, before springing to her feet.

She tossed her head, and her hair whipped about her in a tumbled cascade of curls. 'Well, if you've had your fill,' she barked at him, 'I'd like to go on my ride now.'

He turned on her, eyes still glazed with pleasure, and propped himself up on one elbow to watch as she dressed herself again. 'You really are magnificent, you know,' he drawled languidly. 'And I'm sorry for what I said in the heat of the moment just now. I really do love you. Too much, perhaps, if that's possible. And I really do wish you'd come to London with me. I'm sure it would be good for you.'

Rose flashed him a withering look. 'No.' And then, as an afterthought, she added with frosty sarcasm, 'Thank you.'

Charles raised both eyebrows, and released a sharp sigh through his nostrils. 'As you wish. But . . . you could buy some presents for Christmas. Order yourself some new clothes from the dressmakers.'

'I already have a wardrobe full of good clothes,' she rounded on him as she fastened the riding skirt about her waist. 'And now that my father is dead, I have no one to buy Christmas presents for.'

'Not even me?' Charles questioned wistfully. 'And what about all these friends you are so fond of?'

She frowned at him, smarting under his sardonic words, as once again, he had dominated her. She finished cramming her hair into the finely crocheted snood, grabbed the hat and hatpin she had left ready on the dressing table – pausing for an instant to wonder if she shouldn't jab the hatpin into whatever part of Charles's anatomy she could get at, but thinking better of it – and then stormed out of the room, leaving the door to bang shut behind her.

'Ned!' she yelled imperiously as she hurtled across the stable yard, and almost collided with him as he emerged startle-eyed from mucking out Tansy's loose box, as it was unusual for the mistress to raise her voice. She surprised him even further by demanding that he should bring Gospel's saddle and bridle from the tack room, as she normally did so herself. An instant later, she was pressed up against Gospel's strong, comforting shoulder, her arms about his neck and her cheek resting on his warm, hairy coat to hide her stinging tears. She felt drained, the bravado fled, and in its place, a wrenching misery. She should have stopped to clean herself, to wash away the humiliation Charles, her husband, had heaped upon her, but the only thing she had wanted was to get away from him. She felt used. Physically sick. Her body bruised and aching. She had married Charles for her father's sake, had *made* herself believe she had loved him. She did not regret it. Henry's last months at Fencott Place had been happy ones, and she would have had it no other way. But she had been married in June and now it was the beginning of December, and she had to face the rest of her life tied to a man she could not love. If Henry had survived another few years, it would have seemed far more worthwhile, but just now, as her body throbbed with soreness, it felt as if her sacrifice had been for nothing.

She pulled herself up short as Ned joined her in the box, and Gospel stamped with agitation at the unwelcome intruder. But within five minutes they were out on the moor, crisp and white with a hoar frost. Rose did not consider where they would go until Gospel stopped at a fork in the track, waiting for instructions from his beloved mistress. Rose scanned the horizon, allowing the infinite vastness of Dartmoor to bathe her soul. Her eyes were inevitably drawn to the gaunt buildings of the prison, dominated by the grim and daunting cell block number five, the first of the original constructions to be doubled in ground area and raised to a massive, inhuman, five-storey monster by gruelling convict labour, using stone blasted from the prison quarry. And although the inmates of the new, unheated cell block – already running with damp – shivered through the bitter winter nights, coughing and spluttering and half-starved on the basic prison diet while Rose existed in the lap of luxury, she knew exactly how they felt, incarcerated in a living hell for years on end . . .

It was three days before Charles left for London, three days when the very sight of him brought on nausea. Henry's death had reduced Rose's appetite to that of a sparrow, but now she somehow felt sick and hungry at the same time, and eating something light and refreshing, such as a raw carrot, seemed to settle her stomach. You be turning into a horse, like that animal o' yourn, she could just hear Florrie teasing her. But Florrie wasn't there, was she? Rose nearly gagged on her sadness. She felt so alone . . .

But not quite. She had not dared to sneak out while Charles was still there, though, to be honest, he had never physically prevented her from her lone rides. The truth was that, though she refused to admit it, since the day Charles had forced himself upon her and she had stampeded across the moor in a maddened temper, she hadn't *felt* like going out. But his departure seemed to have given her a new lease of life, besides which there was one exciting event that she could now devote herself to wholeheartedly – and of which Charles, thank goodness, appeared ignorant.

On the fifteenth of December, Molly and Joe were to be married. Charles was not a churchgoer, and so had not heard the banns being read, and as he refused to associate with the people of the lower echelons, there had been no one to inform him of the news. In fact, his life at Fencott Place was fairly insular, and Rose supposed it was one reason for focusing his attentions on his wife with such zeal. He had visited the powder mills once, purely for business purposes and speaking only to the new manager; Mr Frean they both saw on occasion, and Charles had made the acquaintance of the Duchy of Cornwall's agent at Prince Hall. But there were no social rounds as there were in London, and which, to be fair, Charles probably missed. In fact, if she stopped to think about it, Charles had sacrificed much to be with her on Dartmoor, and she bit her lip in remorse, since in her heart of hearts, she recognized that the problems with their marriage were not all one-sided.

No such qualms entered her mind now. For some reason she could not explain to herself, she decided to walk into Princetown rather than take Gospel from his warm stable. The ground was frozen solid beneath her feet, the still, bitterly cold air nipping at her nose and so raw she could almost taste it. The sky was an iron grey, pressing down on her with low, ominous clouds, but she was determined that her visit would bring some respite from the depression that was gnawing at her very core.

She found the sitting room in the new flat in happy chaos. Molly leapt to her feet with a cry of delight and hugged her friend tightly, while her retiring mother came forward with unusual confidence.

'We'm so sorry 'bout your father,' she said quietly.

Rose nodded, and knotted her lips against the lump that swelled so readily in her gullet. 'Thank you,' she whispered automatically, and then jerked her head towards two tea-chests in the middle of the floor. 'You look busy.'

'Yes.' The woman's eyes shone. 'We'm packing some things to go over to Molly and Joe's cottage at Cherrybrook.'

Rose smiled broadly, but somehow the usual vivid light was missing from her eyes. 'Oh, I'm so pleased for you all. And you must be so excited, Molly.'

The younger girl grinned, the joy on her face making her

look even prettier. 'Well, you'm only just married yersel, Rosie, so you should know. 'Tis to be at the chapel, the wedding, but you knows that. And the breakfast, 'tis to be held at the Prince of Wales. Nort fancy, but one up on the Albert Inn, anyways! You will come, won't you, Rosie? You and . . . and Mr Chadwick? I couldn't bear it if you wasn't there!'

Rose felt her heart thud in her chest. There was no way Charles would even contemplate attending such an affair, and no doubt he would do his best to prevent her from going, too. 'You just try and stop me!' she answered, tossing her head and praying Molly wouldn't see the doubt that flickered across her features. 'Now, what can I get you for a wedding present? There must be lots of things you need.'

'Oh, Rosie, you doesn't have to give us a present.'

But the idea sent a thrill of enthusiasm spilling into Rose's troubled soul. 'Oh, of course I do! You must make a list of everything and I'll get it for you.'

'Oh, but, Rose—'

'No buts, Molly! What's the point of being rich if you can't spend some money on your best friend when she's getting married!'

A little voice inside her head grimaced that she earned her wealth in her marital bed, and that frittering away a few pounds of Charles's money on Molly when she knew it would anger him was immensely satisfying. And so she spent the happiest day since Henry had died in the Cartwrights' humble home, helping to make a list and silently vowing to buy the best-quality items and spend as much as she possibly could!

When it was time to leave, Rose kissed Molly goodbye, shivering on the doorstep as the arctic air licked about her slender form despite her warm coat. But there was one more thing she must do before she trod the path home. She crossed over the road, hesitating for a moment by the iron gates to gather up her courage, and entered the churchyard. The gloom at once closed about her aching heart again, the few hours of enjoyment she had spent with Molly dissipated to the four winds. She moved like a spectre, silent and alone, gliding to the slight mound in the grass with the simple wooden cross. No headstone as yet. You had to wait several months for the earth to settle, she had been told by the stonemason, a respectful fellow who had known Henry well. But the memorial she envisaged would be the finest ever made. Not too elaborate, but elegant and skilfully carved. Paid for from Charles's pocket, of course. The bitterness tugged at her lips, the grief searing her throat until she could fight it no longer and tears began to trickle down from her eyes. She knelt, as still as a statue, her head bent as the misery tore at her chest. She wanted to howl, to scream her pain to the heavens so that somehow it might reach Henry and haul him back to the world of the living; that the bottomless pit of her agony might make him appear to her and let her know that in some other way, he still existed, for no daughter could ever have loved a father more deeply than she had. But she knew it would do no good. There was nothing on earth that could free her from the melancholy that held her in its cruel grasp. A good man, perhaps. A better man than Charles. One who understood, who saw her as a person with her own needs and feelings. But Charles was all she would ever have. And the torment of it was suffocating her.

She tipped her head back, lifting her tear-ravaged face to the leaden sky, and the first snowflakes kissed her frozen cheeks.

Fifteen

Saturday week arrived and Charles had yet to return. Rose's heart lifted. The wedding was set for noon and there was nothing to stop her from going. Surely there could be no better medicine for her broken spirit than to witness her best friend getting wed to the lad who had been like a brother to her, a marriage that truly would be made in heaven. The ceremony was perfect, and Rose managed to ignore the barbed pang in her side at the memory of both her own wedding back in the summer, and her father's funeral in the same church not so many weeks before. She shivered as a draught of air brushed her side. Was it Henry? For wild horses would not have kept him from the wedding of his semi-adopted son.

The celebration was a jolly affair. Two fiddlers played lively jigs and reels, and though there was little enough room, the tables were cleared away for dancing. And when, in the middle of the afternoon, Rose knew she must leave so that she would arrive home before dark, she reluctantly said her farewells, and her soul felt refreshed.

'The master be home,' Cook told her in a low, wary tone as she went into the kitchen to order a pot of tea. 'Wanted to know where you was, so I told him. I hope that were all right, ma'am.'

Rose drew in a slow, satisfied breath. She had been to Molly and Joe's wedding. Charles hadn't been there to stop her, and she cared little for what happened next. She had left her wet, slush-coated boots by the door and hurried upstairs to slip into a pair of soft kid shoes. She changed her clothes, too, the hem of her skirts and petticoats being stained with damp. She chose what she knew was one of Charles's favourite dresses, suitable for dining in company on a winter's evening, with long sleeves for warmth, but a scooping neckline to reveal quite enticingly the creamy skin over her collarbones and below the well of her throat. Her hair was already entwined upon her head, and she simply tidied a wayward curl before tripping downstairs again. She paused at the drawing-room door to square her shoulders before she breezed in with a brilliant smile.

'Charles!'

She made herself run across the room to him. He looked up, scowling thunderously, but before he could utter a word, she bent to press her mouth against his, embracing him with all the passion of a young girl.

'Why didn't you come straight in here to greet me?' he said tersely as she straightened up. 'Cook's had time to bring you in some tea.'

Rose glanced across at the tray on the table, and her weary heart sank. Were they to argue already? She didn't have time to answer before Charles barked at her again.

'I hear you've been to Molly Cartwright's wedding,' he growled stiffly. 'You deliberately kept it from me, didn't you, knowing I'd disapprove?'

Rose merely shrugged. 'You weren't here to tell. What time did you get back, anyway? Would you like some tea? I'll fetch another cup.'

She turned towards the door, but he caught her by the wrist. She yelped, for the bruises were still fading from where he had held both her hands above her head in the bedroom when they had quarrelled last. It was a squeal more of surprise, though, than discomfort, and she flicked up her head, the fine line of her jaw lifted stubbornly.

'If I wanted to go to my best friend's wedding to Joe who is virtually my brother, I didn't need your permission!' she hissed at him, her eyes flashing dangerously.

'Oh, yes, you did!' Charles spat, his lips white with anger. 'My wife, hobnobbing with that rabble! I won't have it!'

The bile scorched in Rose's gullet, and it was all she could do to stop herself flying at him with hungry fingernails. Instead, she glared at him steadily, her cheeks colourless with strained composure.

'Nobody possesses me,' she grated levelly. 'If I wish to associate, as you put it, with good, honest, God-fearing folk, you won't stop me.'

'Oh, yes, I will. And may I remind you, madam, that in your wedding vows not so long ago, you promised to obey me.'

'And in all things reasonable I do. Which is more than can be said of *you* when it comes to honouring *me*! You treat me like some whore in bed.'

'Rose! I won't have such a filthy word coming from your mouth!'

He raised his hand, ready to strike her. A rush of fear tingled through her body, and she instinctively wrenched herself away from him. He lost his grip on her wrist, and with the force of her own movement, her feet went from under her. Her head narrowly missed the table as she went down, but her collarbone cracked against it instead. Pain stung across her shoulder, and her vision clouded with black spots as she lay crumpled on the floor, fighting the chasm of unconsciousness that threatened to swallow her. She sensed rather than saw Charles drop on his knees beside her, and she shuddered when he took her in his arms.

'Oh, my darling, I'm so sorry!' his voice shook in her ear. 'I wouldn't have hit you, really I wouldn't!'

She shuddered as she felt him lift her into the air and carry her over to the chaise-longue. Her head swam giddily and when her eyes wandered into focus, Charles's face was looming over her, a mortified picture of concern.

'You don't think . . . It isn't broken, is it?' His lips trembled.

If she hadn't been in such agony, she would have made a verbal attack on him, but as it was, she shot him an acid glance as she tried to look down at the site of the injury. It was too close to her neck to see, so instead she gingerly fingered her collarbone, exposed by the low neckline of her dress. It had already swollen into a tender lump the size of an egg, and she tentatively moved her shoulder in a small circle. It hurt, but over all, the pain was subsiding.

'No, I don't believe 'tis broken.' She found her voice at last, though it was small and shaking. 'So you won't have to explain to the doctor how it happened,' she added with caustic contempt.

Charles's eyes opened wide in his flushed face. 'It . . . it wasn't my fault,' he protested.

Rose glared at him, her eyes glowing like hot coals, and suddenly the resentment, the abhorrence, rose in her like a bore tide. She felt the contents of her stomach lifting to her throat, and with one hand clamped over her mouth while the other arm was held tightly across her chest to protect her injured shoulder, she fled the room and raced upstairs to the bathroom where she retched her heart into the pretty china washbowl.

Rose slowly blinked open her eyes. There had still been some light in the sky when, after a sumptuous Christmas dinner, she had come over so tired that she felt she must have a lie-down. Now, after a short sleep, the room was in total darkness, and she had to fumble with the matches to light the oil lamp on the bedside table. She lay for a few minutes, her gaze meandering over the lovely room. Charles certainly provided well for her, and she *was* grateful, but . . . She exhaled in a profound, weary sigh. If only Charles had continued to be the same man after their wedding as he had been before, she perhaps could have loved him. But he wanted her entirely to himself, to *possess* her in every way, and it was ruining their marriage.

She sat up, wincing slightly as her bruised collarbone was still a little sore, and shivering as Patsy, the housemaid, had not yet lit the fire. Rose had merely snuggled beneath her thick woollen shawl as she lay on the bed, and now she pulled it tightly about her shoulders. Goodness, she had eaten too much, but Cook had excelled herself and Rose's appetite, which had been so poor since Henry's death, had seemed stimulated. Her dress was strained, and the ties around her waist which held the small bustle at the back felt uncomfortably tight. It had been like that for a few weeks now, which was odd really considering how little she had been eating of late. But then her monthly must be due, as her breasts were swollen and tender. She hadn't had the 'curse' as Molly called it since . . . since when?

She frowned. And a little flutter quivered through her body as she cast her mind back. Since her dearest father had passed away, her life had been one appalling black blur. She could scarcely remember the weeks she had spent in London, and the dark days since then had been lost in a mournful haze, all her strength expended in trying to claw her way out of her grief. She simply hadn't considered . . . But now the force of it hit her hard in the chest, stunning her. She had been 'on' when they had arrived in London at the beginning of October.

She only remembered because she had been worried about the long journey and the frequency with which she might be able to find a public convenience. But she couldn't remember anything since. With everything that had happened, her bereaved mind had hardly taken note of . . .

She was pregnant. She must be! Everything pointed to it, the nausea, the thickening of her waist, the tiredness. She sat motionless in the silent room, trying to absorb what had just dawned on her. A child. Charles would be thrilled. And her? Well . . . yes. She supposed so. A tiny kernel of hope was slowly unfurling inside her, hope that the child would heal the deepening rift between herself and Charles. Because she *wanted* their marriage to be a happy one, *wanted* so much the loving relationship that was eluding her. But what if it made things worse? What if Charles wanted to dominate her in all matters concerning the child? It would only make her misery all the deeper.

There was only one way to find out and she got to her feet and went downstairs. As she entered the drawing room, Charles glanced up from the book he was reading.

'Ah, my dear, did you have a nap? You certainly look refreshed.'

At least he appeared in a good mood, and it gave her courage. 'Charles . . .' She came forward and warily squatted down before him. 'Charles, I have something to tell you. I believe . . . I think I may be with child.'

Charles's eyes almost popped out of their sockets and his mouth fell open before spreading into a huge grin. He cast the book aside and dropped on to his knees, wrapping her in his jubilant arms. Her eyes closed as her head lay against his shoulder, and her heart took a little leap in her chest, for perhaps, yes, this would bring them closer together.

'Oh, my darling, *clever* girl!' he murmured ecstatically into her hair before pulling back and grinning almost idiotically at her. And then, bewilderedly, he asked, 'How?'

To witness the collected, dominant Charles Chadwick, businessman of the highest standing, lost for words and quivering, was almost comical and Rose smiled coyly. 'Surely I don't need to tell you that?'

Charles shook his head with a grunt of merriment. 'No, I meant . . . are you sure? I mean. . . when?'

Rose lowered her eyes. 'No. I'm not positive. But I think I must be. I haven't had . . . well, you know, for nearly three months. And I've been feeling queasy for weeks. I hadn't really thought about it, what with Father . . .' Her voice trailed off sadly for just a moment before she came back with a serene smile. 'But just now, I was thinking that I seem to be putting on weight, and it dawned on me that . . . it could be—'

'Oh, I'm sure you're right! Oh, my lovely one! Come now, you must take care of yourself.' He helped her to her feet and sat her down in one of the armchairs like a piece of precious porcelain, fussing over her like a mother hen. Rose felt swamped with relief, for surely he would treat her with kid gloves now that he had what he wanted from her? He had certainly been the perfect, loving husband for the last ten days, ever since the horrible incident on the evening of Joe and Molly's wedding, trying to make up for what he had done to her, she grimaced bitterly, since she considered it was entirely his fault. 'And you must take care of our son.'

He jerked his head towards her belly with a caressing smile, and Rose snatched in her breath. She was giving him a child, but was she giving him a son? She caught her lip, and forced a small nervous laugh. 'There's no need to cosset me. I'm not ill, just pregnant. 'Twas not so long ago that women up north worked down the mines till they gave birth, and then carried on working the next day.'

'Women built like oxen, and they or the child were probably dead within the week,' Charles protested, taking her hand and stroking it adoringly. 'You're more like a fairy, and I won't have anything happen to you or our son. If it wasn't Christmas Day, I'd fetch the physician at once.'

'Oh, I don't think as there's any hurry. Dr Power won't—'

'Dr Power!' Charles's eyes snapped wide. 'You don't think I'm going to let the *prison* doctor see to my wife during her pregnancy, do you?'

Rose's spine stiffened like a mine rod, the glorious hope of the last half-hour crumbling into dust. 'But he's an excellent physician—'

'And looks after the trash of society, the worst criminals in the country, for God's sake! He touches them and their filth, and then you expect me to let him put his contaminated hands on *my* wife!'

'Oh, I see!' she grated sourly. 'He's not good enough to oversee the birth of *your* child, but he was good enough for my father! Is that how you saw my father, then, as some being inferior to your high and mighty self? And am I merely the mare you wanted to service in order to get the son you wanted?'

Charles glared at her, his mouth a thin, tight line and his eyes bulging in his livid face. 'You know that's not what I meant. But you will *not* have the prison doctor attend you. I shall go into Tavistock and make enquiries as to the best and most senior physician in the town.'

'Well, I'd leave it a few weeks if I were you, till the bruising on my shoulder's gone! He might just ask how I came by it.'

She sprang across the room, tears pricking her eyes, unable to remain in his company a second longer. But leaping up with such violence caused the blood to drain from her head, and she made a grab to support herself on the table. As she did so, her arm caught the fine crystal vase on display there and sent it flying into the air. And, just like her splintered heart, it crashed on to the floor and shattered into a million pieces.

Sixteen

Rose stared despondently out of the drawing-room window, not that she could see very much. It was mid-April, and though they had been enjoying some kind spring weather, today it felt as if they had been plunged back to the depths of winter. The day had started mild, but a fine steady drizzle had turned into a thick, grey, bone-chilling fog that sat, heavy and motionless, on the moor like a life-extinguishing blanket. Whether it was a true fog, or whether at fourteen hundred feet above sea level Princetown was merely enveloped in low cloud it was difficult to say, but the moisture hung in the saturated air with not a breath of wind to blow it away, and since midday, visibility had been reduced to no more than twenty yards. It was the sort of day when the unwary traveller could easily lose his way on the moor and become treacherously lost. The best way to survive was to take shelter and wait for the fog to lift, although it might possibly last for days.

Rose turned from the window with a restless sigh. She had heard an explosion earlier, rekindling her appalled memories of the day her father's life had been decimated. It was unlikely to be another such event, and was anyway far quieter. Besides, such sounds were not uncommon up on the moor, a guard firing a warning shot, or blasting either at the prison quarry, the new enterprise at Merrivale, or the massive quarries on Walkhampton Common, so Rose had taken little notice.

That had been some hours ago, and now she sat down in the armchair by the welcoming, cheerful fire, and laid her hand on her swollen abdomen. The baby kicked back, and Rose wondered for the umpteenth time if the child's presence would improve her life, or whether Charles would be as possessive over it as he was over *her*. Or what if the child proved to be as headstrong and domineering as Charles himself?

Oh, she would want to love it, but hadn't she wanted to love Charles, and look what had happened there!

At least this stage of her pregnancy was calm and uneventful, the nausea long gone, and the final month which Mrs Cartwright had told her could be most uncomfortable – and she should know, having brought six children into the world – some time off as yet. Rose wondered amazedly how large she would become, for she already felt enormous. Dr Seaton, whose services Charles had engaged as being the most senior physician in Tavistock, was very pleased with her progress. To her utter relief, he had told Charles that from now on until at least six weeks after the birth – which was expected at the end of June – their marital relationship, as he delicately put it, should cease. There was the possibility that the lady's pleasure could stimulate the womb to go into labour, and the baby's life could be at risk from a premature birth. What pleasure she was supposed to take from Charles's assaults on her she couldn't imagine, but Charles had evidently taken the doctor's warning to heart, and for the child's sake had left her alone.

He had, indeed, treated her like a princess ever since she had announced her condition to him. He had insisted she should not ride Gospel again, but drive everywhere she needed in the wagonette, and she had agreed that this was a sensible precaution. He always wanted to know exactly where she was going – so that he would know both she and the baby were safe was his excuse – and so she had only seen Molly during the two trips Charles had made to London. The second time, a month ago now, Mrs Cartwright had been visiting her daughter, and Joe had managed to spend half an hour with them, so it had been a jolly company. But it seemed an eternity ago, and Rose was champing at the bit to see them again.

She clicked her tongue encouragingly and stretched out her hand, rubbing her thumb across her forefinger in a gesture of beckoning. Amber and Scraggles were lying side by side on the rug in front of the fire, toasting themselves indolently, but the scruffy mongrel at once trotted over to Rose's chair, wagging his unkempt tail nineteen to the dozen as she rubbed his ears. Amber was slower to heave herself to her feet, heavy with the unborn pups Scraggles had given her. Charles had despaired when they had realized what had happened, for God alone knew what the puppies would look like with such a father, and who would want them? Was he to be landed with a houseful of mangy curs under his feet at every minute? But Rose laughed and was delighted. The two dogs behaved like an old married couple, inseparable, Rose considered ruefully as she stroked Amber's golden nose that was resting now on her knee. The sort of relationship Rose herself craved, though Charles had been kindness itself since her announcement on Christmas Day. But that innate understanding, that unspoken intimacy of two fused souls, she knew now could never be theirs. Charles still could not comprehend that sometimes she needed to be alone, out on the freedom of the moors where her heart and her spirit belonged. And his attempts to keep her all to himself were slowly asphyxiating her.

She glanced up carelessly as he came into the room now from his study where he had been dealing with some business correspondence.

'I've ordered some tea, my dearest,' he announced, smiling at her fondly. 'It will be served directly, and I am sure you will . . . What the devil are those two creatures doing indoors?' he thundered, his expression hardening as he rounded the winged back of the chair that had hidden the two dogs from his view. 'Ned reckons she could whelp any day, and I won't have her making a mess all over the carpets! And as for that flea-ridden monstrosity—'

'Oh, Scraggles, what is he saying about you?' Rose crooned, ruffling the endearing animal's ears and raising a teasing eyebrow at her husband.

The annoyance around Charles's mouth slackened. 'I'm sorry, Rose, my love, but you know it makes sense. As soon as Amber's clean again afterwards, she can come back inside. But as for the pups, well, I don't know what I shall do with them!'

Rose screwed her lips into a knot. What *he* would do with them? Amber was *her* dog, and she considered Scraggles was too, and so it followed that the puppies would also be hers. 'I've already promised one to Molly, and another to her brothers and sisters if they're allowed,' she said stiffly, 'so that's two less for you to worry about, and they're not even born yet. Right, come along, you two. Back to the stables.'

She put her hands on the arms of the chair, ready to lever

herself upwards, although she had not yet reached the stage of her pregnancy when it was necessary. It was just that Charles's attitude wearied her, drained her of her natural effervescence. But before she had lifted herself from the seat, Charles had put out his hand, palm outwards in a forbidding gesture.

'No, no, you rest yourself, my darling. I'll take them.'

'Amber's basket is in Gospel's loose box,' Rose called at his back. 'They all like being in together, but make sure you bolt the door properly, or Gospel will nudge it open!'

'Yes, yes, I do know that animal's desire to escape. A bit like his mistress,' Charles added wryly as he ushered the two dogs out of the door.

Rose sat back with a sigh. Poor Gospel. He must be so restless, so frustrated, far more than she was for at least she had the child to slow her down. Normally, Gospel would have been out in the paddock, but being of part-thoroughbred stock, it might not be wise for him to be out in the penetrating damp of such a dense fog as this.

Charles returned five minutes later, holding the door open for the young housemaid who was struggling with the laden tea tray, for though servants were no more to Charles than that, he was not unkind towards them. Although it was only mid-afternoon, the light was fading and it was so depressingly murky that Charles instructed the girl to light the remaining lamps and then stoke up the already cheerful fire to an even more vigorous conflagration. Charles watched approvingly as the maid completed her duties before dipping her knee and backing out of the room.

'Shall I pour, my dear?' This was said with the gleaming silver teapot already in Charles's hand, so Rose nodded absently, accepting both the fragile bone-china teacup and a matching plate upon which he had placed a selection of Cook's delicacies prepared immediately after their fine lunch. They took their tea in silence, since there was little they had to say to each other. Rose ate little, seeing as the kindly Dr Seaton had reminded her that she should eat not for two, but for one small adult, meaning herself, and one baby. Excessive weight would not be good for either mother or child, and in his opinion, if she felt hungry, she should eat extra fruit, vegetables, meat and fish rather than Cook's cakes and biscuits, however mouth-wateringly delicious.

Rose mulled over the elderly physician's visit the previous day. He was not one to beat about the bush, was Dr Seaton, no airs and graces and no being cowed by his wealthy patients. Rose had every confidence in him. Although Dr Power would have been equally competent, she was happy enough to have the more senior physician oversee the birth of the child she prayed would seal her marriage, if not into true love, then at least into a semblance of peace.

She glanced across at Charles now. They had so little in common, except perhaps that he was reading a book as he sipped his tea, and Rose, too, loved to read. The thought made her draw from the pocket in her skirt the letter she had received from Florrie that morning, the postman having delivered it before the fog had closed in, or else she might not have seen it until the weather had cleared again. Which may have made it seem more pleasurable, as the depressing weather had made Florrie's communication seem even more depressing itself, and Rose's eyes saddened as they scanned Florrie's bold and childlike writing for the second time.

> My dear Rose
> I hope you are well and that the baby is going on nicely. I never had no child of my own, as you knows. I had you instead, and that were enough for me. No one could be dearer to me than you, except perhaps your father who I always loved. Though he loved me in return, we was never more than fondest friends. I doesn't know if things might have been different if we had been more than that. All I knows is that I misses him so much and I casn find it in me to come back to the house with him not there. I hopes that time will heal, and that it will for you, too. You was a wonderful daughter to him, but you has your husband and the baby to think of. Tis a great comfort to me staying with my sister and her children, and God willing, I will feel able to come home to you soon. I am well, and so is the family here
> Take care of yoursel, my little maid
> All my love
> Florrie

Rose moistened her lips pensively. Her heart had sunk like a rock when she had first read the letter that morning, as she was hoping desperately that it would contain news of Florrie's return. But Rose understood. Of course she did. Florrie had loved Henry in the same way that Rose had hoped, had believed, she could have loved Charles, and the cruel separation of Henry's death after so many shared years must have been as devastating for Florrie as it had been for herself. She stared into the fire, its dancing flames reflecting in the dark irises of her glistening eyes, seeing and yet not seeing, her mind wandering over her past life at Cherrybrook and her contentment which she had considered would be eternal, but which had been brought to such an abrupt end. It should not have been so terrible. Charles should have brought her comfort, but he never did. Rather she longed for when he was away in London. She looked across at him again now, engrossed in his book. Shut away in a different world. Somewhat as they seemed to live their lives.

She sighed, and went to pour herself another cup of tea, but when she felt the pot it was stone cold and she couldn't be bothered to order some fresh. She didn't really want it anyway. Instead, she went to use the fancy lavatory Charles had recently had installed, a system by which the frequent rainfall kept a massive rooftop tank constantly full of water, which in turn filled the cistern that washed the contents of the decorated pan down into a cesspit beyond the lawn. When this was becoming full, Charles had made an arrangement that it would be collected by a local farmer as fertilizer, suiting them both well. Rose, though, was more interested in the intriguing luxury of a flushing lavatory – just like the one in Charles's London home, but which was apparently quite common in wealthier homes in the capital with its water supply and sophisticated sewer system – and so she welcomed the visits her progressing pregnancy necessitated. Now she washed her hands and went back to the drawing room, reached her feet out to the fire as she lounged in the comfortable chair, and closed her eyes.

She had dozed, the clock showed her, for nearly an hour, Charles still reading, apparently not having moved an inch. Rose stretched languidly, then yawned aloud, which lifted Charles's disapproving head for a moment. Rose's eyes swept about the room. The tea tray had disappeared. The fire still crackled merrily, and Rose was grateful that she was warm and cosy when it was so raw outside. On the mantelpiece were displayed some elegant china ornaments, heavy velvet curtains hung at the windows and the furniture was of fine quality, everything she had carefully chosen meeting with Charles's approval. She admired the room once again, pondering how quickly one became used to such finery. That, to be honest, it meant nothing compared to the true happiness that eluded her. And just now she had nothing to *do*. She was bored. Cooped up like a hen. And she drummed her fingers fretfully on the arm of the chair.

'Oh, Rose, can't you find something to do?' Charles asked with mild irritation. 'Read a book, or . . . or do some sewing?'

'I would if you'd let me make something sensible, like baby clothes,' she answered tartly, though she had done just that in secret. 'Needlepoint just seems such a waste of time.'

'I've told you before, making clothes is not a fit occupation for a lady. You can employ a seamstress for that.'

Rose ground her teeth in frustration, her lips pushed forward mutinously. A heartfelt sigh exploded from her agitated lungs, and before she knew it herself, she was on her feet. 'I simply must get out!' her lips declared, and she found herself glaring at Charles's startled disapprobation.

'Don't be so ridiculous!' he reproached her scornfully. 'You'd be lost in a minute in this fog.'

'No, I wouldn't,' she scowled. '*You* would, but I know the moor like the back of my hand. But as it happens, I'm only planning on going out to the stables, and I'm sure even you can't object to that!' she sneered triumphantly, gloating at the defeated expression on Charles's face.

A few moments later, she let herself out through the back door, pulling her thick shawl tightly about her shoulders. The fog had ushered in an early evening, so Rose had lit one of the storm lanterns from the boot room. She shivered as she stepped across the stable yard. The dense moisture hung in the air in cold droplets that clung to her long lashes and seemed to penetrate to her very bones. It was just like winter again, the line of loose boxes veiled in a misty blur, and Rose hung the lamp on the special hook on the doorpost outside Gospel's stable. The place was deserted, Ned having finished his duties for the day and taken himself off to his quarters above the tack room at the far side of the yard. All he would have left to do was to check the horses before he went to bed, and turn the keys in the padlocks to the stable doors for the night, so Rose slipped into Gospel's loose box unseen.

Scraggles came at once to lick her hand as she turned to bolt the bottom half of the stable door, leaving the top open to allow the uncertain glow from the lamp to enter the pitch darkness inside. The prancing mongrel was a hairy shadow in the gloom, but Amber's golden coat was more distinct as she lay in her basket, not even lifting her head. It was to Gospel's tall, lustrous silhouette, though, that Rose took herself, lacing her arms about his sleek but powerful neck and burying her face against his warm flesh. The animal turned his head, whickering softly in his throat as he nudged his velvety muzzle against her arm. It was too much for Rose, and in the murky silence of the stable, tears began to roll down her cheeks.

'Oh, Gospel, what am I to do?' she whispered brokenly. 'I miss Father so much, and that . . . that husband of mine is . . . Oh, I just *can't* love him.'

Her body was suddenly overtaken with wrenching sobs and she dropped her head, resting her forehead against Gospel's shoulder. Bitterness and grief washed over her in a dousing torrent so that nothing else seemed to exist in the entire world but her own anguish. She did not hear the rustle in the straw behind her, not until the strong hand closed over her mouth, and her desperate tears came to a sudden, shuddering halt . . .

Seventeen

The breath caught in Rose's throat and every muscle in her body seemed paralysed. Only her heart thudded like a hammer, her terrified eyes staring blindly at Gospel's unperturbed flank. For five long, agonizing seconds, neither she nor the owner of the hand moved, and if it hadn't been for the pressure of the arm firmly about her, she might have thought she was dreaming.

'I'm sorry to startle you, miss, but as God is my witness, I mean you no harm.'

The whispered, agitated words reached her as if from another world and might have been in a foreign language for all the sense her petrified, confused brain made of them. But as their meaning slowly filtered through to her, she began to take courage as her innate spirit was released from its stupor. She remained motionless, battling against her taut nerves and trying to rationalize the desperate thoughts that tumbled in her head. The voice that had spoken was that of a man, neither as young as Joe nor that of an older man, but somewhere in between. It was polite, cultured, not local – more like Charles in accent, in fact – and, dear God, it had *trembled* with fear as if its owner was as afraid as Rose was! Indeed, she was aware now that the hand over her mouth was shaking, and the man, whoever he was, was hesitant, uncertain of what to do next, and Rose waited, forcing her reeling mind to think clearly again.

'If I let you go,' the voice quavered as if the words were choking in his gullet, 'do you promise not to scream?'

Rose stiffened, and then nodded, the small sound she made in her throat muffled by his hand. She felt his fingers slacken, and instantly tighten again, as if he had thought better of it.

'You do promise?' he repeated with a slight jerk of his arm. 'Please God, I *beg* you not to scream. Not until you've heard what I have to say.'

There was something in his tone, some desperation, that she recognized, for hadn't she been there, was *still* there, herself?

'I promise,' she managed to mumble through his fingers, and gradually, as the seconds ticked by, his hold reluctantly eased. She was swamped with relief and could easily have slithered to the floor, but some force she could not comprehend kept her upright. She could hear the breath vibrating tremulously in and out of the man's lungs, and once she was sure she was free of his grasp, she had to steel herself to turn round, inch by inch. Her eyes were beginning to adjust to the semi-darkness, and it registered oddly at the back of her mind that the animals seemed undisturbed by the stranger's presence, and Gospel was even munching calmly at his hay net.

Rose dared to look up into the intruder's face, the pulse pounding at her temples. The whites of his terror-stricken eyes glinted in the dim half-light, and she made out the pale shape of a bald head. No, not bald, as it fell into place with a sudden jolt, but cropped. Cropped to the scalp in a convict cut.

She hardly had time to gasp when he let out an astounded, 'Good Lord! You!'

Rose instinctively recoiled, backing up against Gospel's side, and the felon went to step towards her, his hand outstretched – most curiously – as if he would take her arm almost in greeting. But he didn't get that far. As he transferred his weight on to his other leg, it seemed to give way beneath him and with a stifled cry he plunged past her, landing in the thick layer of straw on the loose-box floor.

Rose stood, astounded, numbed by the last few minutes, blinking down at the still figure by her feet. She could scream now, run into the house and raise the alarm. But she didn't. Her eyes had not had as much time as the escaped prisoner's had to adjust to the near darkness, but in that split second she had seen enough of him to spark her memory. It was him, the same fellow who had saved Jacob Cartwright's life, and had been unjustly beaten and kicked by the Civil Guards for his efforts. Who, she had subsequently learnt through Molly, had not only been set upon later by other inmates in retribution for the same incident, but had relentlessly protested that he was innocent of his alleged crime. No. Rose would not scream. Certainly not until she had given him the chance to explain himself.

He groaned, recovering his senses; whether from the fall or a moment's unconsciousness, Rose wasn't sure, but it gave her the opportunity to focus both her thoughts and her vision. In the shadows, she began to distinguish what appeared as several dark, oozing patches on his yellow prison uniform. She knew at once what they were. She realized now it must have been a gunshot she had heard some hours earlier. The somewhat old-fashioned Sniders still carried by the Civil Guard were converted for use with cartridges containing thirteen balls of lead shot rather than bullets, but if they hit in the right place they could still maim or even kill, and this villain's shoulder was peppered with them.

'You're hurt,' she said mechanically, her voice frozen and expressionless.

The man made no attempt even to sit up, but still lying half on his side, he reached down with both hands to his ankle, his face turned into the straw as he writhed in agony. 'I think I've broken my ankle,' he seemed to grate through clenched teeth. 'The surprise of seeing you again . . . made me forget for a second.' He appeared to pull himself together, then, and wriggled into a sitting position, still grasping his ankle. As he looked up at her, even in the dim light, she could see the contorted expression on his face. 'It is you, isn't it? The girl, by the quarry tunnel. All that time ago. You . . . you do remember?'

Rose blinked at him. Yes, she remembered, and her own senses were at once unlocked from their stunned state of shock. 'Yes, 'twas me,' she murmured. 'But I meant your shoulder. You're bleeding.'

He scarcely turned his head. 'I think I can put up with that. It's my ankle I'm really worried about. That's why I had to find somewhere to hide. Otherwise I'd have been halfway across the moor by now. But if it *is* broken, I'm done for. It could take weeks—'

'Let me see.' Rose hardly knew how or why, but she dropped on her knees beside him, all fear dissipated but every nerve on edge, not for herself now, but unbelievably for *him*! She wished vehemently that the light was better, but there was enough to see that he wore no boots and that his coarse woollen socks were in tatters from his flight over the rough terrain.

'I got rid of the boots as soon as I could,' he explained meekly.

Rose nodded. 'The nails in the soles, you mean? In the shape of an arrow?'

'They do leave a pretty distinctive footprint,' he grunted wryly. 'But then my foot caught between two rocks as I was running. If I'd still been wearing the boots, it might have been all right. But I'm sure it's broken. I heard it snap and . . . God, it's bloody agony.' His head went back with a tortured gasp, his face twisted, and when he opened his eyes again, they bore into hers with desperate intensity. 'You won't give me away, will you? Please, I beg you.'

His voice cracked, tugging at Rose's sympathy. But what did she know of him, a complete stranger? A convicted criminal, for heaven's sake, and one of the worst in the land, to merit being committed to Dartmoor Prison!

She lifted her chin. 'And why should I trust you?' she demanded warily, though all the time, keeping her voice low.

He shook his head slowly. 'I can't answer that. Except that I *swear* I'm innocent, and might even be able to prove it, given the chance. Not that it would do me any good. But I just couldn't stand another ten years locked up in that hell-hole for something I didn't do. Surely you can understand that? So, please, help me.' He paused, and in the gloom, she heard rather than saw him swallow hard. 'You . . . you know what will happen to me if I'm caught?'

Rose's heart jerked in her chest, and she lowered her eyes as she nodded. The punishment cells, and then a flogging of up to thirty-six lashes with the cat o' nine tails. They said that the blood ran freely after the third stroke, and by the end of the punishment a man's skin hung from his back in ribbons. Barbaric enough for the likes of the felon who had attempted to split open Jacob Cartwright's head with a stone, but unthinkable for the man who had saved him.

'I know I shouldn't ask it of you.' Rose realized he was speaking again. 'It isn't fair on you, especially with you being . . .' He jabbed his head briefly towards her jutting stomach. 'God knows, I'm sorry for frightening you like that, but I had no choice. You *are* all right? I mean, I didn't realize you were . . . From the back, you don't look—'

'Yes, I'm fine,' she answered, taken aback by what appeared to be his genuine concern. 'A little shaken, 'tis all. And the baby's still kicking.' Which was perfectly true as she felt a foot thrust up under her ribs.

'Thank God,' he muttered under his breath.

'And I'll not betray you.' For how could she live with herself if she was responsible for sending this man, who could well be telling the truth, to a certain flogging? 'But I don't know if I'll help you. I need time to consider it.'

'Of course. I understand.'

'You'll be safe here overnight. Hide yourself in the straw round the corner.' She pointed to the dog-leg of the loose box, which was in complete darkness. 'Ned – that's our groom – he'll check on Gospel again later. But he'll only stick his head in. He and Gospel don't get on, you see. In fact, the only person who can manage Gospel apart from me is Joe.'

'Joe?' he questioned in alarm.

'Oh, he doesn't work here. We only have Ned. But . . . I'm really surprised Gospel didn't make a terrible noise and try to kick the stable down when you came in. He always does with anyone else. Has he not bitten you yet?'

He glanced at her sideways, and then with her eyes accustomed to the mere glimmer of light that entered through the stable door, she saw him smile. 'He's a magnificent animal. I could see he was spirited, so I just talked to him, and he let me in.'

Rose was about to express her astonishment, but the stranger – for somehow she could not think of him as the escaped convict – must have shifted slightly and threw up his head with a gasp of agony. His hands went down to his ankle again and he drew a trembling breath through his gritted teeth. Without a second thought, Rose leaned forward and gently peeled the remains of the sodden sock – as one could never go far on Dartmoor without getting one's feet wet, especially when running for one's life – while he held his foot as rigid as possible. She sucked in her cheeks. Though she had no experience of such things, it was quite obvious the bone was broken. The ankle had swollen up like a football – or at least like one of the inflated pig's bladders that boys kicked about the streets of Princetown – and even in the shadows Rose could see it was turning a horrible shade of purple. She reached out her hand and met the fellow's eyes. He turned his head away, biting on his knuckles, and she heard the guttural choking sound he made as she stroked her fingers lightly over the swelling. Dear Lord, she could actually *feel* the break about three inches above the protruding mount of the ankle bone on the outer side of his foot.

'You need a doctor,' she murmured at once, quite horrified.

'No. It's too risky.'

She stared into his stricken face, pursing her lips. 'My own physician, from Tavistock. He's a good man. He should be calling tomorrow. Perhaps I can persuade him—'

'I need to do something about it *now*. It'll be a Pott's fracture. The tibia's probably broken as well, further down on the inside. Or the ligament will have torn. Either way, it's pretty serious. Would you mind . . . Could you see if you can feel a pulse below the break? Look, just here. I can feel it myself, but that can be unreliable. I might just be feeling the pulse in my own fingers. That's stronger, you see.'

Rose, quite frankly, was so amazed at his anatomical knowledge that she obeyed at once. She all but rejoiced when she felt the rhythmical vibration beneath her touch. 'Yes, I can definitely feel it,' she told him.

He released a heart-wrenching sigh. 'Thank God.' He dropped his head forward for a moment, then turned to look at her, his lip caught between his teeth. 'This doctor. Could he . . . could he be trusted?'

Rose hesitated. 'I can't say for sure, but I should think so. But 'tis a chance I think you've *got* to take.'

She heard him breathe in, and then exhale heavily. 'You're right. No matter what happens, I don't want to end up losing my foot.'

'Should we try and strap it up for now?'

'It might help. If you can find something to do it with.'

'Yes,' she answered, her mind racing. 'And I'll bring some dry clothes. Yours are wet through.'

'Oh, I'm used to that,' he snorted bitterly. 'But they are somewhat of a giveaway. And . . . do you think you could smuggle me out a glass of water?'

'I'll try. But I don't know how long I'll be. I'll have to be careful. My husband . . . I'm sure he'd turn you over to the authorities at once.'

She rose awkwardly to her feet, and as she hesitated for a moment, she felt his grip on her hand. 'Thank you.'

She barely acknowledged him, since her sharp wits were preoccupied, planning, scheming. 'Hide yourself round the corner,' was all she mumbled, and then she was back across the yard, taking the lamp with her as everything must appear normal. She went inside and, though her heart was pounding, she made her way with what she hoped was a casual air to the two rooms Henry had occupied and which had not been touched since his death, but which Charles was planning to convert back into a morning room. Rose need not have worried. Cook and Patsy, the maid, were busy in the kitchen preparing dinner, and Charles was probably still in the drawing room despairing of his self-willed wife.

Rose went straight to the cupboard where Henry's bed linen was kept. He had preferred the worn sheets they had brought with them from Cherrybrook as they were softer when his skin was sore from his immobility, and now they were perfect for Rose's needs. A little nick with some scissors on the edge she had hemmed herself years ago, and they tore easily into long strips. A set of clothes, then. Her father had been quite tall so they should more or less fit the man hiding out in the stable. But how could she carry them without arousing suspicion? She rolled her eyes to the ceiling as if seeking inspiration, and in her mind she could see her father smiling down on her. Of course! She could say she was beginning to find the courage to sort Henry's effects! What could be more natural? If someone met her with them outside, she could say she was going to offer them to Ned.

With the makeshift bandages – and, as an afterthought, the small bottle of laudanum that still sat on the bedside table – stuffed into the ample pocket of her skirt, she carried the bundle of clothing to the table in the boot room and placed it next to the storm lights. Then she went to the kitchen to fetch *herself* a glass of water, unthinkable for the master to do so, but the young mistress would often come and help herself to whatever she wanted rather than ringing for the maid! So with the garments tucked under one arm, the lantern in one hand and the glass in the other, she was back out in Gospel's loose box within twenty minutes.

''Tis only me,' she whispered urgently.

In the inky obscurity of the dog-leg, there was no sign of the convict and she wondered for a second if he had not decided to hobble off into the fog. Disappointment twinged at her heart and she frowned with bafflement, for what was he to her, anyway? But then the heaped straw moved and he slowly emerged from its shelter, and she somehow felt relieved as she handed him the glass of water.

'Thank you so much,' he croaked back, and she could not help but wonder how a supposedly fiendish criminal could behave with such natural civility.

'I've brought some laudanum if you want it.'

'Laudanum?' He sounded surprised. 'Oh, God, I'd love to take some, but I'll need all my wits about me if anyone else comes in. But thank you all the same.'

Rose sank down in the straw beside him. 'I can virtually guarantee that no one will, and what could you do anyway? You can't exactly run off, can you?'

He bowed his head. 'No. I don't really know how I managed to get *here*.'

'Then take a few drops. 'Twill take the edge off the pain.'

'All right, I will. And thank you again.'

She unscrewed the bottle and with the pipette attached to the lid, released a few drops into the glass. He hesitated before drinking down half the water in several thirsty gulps.

'And where exactly is here?' he asked as he paused for breath.

'About two miles from Princetown.'

'Two miles? Is that all? Christ, they're bound to come looking! Oh, I'm sorry,' he added sheepishly. 'I've forgotten what it is to be in the company of a lady.'

But Rose shook her head. Under the circumstances, she felt the oath was understandable. 'With your ankle and in the fog, I expect it seemed further. But just as well. If you'd wandered out on to the moor from here, you might've come upon Fox Tor Mire, and you wouldn't have been the first to be sucked under. You don't know the moor, I suppose?'

'Only the prison farmlands,' he answered, his voice vibrant with bitterness. 'But it sounds as if God was on my side, for once, when He guided me to you.'

'I'm not promising to help you,' she reminded him tartly.

'But you already are. And you'll never know how grateful I am.' He smiled at her then, for though his face was in shadow, she saw the flash of his white teeth, and she wondered fleetingly what he really looked like, as even during the ugly incident at the quarry tunnel she had only caught a glimpse of his face. She watched while he finished the drink, his back propped against the wall and his injured leg stretched out before him.

'I'd best bandage your ankle,' she said swiftly. 'If I'm too long, I'll be missed. 'Twould perhaps be better if you changed first. I've brought you some clothes.'

'I can't thank you enough. You have no idea what it means to have someone *listen* to me after all this time.'

'You haven't actually told me your story yet,' she observed sharply.

He had struggled to his feet, hopping about on one leg as he began to strip off, and Rose discreetly averted her eyes.

'No. But I will. I must tell you everything.' He stifled a gasp as he was obliged to put his weight on his ankle for a moment, and Rose's caution, her disbelief at what she was doing, was instantly washed away yet again by her natural sympathies. He sat down again beside her, wincing as he pulled off his upper garments.

'What about the pellets in your shoulder?' she murmured.

'They'll have to stay there. At least until morning. It'll need a good light. And some tweezers. That is . . . if you wouldn't mind?'

Rose chewed on her lip. She really wasn't sure . . . 'If I can,' she said reluctantly. 'But let me see to your ankle first. If you can roll up the trouser leg.'

'Yes, of course. Oh, God, I'm feeling light-headed already.'

'But it has eased the pain?'

'A little, yes.'

Nevertheless, she felt him stiffen as she set to work. As for herself, having a task to concentrate on pushed the serious doubts to the back of her mind. She worked as quickly as possible, presuming she should strap his foot quite firmly, but constantly aware that she must be hurting him. 'If I'm taking such a chance, helping you like this,' she whispered as her nimble fingers wound the lengths of sheeting about the limb, 'don't you think I should at least know your name?'

'My name? Dear Lord, I'd almost forgotten I had one. You just become a number once you're in there . . .' His words had ended in a thin, rueful trail as fatigue, the tension and the pain of the afternoon's events caught up with him and were over-whelmed by the sedative effect of the laudanum. 'Collingwood,' he said with a sudden start, 'Seth Collingwood.'

Rose raised an eyebrow. 'Right, Mr Collingwood, that's done. And I really must go.'

'Call me Seth, if you wouldn't mind. Just to be treated like a human being again . . .'

She heard the catch in his voice, and instinctively reached to touch his arm. 'I'll try and bring you some food later, but I can't promise. Bury yourself in the straw again, and hide your uniform. Don't destroy it, though. If you're caught, you'll be punished for that, as well.'

'Well, thank you for that. And thank you for everything.'

He sounded exhausted, half asleep from the laudanum, and as Rose hurried back across the yard, she wondered yet again at the temerity, the foolhardiness of what she was doing. No one appeared to have realized where she had been. When she returned the glass to the kitchen, Cook barely looked up from her labours except to assure her young mistress that dinner would be served punctually at seven thirty, as usual.

Rose went upstairs to change for the evening meal, a ridiculous charade she had grown used to. Her wardrobe was more limited now, as it seemed a waste to have too many voluminous garments to accommodate her growing stomach. But it always seemed to please Charles if she adhered to these society customs, and just now she wanted to keep him as sweet as possible.

'Ah, there you are,' he declared as she entered the drawing room. 'Enjoyed our afternoon spent with our confounded animals rather than in the company of our husband, have we?'

His voice rang with sarcasm, and Rose stopped in her tracks. In that instant, her mind was made up. Charles would be galled and horrified if he knew that she was protecting an escaped convict, and if she could do so under his very nose, oh, what joyful satisfaction that would bring her! Hopefully, Charles would not discover her deceit, and would never be aware of how she had defied him, but it didn't matter. Her triumph over him would be enough! What she was doing was illegal, but she didn't care. And if what Seth Collingwood claimed was true – though of course she had yet to hear his story – then the law was an ass, and what heed did Rose Maddiford ever pay to rules and regulations anyway?

She bounded across the room to her husband in as dignified a fashion as her protruding belly permitted, and on her face was the sweetest, most angelic smile she could muster, and one which evidently won over Charles's displeasure at once.

'Oh, Charles, I'm sorry.' She slid on to her knees at his feet and rested her cheek against his thigh a little akin to an endearing kitten – though could he have seen her eyes at that moment, he would have been appalled to see them gleaming with the cunning of a tigress. ''Tis just that I miss Father so much that sometimes I just need to be on my own for a while. And what with not riding again until after the child is born, I get so restless at times.'

She mentally crossed her fingers, and then complacency stirred in her breast as she felt him entwine his fingers in her tumbling locks. She had twisted part of her hair into a knot on the crown of her head, deliberately leaving the remainder to hang down in a waving curtain of silk that she knew Charles would find irresistible. He had fallen for it, and she turned her head, lifting her pleading velvet eyes to his face.

'I must apologize, too, my dear,' he admitted warily, 'but I do worry about you so. And the baby.'

'Oh, there's no need, Charles!' she assured him. 'I'd never do anything that could jeopardize the baby, I promise. And I will be a good mother, I know I will.'

She knelt up and threw her arms about his neck as far as her bulge permitted, all the while laughing up her sleeve at him. He might think she was submitting to his will, but little did he know!

'I know you will, sweetheart, and our son will be blessed! My only regret at present is that I have to keep away from you at night. It really is quite frustrating, but I'm sure this wouldn't hurt.' And so saying, he slipped his hand inside her bodice and began to stroke her swollen breasts.

Rose gritted her teeth as her stomach turned over with revulsion. He couldn't leave her alone even now, could he? He was disgusting, and she was tied to him for life, though it was her own doing and she only had herself and her ignorance to blame. But surely, if he were to show her some consideration, guide her body instead of using it entirely for his own gratification and then turning his back on her, she might learn to love him. But could he ever change? She very much doubted it.

Dinner was served and Rose ate daintily, feigning good humour and politely deploring the fog, when all the while she was engulfed in her contempt for the man who sat at the opposite end of the table. If only Florrie was there! But perhaps it was as well she wasn't, for Florrie would not so easily be deceived, and Rose would not want her to be involved with the escaped prisoner. Florrie would have thrown her apron over her head in horror – Rose could visualize it now – and the game would be up in minutes.

'I'm just going to feed the dogs,' she announced some time later, since no other ruse had sprung to mind all evening.

'Didn't Ned do that?' Charles glanced up in surprise.

'Probably. But I expect Amber could do with a little extra, and I want to say goodnight to her, anyway. What if she has the pups in the night? And I think I'll take out an old blanket as well, just in case,' she added as an afterthought.

'Go on, then,' Charles chuckled. 'But change out of your gown first, and be careful out there in the dark.'

'I will.' And though it burned her lips to do so, she planted a fleeting kiss on his cheek.

Having hurried upstairs to change again, she took two blankets from the cupboard in Henry's room. No one would miss them, worn in places and greying, just as they had been brought from the house at Cherrybrook, but of thick good-quality wool. The loose box always stayed warm from the body heat of the animals, but lying down asleep was a different matter, and with his broken ankle and the lead shot in his shoulder a little comfort would not come amiss to the convict on this dark April night.

Rose sauntered into the kitchen, smiling, and with a vivid light in her lavender-blue eyes, though inside she was trembling. But, she told herself, she was mistress of the house and had every right to be there, and indeed often was, so this visit would not be unusual. She cadged from Cook a large bowl of leftover casserole, saying it was extra for the dogs, and taking a mug of hot, sweet tea *for herself*.

She grimaced ruefully to herself. The deception was beginning to come so easily! She even slipped a spoon – how else would the fugitive eat the stew? – and a couple of rolls into her pocket when Cook was looking the other way. And so, armed with everything she thought Seth Collingwood would need, she boldly made her way out to the stables.

At her voice, he appeared cautiously from beneath the heaped-up straw like a badger emerging from its sett at dusk. Rose sensed at once the change in him. He was shaking, his very breath quivering, and she knew instinctively it wasn't just from the cold. His injuries, the shock and fear were taking their toll, and somehow his vulnerability gave her strength. He fell on the mug of hot tea with a grateful nod, warming his hands about it and sipping the scalding liquid while she draped the blankets over his shoulders. The casserole was only lukewarm, but it seemed to give him strength. He seemed to force down the first few mouthfuls, but the rest he swallowed more normally, washing it down with the remains of the tea and then leaning back gingerly against the stable wall.

'That was the best food I've tasted in years, since I was—' He broke off with a shuddering sigh, and let his head fall back dejectedly, his eyes shut – at least, in the shadows, Rose believed they were. 'It really is good of you,' he muttered, 'but you do realize what a risk you're taking?'

Rose felt her heart trip. Yes, she knew. But how could she betray this man who, just as he had by the quarry tunnel all that time ago, had once again thrown her innermost self into a confused turmoil? And now he was hurt, was in what must be excruciating pain after continuing to run on his ankle after it was broken, yet he was suffering it in silence and was showing more concern for *her* than for himself.

'Let *me* worry about that,' she whispered back, remembering that she must keep her voice low. 'Do you feel any better now?'

'Feel?' He seemed to start, and then shook his head with an ironic grunt. 'It's such a long time since anyone's asked how I feel that I've forgotten how to ask myself. I've just learnt to get on, no matter what. But, since you ask, I feel pretty rough, though the food and drink has helped. Thank you. But how did you . . .?'

'I said 'twas for the dogs. Amber especially. She's about to whelp.'

'Yes, I can see.'

Rose tipped her head, wondering for not the first time how he seemed so knowledgeable, as Amber's condition was far less noticeable than her own. But now didn't seem the time for explanation. 'I've got these as well,' she told him, producing the rolls from her pocket.

'Thank you. Again. I'll save them for the morning. Unless I'm discovered in the meantime. That fellow – Ned, I think you said – looked in. I was half asleep from the laudanum and it gave me one hell of a shock. But like you said, he didn't actually come in.'

'No. But he will padlock all the stables before he goes to bed. So you will be locked in for the night. But you'll be safe, so try to get some sleep.'

'Yes, I will. Just now I'd like to go to sleep and wake up to find the last couple of years have just been a nightmare.'

'Yes, I'm sure. But there's nothing to be done overnight, so enjoy the peace while you can. And I suggest you take some more laudanum.'

'It can't hurt, I suppose. Huh! Perhaps I should take the whole bottle and my worries would be over for good.'

Rose snatched in her breath as her heart contracted with horror. 'No!' she gasped with a vehemence that astounded and bewildered her. 'Even if you're caught and you go back to prison, you'll be released in . . . how many years did you say?'

'Another ten,' he groaned in despair.

'But you'll still only be . . . what?' she demanded, amazed at the sudden force of her feelings.

'Just turned forty. I've worked it out often enough.'

'With a long life still in front of you, then.'

'Hardly,' he scoffed. 'Besides, who knows if I'll survive that long in that place. There's plenty who don't. But it's unfair of me to talk like that. You've been so good to me, and I really appreciate it. But . . . perhaps I won't have another chance to know the name of my benefactress.'

'Rose Chadwick. *Mrs* Rose Chadwick,' she repeated, though she shied away from the title. 'But if I am to call you Seth, you must call me Rose.'

'That seems . . . impolite.'

'Then impolite you must be. And I must return these things to the kitchen before Cook comes looking for them!'

She clambered to her feet, gathering up the used crockery. 'Whatever happens, good luck.'

'Thank you. And thank you for everything.'

And with a pat to the horse and the two dogs, Rose let herself out of the loose box and bolted the door firmly behind her.

Eighteen

They came for him first thing the next morning.

Having taken some time to get to sleep, Rose woke again to hear the dawn chorus of the moorland birds, and her thoughts instantly sprang to the injured man hiding in Gospel's stable. Charles lay beside her on his back, mouth open and his regular breathing so heavy it was verging on a snore. Rose glanced at him with a scornful eye and sighed. Charles was good-looking, attentive and a gentleman, and should have made her an excellent husband. Indeed, he could have made the perfect husband for many a young woman, but not her. Not Rose Maddiford, who had a will and a purpose of her own, and would not be down-trodden and crushed by any man!

How different he was from Seth Collingwood. How different he made her feel! With Charles, she felt she had to be constantly on her best behaviour, like a child paraded before a visiting maiden aunt. Whenever she was herself, her *true* self, it always ended in a row. But, after the initial shock of encountering the escaped prisoner, she had at once felt at ease with him. It was ludicrous, she knew! He was a criminal convicted of God alone knew what heinous crime, and yet . . . she had to admit it to herself, she *liked* him. He was hurt and in pain, and perhaps her condition had made her more sensitive to the distress of others, but it was more than just an arousal of her sympathies. Helping him was not only reckless and insane, it was illegal. She bit down on her lip as her mouth twisted in anguish. *She should not be doing this!* It was pure madness! But she *wanted* to do it. It was an adventure, exciting, and not just a supremely satisfying way of hitting back at Charles. If the fugitive had been a foul-mouthed, threatening, uncouth brute it would have been a different matter, she recognized that. But Seth Collingwood was polite, refined, concerned for herself and the risk she was taking for him. She couldn't believe he could have committed some dreadful offence that had warranted confinement in what everyone knew was the worst prison in the land, dedicated to the punishment of the most dangerous, bestial felons. She knew from Molly's father that he had been protesting his innocence – in vain, for what good could it do him? But last night he had spoken of proving it, and his voice had been choked with what she believed was genuine emotion. Unless he was a talented actor, of course, but her instincts told her otherwise.

She turned over again and shut her eyes, attempting to go back to sleep, but the darkened interior of the stable kept creeping back into her mind. She hadn't been the least afraid, at least not after those first few minutes. And of course, when she realized who he was, that he was the very same unfortunate prisoner who had saved Jacob Cartwright's life – and paid dearly for his pains – the panic had fled. He could have played on that, saying that she could trust him because she had seen for herself that he was really a decent sort. But he hadn't even mentioned it. It had been her by the tunnel, was all he had said. No more. Of course, he didn't know that the warden in question was her best friend's father. That she had discussed him with Molly, and that she knew about his claims of innocence. Nonetheless, if he had been a cunning villain, he would surely have used the incident to convince her. But he hadn't, and it all led her to believe him.

She realized her eyes were open again, the room fully light now and her body and mind wide awake. Had Seth managed to get some sleep, or had he been too afraid or in too much pain to rest? She had never broken a bone – to say nothing of being shot – but she imagined he must be in agony. She wanted to bring him inside, put him in a proper, comfortable bed, fetch the doctor to have his leg correctly set and his wounds properly tended and kept clean. But she would just have to do what she could for him on the hard floor of the stable, and pray that the increased risk of infection would not be a problem.

And that was another thing. Gospel. Who seemed to have an inborn sense about people. He behaved like a lamb towards her, Joe and even Molly, though the poor girl was terrified of him. He disliked Ned and was distrustful of any stranger, and yet he had peacefully allowed Seth to enter the loose box when he would normally have created such havoc it would have had them all running! What was it Seth had said? He had *talked* to Gospel. Did he have a natural affinity with animals, since the dogs had accepted him in the same way? Amber was so placid she would greet anyone with a calmly wagging tail, but Scraggles always became overexcited and barked with joy, and yet somehow Seth had silenced him. So he *must* be used to animals, and to horses in particular. And you only gained that kind of experience if you were a groom – and by the cultured way Seth spoke that hardly seemed likely – or if you came from a good-class, *moneyed* family.

So how had he ended up serving a lengthy sentence in Dartmoor gaol?

It did not add up! In Rose's mind, the only possible explanation was that he was indeed innocent! Unless . . . could he have attempted to murder his own father or some other relative in order to inherit a fortune more quickly? Surely not! He seemed far too gentle for that. Such a wicked crime would surely have been reported in the papers no matter where it had taken place, and she and Henry had always read the nationals as well as the *Tavistock Gazette*, which reported not only local news, but national and even international events as well. Besides, although she was no expert in the law, would he not have hanged for such an attempt? No. Everything pointed to the fact that Seth was telling the truth, although she would insist on hearing his story at the very first opportunity. She was well aware that she was taking a tremendous risk, that she was being rash and foolhardy, but then, when had that ever stopped her? And she had considered the matter long and hard, agonizing over the situation, and she *still* believed Seth Collingwood was blameless.

Beside her, Charles stirred. She opened one eye to glance across at the clock, and then pretended to be still asleep. Twenty past six. It was quite usual for Charles to wake at this time, tossing in the bed until it disturbed her sufficiently for him to demand his marital rights. Recently, of course, Dr Seaton had advised against it, and for the child's sake, at least, Charles had acquiesced, taking himself downstairs so that Rose more often than not dozed for another hour or so, enjoying the luxury of lying in bed without Charles pawing at her. But this morning Rose felt differently, and no sooner had her husband donned his dressing gown and padded quietly out of the room in his slippers so as not to wake her – showing the consideration he was capable of at times and which mortified her – than she was out of bed and into the bathroom. There was only cold water in the jug, since Patsy was not expected to bring up the hot until later, but Rose hardly noticed as she quickly washed and then dressed herself. For her mind was occupied with the desire to see Seth Collingwood again at the earliest possible moment.

Charles raised his eyebrows in surprise as she entered the dining room fully dressed. He was sat at the table, leisurely sipping at a cup of coffee. The aroma of it mingled mouth-wateringly with the fragrance of the rolls and bread that were baking in Cook's oven and that would be served with breakfast in half an hour together with eggs, bacon, sausage, mushrooms and anything else that was available in Cook's well-stocked store. Rose poured herself some of the dark, steaming liquid and topped it up with thick cream before sitting down opposite her husband.

'You're up early, my dear. I hope you're getting enough sleep.'

'Oh, I was restless,' she answered, which was no lie. 'Baby was kicking and, I don't know, I just felt the need to get up. I can always put my feet up this afternoon. 'Tis only to be expected.'

Charles smiled benevolently, making her feel somewhat guilty. 'Never mind. Only, what is it, ten more weeks? And the little chap will be in your arms and it'll all have seemed worthwhile.'

Yes, in ten weeks' time, the child, be it boy or girl, would be putting in an appearance and changing their lives, healing, she prayed, the rift between them that for most of the time Charles appeared to ignore. And by then, in one way or another, Seth Collingwood would be gone, never to be seen again, and the idea strangely saddened her.

''Tis a better morning,' she observed absently.

'Yes. The mist's lifting and I think the sun's trying to break through. Let's hope it'll warm up a little.'

And there the conversation, such as it was, ended. At that precise moment there was a loud banging on the front door, so insistent that Charles was already in the hallway when the maid answered it. The hairs on the back of Rose's neck stood on end for she knew instinctively who it would be. She sidled out into the hall. Patsy was still fumbling with the locks and bolts of the door, which had not yet been unsecured that morning, and Charles was striding up behind her, demanding who the devil was disturbing his privacy at that unholy hour. Rose slipped behind them both unseen and, borne on a tide of fear, let herself out through the back door, already open for the servants' use, as it was laundry day and the woman from Princetown who came once a week to do the washing would be arriving at any moment.

Rose hurried across to the stables, her fine shawl pulled tightly about her shoulders, as she was shivering with apprehension. The upper half of each stable door was fixed open and Gospel's sleek black head and next door but one that of Merlin, the roan who pulled the wagonette, were poking out, eagerly awaiting their morning feed. Ned appeared from the store, and at the sound of the clinking buckets, Tansy's bright chestnut face came to look patiently out of her loose box between her two friends.

'I'll take Gospel's.'

Rose hadn't thought what she was going to do, acting purely by instinct. Fortunately, the bucket wasn't heavy, containing only a small supplement of oats, and she emptied it easily into the feeding trough, and then, satisfied that Ned was occupied in the other stalls, she stepped round the corner of the loose box. In the light of day – though of course the dog-leg was in shadow – she could see clearly the mound of straw in which Seth lay hidden, but, her swirling mind demanded, would it be obvious to anyone searching for an escaped convict?

'Seth!' she hissed, burying her hands in the straw and shaking whatever part of his anatomy she had got hold of. The mound stirred, and she pushed him back down. 'The Civil Guard are here!' she whispered frantically. 'Lie as still as a mouse!'

He did. And she heaped the straw over him in what she hoped was a more natural fashion.

When the guards came to the door of the loose box, what they saw was a young woman kneeling down by a pretty golden dog while another bedraggled specimen leapt playfully about her. When she rose gracefully to her feet and turned to them, revealing the obvious dome of her pregnancy, a soft and enquiring expression in her beautiful violet-blue eyes, they stepped back in humble deference, stunned by the unexpected vision of loveliness with her dark, loosened hair cascading about her shoulders in a glorious, shining cape.

'Yes, officers?' she asked, not needing to put the alarm in her voice as it was already there! 'Is there something wrong?'

The most senior of the group, for there were several of them swarming over the yard, cleared his throat and put his hand up to the brim of his soldier's hat. 'An escaped prisoner, ma'am, I'm afraid.'

The gasp that came from her throat was genuine. 'Oh, dear!' she choked, and turned her eyes desperately on her husband, who had come up behind the guard. 'Oh, Charles, how dreadful!'

'No need to be alarmed, ma'am. We'll catch the devil soon enough!' the sergeant assured her, preening himself proudly. 'Always do under my command. Ran off from the prison farm yesterday. Crafty bugger . . . if you'll excuse my language, ma'am. Always pretended to be the model prisoner, and then when that fog came down yesterday, he was off! My men shot at him, though,' he smirked gleefully, 'and one of them got him. Unfortunately, only winged him in the shoulder as far as we know, but it'll slow him down. Trouble is, though, we've been searching all night and haven't found a trace of him.'

'Perhaps he were swallowed up in Fox Tor mire,' Rose suggested with a frown. 'Either that, or he's well away across the moor by now.'

'More like hiding somewhere and licking his wounds. Which is why we must search everywhere, ma'am, so if you wouldn't mind standing aside . . .'

Rose's heart lurched into her throat, and for one horrible, sickening moment, she thought she was about to faint, but then Amber lumbered against her leg and pushed her snout into Rose's hand.

'I'd rather you didn't, officer,' she heard herself say. 'You can see my dog,' and here she smiled sweetly down at Amber, 'is about to have her puppies, and I should rather she wasn't disturbed. I'm certain I'd know if there were someone in here.'

Dear God, her heart was positively bucking in her chest,

and she was sure that the fellow must be able to hear its thunderous beat. But he seemed to hesitate. 'Well, I really ought to . . .'

'I'm sure my wife is right, officer.'

Rose stared in amazement. Charles, unwittingly, was defending Seth Collingwood, whom he would have kicked into the gutter if he'd known the truth! The irony of it was astounding, but there was no need for any further deliberation as Gospel, objecting to the stranger who as far as he was concerned was molesting his beloved mistress, stamped up behind her and stretching his long neck over her shoulder, ears laid back and eyes rolling, proceeded to bare his huge teeth and aim them at the guard's person. The man leapt back, a flush of terror and embarrassment colouring his face.

'Er, well, of course, sir,' he muttered, and Rose had the desire to laugh, though she knew she mustn't.

'Is this prisoner dangerous?' Charles was asking, his face a picture of consternation.

'Very much so, sir. And certainly a slippery customer. So be on your guard. And you, too, ma'am.'

He dipped his head at the magnificent young woman and the great horse beside her that shook its head irritably and looked as if it was just waiting for another opportunity to try and take a bite out of him! His dignity, though, was rescued in the nick of time by one of his men reporting that there was no one lurking about the house, its gardens or outhouses, and with another polite warning, the group of guards took their leave.

Rose felt her knees weaken as the bravado drained out of her, but it was far from over yet.

'You'd better come inside, Rose, if this felon's on the loose,' Charles was insisting, and Rose's desperate mind spun in a nauseating spiral.

'Yes, of course, Charles,' she answered, her voice anxious, though not for the reason Charles believed! 'I'm just going to move Amber's basket round the corner out of the way, so as Ned won't disturb her when he comes to muck out,' she told him loudly so that Seth would hear her. ''Tis quite clean round there. So it doesn't need doing.'

'Let me do it, then. It's too heavy for you.'

Rose's heart nearly exploded as Charles stepped into the

loose box, eyeing Gospel warily as the massive animal stamped his hooves in agitation. What if Charles . . .?

'Don't be silly!' she laughed nervously, for indeed he did look somewhat comical. 'You're still in your dressing gown, and you don't want to step in something nasty in your slippers! Look, I'll just drag it.'

And firmly grasping one end of the basket, she did just that, leaving it across the dog-leg, effectively barring the entrance to where Seth lay. It was still taking one hell of a chance, but what else could she do? Her face broke into its most enchanting smile as she came back to her husband, and though it seared at her to do so, she deliberately took his elbow, leaning her head against his shoulder as if craving his protection. He responded at once, putting his arm defensively about her.

'Oh, Ned!' she called casually as the young man appeared from the tack room, nodding his head politely at his master. 'When you muck out Gospel's box, I'd be obliged if you don't go round the corner. I've put Amber's basket there. She's behaving so oddly this morning, I think she must be about to have the puppies.'

'Knows her time's coming, I expect, Miss Rose . . . er, Mrs Chadwick,' he corrected himself under Charles's stern gaze.

'And will you be turning Gospel out into the field later? 'Tis a much better day than yesterday.'

'Yes, I were going to, ma'am, if he'll let me put his halter on.'

'Well, just call me if he gives you any trouble.'

'Will do, ma'am.'

They turned back to the house, Rose almost sagging with relief. The first hurdle was over, but it was only the first. And the Civil Guard might return at any time over the next few days, few weeks even. Dear Lord, what had she got herself in to? Why was she putting herself at risk, trusting this stranger about whom she knew next to nothing? Following her instincts alone?

And as they went into breakfast, she found she had very little appetite indeed.

Nineteen

'My dear, I really ought to go into Princetown and send some telegrams,' Charles frowned with a heavy sigh as he flicked over the correspondence in his hands some time later. 'But I don't like leaving you, not with this felon still at large.'

'Oh, 'tis not as though I'm alone,' Rose shrugged, her mind leaping at his words, for she hadn't yet found an opportunity to go out to the stables again. 'Cook and Patsy are here, and Mrs Robbins today. And there's always Ned. And Dr Seaton is due to see me this morning. Besides, I don't imagine any escaped prisoner would stay around so close to Princetown. You wouldn't if you were in his shoes, would you? He'll be well away by now.'

'All the same.' Charles raised a sceptical eyebrow. 'You heard what the sergeant said. He's highly dangerous.'

'Oh, I'm sure we'll be perfectly safe. You'd keep away from people during the day, wouldn't you? You can't neglect your business affairs on the off-chance that this fellow will turn up here when there's over three hundred square miles of Dartmoor to hide in! No, you go. How long do you think you'll be?'

'Yes, I suppose you're right. I'll take Tansy to be quicker, but I will need to await replies, so I could be a little while. But promise me you'll stay in the house.'

'Absolutely,' she assured him, though she had no intention of doing so!

'I'll tell Ned to saddle Tansy, then.'

'Yes, dear.'

She caught his hand as he passed her, kissing it softly and looking up at him with her dazzling smile. He smiled back, squeezing her shoulder before striding out of the room, and Rose leaned back in her chair, releasing her breath in a steady stream. So far, so good. Ned must have mucked out the stables by now, and there had been no sudden cries of discovery, but it was a daily task, and how long would Seth have to wait for his broken ankle to mend? Six, eight weeks? Dear Lord, could he possibly remain there in secret for so long?

Rose watched from the window as Charles cantered off down the driveway, and before he had turned out of the gates she was skating into the kitchen. There was some bacon left over, which she took on the pretext that it was for the dogs, and then she poured a mug of coffee for herself, or so she told Cook.

'There's just a drop of cream left to put in it,' the kind woman said. 'I could really do with some more, mind.'

Rose's face lit up. 'I'll send Ned.' And then, armed with the coffee and the bacon, she stepped out into the spring sunshine.

Ned was crossing the stable yard, whistling tunelessly, his hands in his pockets, believing his morning's work was over.

'Ned!' Rose called, and he came over, ever hoping – though in vain – that his luck might be in with her. Still, this was a good job, and he was in no hurry to lose it! 'Did you have any trouble with Gospel?'

'No,' he answered, taken aback. 'Good as gold he were this morning. He and Merlin are romping round the field like a couple o' rabbits now!'

The smile that shone from Rose's face shimmered in her eyes – as she had meant it to. 'Good! Now, be an angel and walk over to Tor Royal for some cream, would you, please, Ned? Ask the dairymaid to put it on our account.'

Ned went to scowl, but then remembered that the dairymaid was a pretty wench, not slight as a cowslip like Miss Rose normally was, but a homely, buxom sort, and he was not averse to that! 'But what 'bout this yere convict? Maister said I'm to protect all yer women folk.'

'Oh, get away with you, Ned Cornish! He's hardly likely to come here, is he? And I promise I won't tell the master if you won't.'

Ned seemed to consider for a moment, a moment in which Rose felt her nerves jangle on a knife-edge, and then he was pulling on his worn jacket and striding away with a noticeable skip in his jaunty gait.

Rose was in the loose box within seconds. The door had

been left open so that the dogs could roam in and out, and clean straw had been shaken out over the floor. Scraggles was scampering about at Rose's feet, but as she came round the corner, Amber hardly lifted her head from the basket, which hadn't been moved.

'Seth, 'tis all right,' Rose whispered as she stepped around the dog's bed. 'You can come out now.'

She waited as Seth moved slowly and stiffly, cautiously pushing his head up through the straw and brushing it from his face. 'Are you sure?' he croaked.

'Yes. My husband's gone out and I've sent Ned on an errand, and Cook and the maid and the laundry woman are all busy in the house. And 'tis not one of the gardener's days, so we're quite safe.' She paused for breath, realizing her tongue was careering as fast as her racing mind. 'But we've no time to lose. Sit up and drink this, and I'll fetch the things to take the shot out of your shoulder. And here's some bacon. 'Tis cold, I'm afraid, but 'twas the best I could do.'

He glanced up at her, his forehead pleated with anxiety as he shifted position. A tormented wince escaped his lips as he leaned back against the wall, and Rose's heart squeezed with sympathy.

'Thank you, ma'am,' he said, but as he took the cup from her, she saw that his hands were trembling and his face was shadowed with agony. He took a gulp of the coffee, then dropped his head back, his eyes closed. 'Oh, that tastes good.' He seemed to savour the moment for several seconds before looking up at her again. 'God, I've never been so terrified in all my life as when those guards came in. I really thought they'd find me. You were wonderful! And then when your Ned was mucking out, well, he only needed to be a little more thorough. I hardly dared to breathe.'

'Well, you're safe for a while now,' she assured him. 'You get that down you, and I'll be back in a few minutes.'

'You know . . . you don't have to do this. I'd fully understand if—'

His voice cracked with emotion, and Rose felt her heart tear. 'But I want to,' she answered simply, and as she spoke the words, she knew it was the truth.

It only took her a few minutes to collect up all she needed and hurry back to the stables. The yard, as expected, was deserted, but she shut the lower section of the door so that if anyone should happen to cross the yard they wouldn't be able to see in unless they deliberately peered into the loose box.

'Seth, you'll need to come round the corner into the light,' she told him as she set the bowl on the floor.

She heard him draw in a shaking breath, and then he was dragging himself across to her. As he emerged from the shadows, she saw his teeth were fiercely gritted, and his face, which she could see now was strikingly handsome despite the convict crop, was ravaged with pain.

Rose frowned deeply. 'Is it worse, your ankle, I mean?'

He nodded, looking up at her beseechingly. His eyes were large and expressive, a soft hazel with darker flecks near the edges which merged into a brown outer rim. They seemed to reach into her, touching some depth in her soul that had lain undisturbed all her life and which now burgeoned and blossomed in an instant. A warm tide flowed into her, calming and yet tingling with excitement. She turned away, driving the sensation from her mind, recognizing the same intense feeling she had experienced by the quarry tunnel, confused and bewildered . . .

'Turn your back to the light.'

Her voice was so small, quavering, as she watched him struggle out of her father's clothes. When he got down to the shirt, it had stuck to the oozing wounds and she helped him ease it away, forgetting the strange, unwanted emotions that had gripped her as the overriding sense of sympathy engulfed her again. His shoulders were strongly muscled, but he was so thin his ribs showed beneath his skin. Half-starved and expected to work like dogs, she'd heard Jacob Cartwright complain in the privacy of his own home. Now she could see for herself exactly what he meant.

'Hold very still,' she ordered as she took from her pocket the tweezers she had carefully washed and wrapped in a clean handkerchief. 'I'll try not to hurt you.'

'Are you sure we're safe?'

'As sure as I can be.'

'If we're caught, I've frightened you into helping me. Understand?'

She paused, tweezers poised. Even now, he was thinking of her rather than himself. 'Yes,' she muttered, steeling herself as she laid the tweezers against the first small hole. 'Ready?' she whispered.

He nodded, and she saw him tense rigidly. Her own mouth knotted as she worked the tweezers into his flesh, and he arched his back, choking on a stifled gasp. Rose's hand was quivering and she bit down hard on her lip as fresh blood trickled down from the wound. Extricating the small ball of lead shot was not an easy task and it took her three attempts before she finally pulled it out. Blood was flowing freely down Seth's back, but she wet a piece of the bandaging left from the previous evening and twisted a corner of it into a probe to clean out the wound. She knew there was danger of infection from any dirt or fragments of material the shot had taken with it, infection that could kill the strongest man, as could either gangrene or something called lockjaw that often developed in puncture wounds. Both were invariably fatal. And though she felt sick at the torture she was causing him, she knew it had to be done, though even so there was no guarantee.

'There,' she announced encouragingly as she finally pressed a fresh cloth over the wound to staunch the bleeding. 'One down and only five to go.' Five more. Oh, dear Lord, she didn't know if she could do this! But she *had* to. There was no alternative. 'Thank goodness some of them missed you,' she murmured hoarsely.

Seth hung his head, snatched breaths shuddering in and out of his lungs. 'And thank God I was almost out of range, or they'd have gone in deeper. And if the guards were armed with the new Martini-Henry rifles instead of those converted Sniders, I'd probably be dead.'

Rose faltered as she took up the tweezers again, but perhaps talking would help to keep both their minds from the harrowing procedure. 'You seem to know a great deal about guns,' she observed, and a twinge of caution tugged reluctantly at her conscience as she inserted the instrument into the second hole. He let out a quickly muted cry, holding his breath and then releasing it shakily. 'Are you sure you won't take some laudanum?' she pressed him.

He grunted bitterly, shaking his head. 'I don't think laudanum would do much against this. And I want to keep my wits about me. No. Just get on with it as quickly as you can. The sooner I can hide again, the happier I'll feel.'

'I'll do my best.'

She worked on, bracing herself against the cold sweat that flushed over her in waves. It seemed to take an eternity, and by the time all six lead balls had been removed and the wounds cleaned, Rose was drained and exhausted. She was ready to slump down on her bed, weep away her anguish, but there were still tracks to cover.

Seth groaned as he reached for Henry's shirt, and she could see he was shivering.

'Wait a few minutes. That last one's still bleeding. I'll slip across and get you a clean shirt.'

She went with more confidence, but then checked herself. She must be on her guard at all times, and it wouldn't be long before Ned was back. But as yet there was no sign of him, and she could hear the busy goings-on in the kitchen. By the time she returned to the stables, Seth had moved back into the relative safety of the darkened dog-leg and half hidden himself in the straw. She inspected his shoulder again. The bleeding had virtually stopped, so she gently wiped it clean and then used the last of the bandages to bind up his wounds. Rose could see his face was grey as he lay down and she covered him with straw. She felt so frustrated. So angry! He should be in a proper bed, being carefully nursed, taking laudanum to ease his pain and help him sleep through the healing process. But here he was . . .

'I imagine 'twill hurt worse now,' she mumbled as she cleared away the bloodied rags.

'Yes. But it should settle down soon. And thank you, Mrs Chadwick. That was very brave of you.'

'Call me Rose, please.'

The hint of a smile flickered over his generous mouth. '*That which we call a rose by any other name would smell as sweet.*' His eyes fleetingly met hers, and she was once again overwhelmed by the loveliness, the sensitivity in them that seemed to speak to her. And a convict who quoted Shakespeare with such feeling . . .

When Rose took the mug back to the kitchen, Cook was busy preparing a thick, tasty soup for lunch.

'How's the dog, ma'am?'

'Behaving strangely. I think we'll see the pups any day.'

'New life's always good, ma'am. Though pups I can do

without. 'Tis that babby o' yourn I'm looking forward to, if you doesn't mind us saying so, ma'am.'

'Not at all!' Rose grinned, and even Patsy gave a shy smile.

There! All quite natural. No one suspected a thing. And ten minutes later when she saw Ned turning the corner of the house carrying the canister of cream, she knew they were safe.

For now . . .

'Charles, I'm just taking Dr Seaton over to have a look at Amber,' Rose announced as she poked her head around the door to his study.

'Forgive me if I don't come with you,' Charles replied as the elderly physician's head appeared over his wife's shoulder. 'I went into Princetown earlier to send some telegrams, and now I have a deal of correspondence to deal with. But tell me, how is she, and the baby, of course?'

'Blooming!' Dr Seaton reassured him. 'She seems to have the perfect balance between rest and exercise, and the baby is growing and has a strong heartbeat. Now let me see this dog of yours, Mrs Chadwick.' He smiled indulgently, for who could resist the charms of this vivacious young woman? He was semi-retired now, travelling in a horse-drawn trap rather than on horseback as he once had. He wouldn't normally have agreed to take on a patient as far out as Princetown, but Mr Chadwick had been very persuasive and his wife was a delight. She was like a breath of fresh air. No. More like a whirlwind, and he looked upon her as he might a wilful grandchild.

She skipped along beside him now as they crossed the yard, having insisted that he bring his medical bag in case the dog needed anything! But now, below her finely shaped eyebrows, her arresting violet-blue eyes fixed him with their piercing clarity.

'Dr Seaton,' she began torturedly, and had he been taking her pulse at that moment he would have felt it accelerate alarmingly, 'isn't there some sort of promise that doctors make? That they'll treat a patient no matter who they are? And that they must keep all details about their patients confidential?'

The physician's grey eyebrows swooped into a frown. 'The Hippocratic Oath, you mean? Well, it's not as straightforward as that, but broadly speaking, yes.'

'And,' she went on, her heart doing its level best to escape from her ribcage as they stepped over the threshold of Gospel's loose box, 'what would you say if . . .' She hesitated, her dry throat closing up. Dear God above, could she trust this kind, elderly man, or would everything she had done for Seth so far have been in vain? But there was no doubt in her mind that Seth's ankle simply *must* be seen by a physician. 'What if the patient was an escaped convict?' she rasped in a whisper.

Dr Seaton stopped in his tracks. He glanced furtively about him, then glared down at the agonized expression on her face. 'I don't think I'm going to like what you're about to tell me, Mrs Chadwick.'

Rose drew him into the loose box, ignoring Amber, who seemed disinclined to move from her basket. Rose felt so scared, more than at any other time in her life, and her knees were like rubber beneath her. 'Please, Dr Seaton,' she begged, her voice trembling. 'He escaped because he's innocent. And before you say that's what they all claim, I believe him. But he's broken his ankle, and he was shot.'

Dr Seaton paused and drew in a long breath. 'And you want me to help him?'

She nodded, and tears were glittering in her lovely eyes.

'And am I to assume that your husband knows nothing of this?'

She nodded again, dancing on the spot, perspiration oozing from every pore. The doctor hesitated, contemplating the compassion that creased her face.

'The Oath only goes so far, you know,' he finally answered, his voice low. 'I should turn him over to the authorities at once. You do realize what you're asking of me?'

'Yes. But *please*! I beg you. If you talk to him, you'll see he's . . . *different* from most of the other felons at the gaol.'

The doctor shook his head, and for one horrible, stomach-churning second she thought . . . 'All right. I'll take a quick look.'

'Oh, thank you!' She almost collapsed into his arms. 'He's just here. Behind us. Seth. Seth?'

The doctor's lined face jerked in surprise as the mound of straw moved. 'You've got him well hidden,' he confessed in amazement, and at once he was the professional physician, kneeling by his patient while Rose kept an anxious lookout, her heart in her mouth. 'Let's have a look at you, then.'

Seth's eyes stretched wide. 'Thank you, Doctor, for not

betraying me at once. It's my ankle and I took some shot in my shoulder, but Mrs Chadwick got it out for me this morning.'

Dr Seaton raised an eyebrow. 'Did she, by Jove?'

'There were six pellets,' Rose whispered over her shoulder. 'And I cleaned the wounds as well as I could.'

The doctor gave an enigmatic grunt. 'I thought they were supposed to aim for the legs. To stop you running.'

'They are,' Seth grimaced. 'But Sniders aren't amazingly accurate. And I was almost out of range, so they'd lost their velocity.'

'Hmm. You speak like a man of the army yourself.'

'I am. Ex-army. And I'm not a deserter, if that's what you think. I resigned my commission.'

'Officer, then?'

'Yes. But perhaps if I'd stayed in the army, I wouldn't have got myself into this mess.'

Rose's ears had pricked up like a fox. It was the first she really knew of Seth's background. But they were wasting precious time. 'What about his ankle?' she almost hissed in her apprehension.

'Yes, of course. Let me see.'

The pulse was thundering at Rose's temples as she stood guard, Amber gazing dolefully at her mistress, not understanding why she wasn't being patted and stroked when something very strange was going on in her belly. But Rose had other, more desperate matters on her mind.

'The fracture's slightly displaced,' she heard the physician pronounce.

'Can you splint it?'

'I can do better than that. I'll use plaster of Paris.'

'Have you got some? No disrespect, but I wouldn't have expected a provincial doctor—'

'Oh, I keep up to date, lad. And it *has* been in use for several years, you know. But I'll have to reduce the break. Put it back into place. Now let me tighten this around your arm and see if we can get a good vein for some morphine.'

Seth's reply was instant. 'No. If I'm caught when I'm out cold, it'll be too difficult to explain, and then *you'll* be in trouble, too.'

'And I refuse to do it without morphine. I'd prefer to put you to sleep with chloroform, and you'd come round quicker afterwards, but I've only got one pair of hands and I'll need Mrs Chadwick's help at this end. But I can guarantee that without one or the other, you'll scream and bring Mr Chadwick running. Besides, how would you explain the plaster cast? I'm implicated already.'

'I stole the plaster from your medical bag,' Rose put in. 'You thought you had some, but it wasn't there after your rounds. Anyone could have taken it. And you weren't sure, anyway.'

She heard Dr Seaton inhale deeply. 'All right. But I'll need a bucket of water and an empty one, too. And if you can help me, please, Mrs Chadwick.'

Rose reluctantly left her post, but there was nothing else for it. If they were caught now, they could make excuses, say they had only just found him. At least Seth's ankle would have been tended, and someone on the outside would have some care for him. Perhaps she could even pay him a prison visit. But Rose couldn't bear the thought of what would certainly happen to him . . .

She worked on, obeying the doctor's every instruction, but with one ear constantly on the alert. At one point there was a patter on the loose-box floor, and her heart literally stood still. But it was Scraggles returning from some errand – only he knew what. Rose felt faint from relief, and was infinitely glad the morphine had put Seth to sleep, though it wasn't a full anaesthetic like chloroform and he groaned when the good doctor pulled his ankle back into place, making a grating sound that set Rose's teeth on edge. But the process took surprisingly little time, and as she buried Seth's limp body in the straw again, Dr Seaton washed the residue of the white powder from his hands and rolled down his sleeves.

'Keep an eye on his foot,' he told her quietly. 'Make sure he can wriggle his toes and that they stay a good colour. If they start turning blue or cold, you must turn him in at once. The swelling should go down in a few days, but if the opposite happens, he *must* have medical attention. Ideally, I'd like to re-cast it in a week. The plaster will become loose as the swelling reduces, you understand. And there's almost certainly damage to the ligaments. It could take months to heal.'

'Months?' Rose's eyes stretched with horror.

'I really would strongly advise him to give himself up. At least he'll have the medical care he needs.'

'And then he'll be flogged,' Rose muttered bitterly under her breath.

Dr Seaton looked at her, and his mouth twisted with compassion. 'As he said, he's got himself into a mess. Though if he *is* innocent, he has my every sympathy. Anyway, I'll leave you this. It's phenol. A few drops in a bowl of water to bathe the shot wounds. A mild infection he can stand, but again if he becomes feverish, well, you know my opinion. Or if his speech becomes slurred, or his muscles start to stiffen. Though God knows there's little anyone can do if he develops lockjaw.'

Rose's heart had sunk like a lead weight. Dr Seaton's words had really brought it home to her that Seth's life could be in danger. Perhaps she should betray him for his own sake. But how could she? He had put his trust in her, as she had in him. In the short time she had known him – heavens above, was it less than twenty-four hours? – some invisible bond had developed between them. It would be cowardly, dishonourable even, to expose him while he slept off the effect of the morphine. No. She must wait. But if he became seriously ill, she would do her utmost to persuade him to give himself up.

But they both knew what would happen when he was recovered.

In the event, Rose missed the birth of the pups altogether.

She managed to slip out to the stables after she and Charles had shared a light midday meal, but Seth was still sleeping, and so she waited several hours as she didn't want to arouse any suspicion. It gave her the opportunity to put her feet up and relax. She was confident no one would enter Gospel's loose box, and whatever happened, Seth's injuries had at least been properly tended.

It was late afternoon when she sauntered casually over to the dogs carrying a glass of cool water, for she was so thirsty, she told Cook. It must be the baby, she had proclaimed, and the older woman had nodded in agreement! Seth would be parched, she was sure, but she knew from nursing her father that morphine induced nausea, so he must sip the water slowly no matter how dry he was. But just for a moment as she entered the stable, her concern for the fugitive was interrupted.

Snuggled up against Amber's golden flank were four tiny bundles of wet fur, eyes closed, ears so small they were hardly visible, and bald pink button noses twitching as they instinctively searched for their mother's teats. The detritus of birth lay about them, and Amber ceased her tender licking of each of her pups to glance up proudly at her mistress, while Scraggles nudged his offspring with bemused curiosity.

Rose held her breath, spellbound, as she gazed down on the minuscule creatures, two of them the image of their beautiful mother, and the other pair black and white like their father, and all of them squeaking plaintively as they made their first attempts to gain sustenance for their empty bellies. Rose hardly dared move in case she disturbed the wondrous vision, or caused the new mother any distress, but simply stood in rapt amazement.

'This one's not doing so well.'

Seth's low voice destroyed her reverie, and a shiver ran through her body as she remembered why she was there. She peered into the shadows around the corner, and though Seth was buried in straw from the waist downwards, he was sitting up, totally visible, as his attention was concentrated on some minute scrap that lay in the palm of his hand.

'Seth, you'll be seen!' Rose hissed at him in alarm.

'I couldn't let this one die,' he answered, and she saw that he was gently rubbing whatever it was with a hank of straw. 'The runt of the litter.'

He changed what he was doing then, and she was able to make out that he was holding the little damp bundle upside down, shaking it firmly until a string of mucus dribbled from what she realized now was a diminutive snout. Whipping the debris away with his free hand, Seth proceeded to blow softly into the tiny mouth, which he held open between his thumb and little finger, and after two or three attempts he looked up at Rose with a grin so delighted and so stunning that the breath seemed to leave her body.

Her senses reeled away from her and she might have fled back across the yard, but she didn't. She was confounded. Baffled. And she sank awkwardly on to her knees in the straw beside this supposedly dangerous criminal, her pulse drumming steadily at her temples as, heads together, they contemplated the indescribable miracle of new life.

'Oh, he's beautiful,' Rose breathed, for indeed the puppy was a striking mixture of caramel and copper with a little white face and one black sock.

'He's a she, actually, and I suggest you put her with her mother. She'll take care of her now.'

Rose put down the glass and cupped her hands to receive the tiny creature. 'Oh, thank you so much for saving her.'

'Little ones are always wonderful.' And then somehow his face closed down as he muttered under his breath, 'As you'll soon find out for yourself.'

Rose frowned as she carefully placed the little animal among its siblings. This enigmatic stranger had such a curious effect on her that she couldn't fathom it out. His past life was still a mystery to her, and she was anxious to be enlightened, not just for his sake, but for her own. But first things first.

'How are you feeling now?' she whispered, for having handed her the puppy, he had instantly lain down again as if in exhaustion.

'Still groggy, to tell the truth.'

'What about your ankle?'

'It still hurts, but it's definitely more comfortable than it was. I didn't really get to thank your doctor properly. It was good of him to take such a risk.'

Rose nodded. 'He's a good man. You know, Charles – my husband – insisted on finding another doctor for me. My father and I always had Dr Power—'

'What!' Seth lifted his head in horror. 'You mean—?'

'The prison doctor, yes. I was furious at the time. 'Twas as if he was good enough for my father, but not for Charles. But I'm glad now. Not that Dr Power isn't an excellent physician, but he'd have been obliged to turn you in. 'Tis ironic, really,' Rose snorted. 'Charles would hand you over without a thought, and yet because of him, you were able to see a doctor in safety.'

Her voice was laced with bitterness, and Seth raised his eyebrows at her. 'Forgive me for saying so,' he faltered, 'but I have the impression you're not too happy in your marriage.'

Rose's head jerked backwards on her neck. Molly was the only person to whom she had ever confessed her misgivings over her marriage to Charles, but her dear friend was so enraptured by her love for her own husband that she did not seem to appreciate the strength of Rose's feelings. But apart from Molly, no one had ever gained the least impression that she regretted her marriage to Charles, and yet this man, this *convict*, whom she scarcely knew, had seen straight into her very soul. She wanted so much to unburden herself, but it hardly seemed right and she reared away from it.

'Drink the water,' she commanded instead.

The flicker of a frown creased Seth's broad forehead, but he said nothing, propping himself on one elbow as he sipped from the glass. She noticed him wince slightly as he moved his shoulder, bringing her own thoughts back to reality, and she bent to feel the plaster cast through the pile of straw.

'It feels a lot drier,' she said automatically.

'It'll take twenty-four hours at least to dry properly. And I can move my toes, so it all seems good.'

'I'll bring out a bowl of water later if I can to bathe your shoulder, and you can have a wash. I can say 'tis to clean up the puppies.'

'That would be good. Thank you so much.'

'Rose! Rose, my dearest, where are you?'

Rose was convinced her heart had stopped beating, and then it seemed to catapult forward with the force of a sledgehammer. Her knees felt weak and trembling as she turned to look, wide-eyed with terror, over her shoulder.

'Quick!'

Seth's frantic whisper galvanized her brain into action and she was wildly heaping straw over him, tossing it over his head – she prayed to God that he could still breathe – and then patting it down so that she hoped it didn't appear as what it was, a disguise for the human form hiding beneath it. She swept up the almost empty glass, standing solidly between the dog basket and the hump of straw, spreading her voluminous skirt out sideways. When Charles ambled into the loose box, though her heart was thudding savagely, she met him with an enchanting, enraptured smile.

'Look, Charles! Amber's had her pups!' she cried in jubilation. 'Aren't they gorgeous?'

'Indeed, they are, my dear.' Charles's words were stiff, and he barely glanced down. 'How many are there? Oh, good. Only five, I see. And that little runt probably won't survive, so that'll only be four to dispose of.'

Rose felt the barb cut into her side. Seth had risked his own safety to revive the fragment of life that was the ailing newborn pup, while Charles dismissed it as some vile, unwanted thing that he would prefer to be dead, as he would clearly have liked the others to be as well! The gall burned into Rose's throat, but she stepped forward with a fixed smile, taking Charles's arm and turning him away from both the animals and the obscured man.

'Come, Charles, I should like to take some tea now. To celebrate. This water has quenched my thirst, and now a cup of tea would go down very nicely.'

They were out in the spring sunshine again, and the warmth penetrated her shivering flesh. Charles patted her hand as it lay cradled in his elbow, and the rancour stung deeper into her soul.

'You go and tell Cook or Patsy to make the tea,' she smiled sweetly up at him. 'I just want a word with Ned about the puppies.'

'All right. But don't be long.'

She waited to make sure he had gone back inside, and then she went in search of Ned, for an idea had just struck her that filled her with relief. She found him in the tack room, lounging in the chair with his feet stretched out before him, scarcely bothering to move when she put her head around the door.

'Ah, Ned, there you are. Busy as ever, I see,' she observed scathingly. 'Well, I've a job for you. When you've time, of course. Amber's had her puppies, and I'm worried that Gospel might step on them, so I want you to put him in the spare box when you bring him in. So will you get the box ready for him, please. And I don't want anyone going in to Amber and the puppies until I say so. I'll put down some newspaper for them and see to all that sort of thing. I'm still quite capable of that, so there's no need for you to do anything. I'll just put everything in a bucket by the door, and you can empty it into the incinerator with all the rubbish.'

'Right-ho, Miss Rose,' Ned grinned indolently. And as she turned away, she heard him mumble to himself that he didn't want to have anything to do with the bloody things anyway. And that suited Rose down to the ground! It had crossed her mind that she would have to think of something for Seth's personal needs, too, and this would kill the two birds with the one stone.

And feeling quite pleased with herself, she went indoors.

Twenty

'Rose, my dear, I need to go to London, and I really would rather you came with me. The change would be good for you, and they haven't caught this escaped convict yet.'

Rose's hand was poised in midair as she lifted a spoonful of Cook's sumptuous dessert towards her mouth. Her heart took an almighty bound and it was with the greatest effort that she made her hand continue its journey and she calmly swallowed the delicious morsel, allowing her frantic brain time to think. The last few days had not been at all easy, and if it hadn't been for the excuse of checking on Amber and the puppies she would hardly have been able to slip out to the stables at all. Seth's appetite was surprisingly poor, but Rose knew the importance of a sufficient supply of fluid. The wounds on his shoulder were sloughing and should have been bathed daily, but she had only managed one opportunity to do so as yet. And if she had to go to London, well, the game would be up. Without her help, Seth could not survive, and he would have no choice but to give himself up.

'Oh, Charles, that would be nice,' she replied with a pretty smile, 'but I really think I'd find a whole day on the train too much. I'm beginning to get backache and I feel so uncomfortable, I really should prefer to stay here.'

'It would be your last chance for some time,' Charles argued. 'And once the baby's born—'

'Yes, I know.' She deliberately released a profound sigh and was quite pleased how natural it sounded. 'But then I'd have the whole journey to do in reverse, and I don't think 'twould be a good idea.'

'You could stay in London. Have the baby there.'

'No!' She was genuinely horrified, her voice trembling at the very thought. 'I want it born here! Dr Seaton has been so kind and I have the greatest confidence in him. No, Charles. I'm sorry, but I will stay here.'

She met his gaze defiantly across the table, her eyes glinting that deep heather he knew so well and her fine jaw raised stubbornly.

'But you will take care of yourself while I'm gone?' he conceded with reluctance. 'I really am concerned about this prisoner.'

'Didn't you say someone answering his description was seen over Ivybridge way?' she prompted.

'That's true. The Civil Guard are concentrating their search over there.'

'Well, there you are, then! And if 'twasn't him, then I expect he'll have perished out on the moor by now. Hopelessly lost, sunk into a mire, anything can happen out there. The moor's a treacherous place if you don't know it, and 'tis still cold enough at night to kill.'

'Yes, I suppose so.' Charles's lips contorted into a grimace. 'All the same—'

'I'll be fine!' she assured him. 'I've lived here all my life almost and there's never been any problems with the prisoners. 'Tis more important you sort out your business affairs so as you can be here when the baby's born.'

'Good Lord, I won't be that long! About ten days should do it.'

'And when will you go?' She was trying to sound casual, but her stomach was churning nervously, so much so that for a horrible instant she was worried about the baby, and relieved when it suddenly kicked hard under her ribs.

'The day after tomorrow, I should think.'

'Oh, so soon?' Heavens above, it was becoming so easy to play-act, to lie and deceive, but what choice did she have? Besides, she was finding Charles more irritating by the day, just inconsequential, trivial matters, but ones that were growing into an increasingly tall pile. While out in the stable, the convict, the *dangerous* criminal she scarcely knew, was drawing her curiosity and, dare she say it, gaining her trust more surely with every day that passed.

* * *

She saw Charles off first thing in the morning, waving from the front door, as Ned drove them away in the wagonette. The second they were out of sight, Rose hurried up the stairs as quickly as her bulging abdomen permitted. The train left Tavistock shortly before nine o'clock, and the round trip to the station and back would take Ned the best part of three hours. Three precious hours which she intended to spend with Seth Collingwood. She had prepared a list of extra jobs to keep Cook and Patsy busy, and if she wanted to sit out in Gospel's loose box watching the newborn puppies of her beloved dog, no one was going to question it.

She had breakfasted early with Charles, so having washed and dressed, it seemed quite acceptable to ask for a cup of chocolate to take out to the stables with her. Some extra scraps for the lactating bitch, well, it was the best she could do without arousing suspicion, and she had rescued a jug of tepid water, for she must take the opportunity to bathe the wounds on Seth's shoulder.

She could see he was stiff with cold as he dragged himself from his hiding place and he fell on the steaming drink like a drowning man grasping at a rope. He was shivering, and Rose tried to tuck the two blankets around him, but they, too, were damp to the touch.

'Thank you,' he murmured as he glanced sideways at her, and she was alarmed when he clearly held back a rasping cough.

'You look dreadful,' she told him, biting on her bottom lip.

'I don't exactly feel on top of the world. But you get used to that,' he added with a rueful grimace.

Rose's mouth fined to a sympathetic line. 'How's the ankle?'

'A little more comfortable, I'm pleased to say.'

'And your shoulder?'

He dipped his head slightly. 'Worse. I can hardly move my arm it hurts so much.'

Rose felt her heart constrict. 'I'll take a look and bathe it with the phenol. And I've brought some fresh bandages.'

He nodded as he began to struggle out of her father's clothes and she unwound the makeshift dressings from his shoulder. He winced agonizingly as the stained material pulled away from the angry, suppurating wounds, two of which had swollen dramatically and were leaking with thick, foul-smelling pus.

'Oh, God, I don't like the look of this, Seth.'

He instantly jerked up his head. 'But I'm not giving myself up. To be frank, I'd rather die than go back. If I was guilty and deserved it, I'd serve my sentence like a man. But I'm not, and I might as well be dead as spend ten more years there.'

Rose said nothing, but met his gaze in silence. What he said appalled her, though she could understand how he must feel. Life in the prison must be unimaginably harsh, and must seem so unjust for someone who was innocent. 'Let me see to your shoulder,' she said instead, 'and then you can tell me your story.'

She tried to be gentle as she tended his injuries, but it wasn't easy, Seth holding himself tense but not uttering a sound until she had finished, even though she knew it must be torture for him. She had done her level best, but heaven alone knew if the cleansed wounds would now improve.

'I think getting some air to them might help to dry them up. If I arrange the blankets around you . . .'

It took some minutes for him to shift into a suitable position, encumbered as he was by the plaster cast, and then Rose had to get herself comfortable, which was becoming increasingly difficult. She sat on a bale near Amber, stroking the animal's silky, domed head and looking down on the five puppies that were nestled against their mother's flank in a peaceful confusion of sparsely haired bodies and little round tummies that were becoming fatter by the day.

'Lovely, aren't they?' Seth whispered, following her gaze, and when she turned to look at him, he was smiling through his strained expression. The breath quickened in her throat. The even set of his strong teeth was a long white slash in the stubble of his unshaven jaw, his eyes shining softly with a deep tenderness. Beneath them were the dark smudges of a man who hardly slept, who passed every minute in fear, and Rose had deliberately to shy away from the emotion that stirred mysteriously in her breast.

'Yes,' she gulped, and had to clear her throat. 'Now, whilst we have the chance, you'd better tell me what happened.'

The enchanting smile at once faded from Seth's face and his eyebrows arched. 'It was the twenty-second of October 1874,' he began slowly, bowing his head to concentrate his thoughts. 'I think that date will be printed on my mind for

ever. I'd been out of the army for about six months, just travelling around the country wherever I fancied. I worked as and
when, casual labour, whatever was available. I didn't really
mind. When you're used to army conditions, it doesn't really
matter. During that summer I slept in an inn, a barn, under a
hedge. Just the freedom of the open road, not having to obey
orders, to *give* orders to my men I didn't want to give.
Everything I owned was slung over my back in a kitbag. I
only had myself to please—'

'Do you not have any family?'

He jerked up his head and his eyes flashed. 'No!' he barked,
his face taut. 'Not that I wanted anything to do with.' But then
his expression softened. 'I'm sorry. That must sound dreadful,
but I'm afraid it's true.'

'And I'm sorry you feel that way. My father meant the world
to me. Since he died, my life's not been the same . . .'

Her voice trailed off in passionate sadness, but the silence
that followed didn't seem awkward.

'You have a husband. And a child to look forward to,' Seth
finally said.

'Ah.' Rose breathed an enigmatic sigh and a wistful smile
lifted the corners of her mouth. 'But we're supposed to be
talking about you.'

'Yes. As you wish.' And she was relieved when he didn't
press her. He clasped his hands, staring down at his intertwined
fingers. 'I'd spent a few weeks working as an assistant drayman
for a brewery in Exeter. I'd always jump at the chance to work
with horses, you see. The chap had hurt his back, so I was
just helping out, really. When he was better, I made my way
to Plymouth. I still had some army pay left as well, so I was
in no hurry to find work straight away. I'd had the idea that I
might try and get on a ship. Work my passage to America,
perhaps, and start a new life there. I'd been in Plymouth about
a week, trying to decide what to do and making a few enquiries,
but I was so near to Dartmoor and wanted to see it properly.
Everyone said Tavistock was a good place to see it from, so
I decided to walk there. I took two days over it, and arrived
on the second evening. I thought I'd call in at a public house
and ask about lodgings for a few nights. But I tell you, I wish
to God I'd never set foot in the place! If I'd chosen a different
establishment, I wouldn't be in this mess now!'

His voice had risen to an anguished crescendo, and Rose put out a hand to calm him. 'Sssh,' she warned. 'Ned won't be back for some time, but all the same.'

'Yes, of course. It was the Exeter Inn,' he went on, resuming his story. 'I couldn't have told you the name then, but I certainly know it *now*. It's a coaching inn, so I didn't want to waste money staying there, and I asked the landlord if he could recommend somewhere cheaper and he told me of a lodging house in a back street around the corner. I bought a mug of ale and sat down on my own in a corner to drink it. Naturally, there were other customers, including one obnoxious fellow, drunk as a lord and annoying everyone else. He was obviously known to the landlord, and he warned him about his behaviour. He was boasting about how much money he had in his pocket. Even took it out and counted it for everyone to see. Said he'd won it gambling. Anyway, at one point he came over to me. Singled me out as a stranger drinking on my own, tried to taunt me, that sort of thing. It was all rather ugly, and I just let him get on with it. I've dealt with drunken privates often enough before, and they usually just run out of steam. I stood up to go and buy another drink, and he came up to me again. I was getting fed up with him by then, and suggested to him that he'd had enough to drink, and with that, he decided to give me a bloody nose for absolutely no damned reason. There were plenty of witnesses to the fact that I didn't retaliate. The landlord refused to serve him then and had him thrown out, but he was still shouting at me and saying it was my fault he couldn't have another drink. The landlord apologized profusely to me and gave me a glass of brandy on the house. I thought no more about it. I didn't stay long. I was a stranger and it was dark, and the sooner I found somewhere to stay, the better. I'd been directed into what I believe is the very old part of the town. I expect you know it. Dark, narrow streets. I hadn't gone very far, less than a hundred yards probably, when it happened.'

He paused, and when Rose glanced at him, she saw him swallow hard, as if summoning the courage to relive whatever it was had caused him to be detained at Her Majesty's pleasure. 'Go on,' she urged, aware that the time was ticking away.

He took a deep breath. 'I saw two figures struggling in the

shadows. And then I heard a cry. One of the figures collapsed on the ground and the other pounced on him. It was dark, but there was enough light coming from the windows of the houses for me to see that he was rifling through the other man's pockets. There was a couple walking down the street, elderly I think, but they just stood back and watched. Didn't want to get involved. God knows, I wish I'd done the same.'

'So what did you do?'

'Well, I shouted out and started running towards the attacker. It frightened him off and he disappeared into the darkness. It would have been pointless to give chase, and I was more concerned about the chap lying in the street. He'd been stabbed in the side, blood everywhere, and I was trying to stop it. I gained some knowledge of how to deal with wounds in the army, you see. I called out for help. For someone to fetch a doctor. But the couple hurried off round the next corner. I vaguely remember seeing someone else come along and then he, too, disappeared. I'd stopped calling out by then. I was just concentrating on saving the fellow's life, he was bleeding so much. I was loosening his clothing, trying to make sure he was still breathing. The next thing I knew, I was being dragged away by two constables and was locked up in the police cells.'

Rose could feel her heart pumping nervously in her chest. 'You mean they thought 'twas you who'd attacked him?'

'Exactly,' he grated with such vehemence he had at once to subdue another cough. 'The other passer-by had evidently seen me loosening his clothes and assumed I was robbing him, and went off to the police station, which I'm sure you know is just round the corner. The knife was still in him, and as you might imagine, I was covered in his blood, and they put two and two together.'

'But . . . but surely . . .' Rose stammered, her eyes wide with horror, 'surely they couldn't convict you on that?'

'Oh, it wasn't the only so-called evidence,' Seth scoffed. 'It turned out the victim was the drunkard from the inn. And . . .' He paused, and drew in a long, slow breath. 'The bastard swore it was me.'

Rose stiffened, and her hand went over her open mouth as she found herself trembling. 'Oh, Seth, no. But surely 'twas his word against yours? I mean—'

But Seth shook his head. 'There were so many other factors

as well. At the inn, there were plenty of witnesses to his punching me in the face, and it was reckoned I'd followed him out to have my revenge. If only I'd flattened him there and then in the inn, which I could have done easily, none of this would have happened. The money he'd been boasting about was gone, of course, and I had a virtually identical amount in my pocket, when minutes before I'd been asking for a room somewhere cheap. I can't blame the landlord for testifying to that when he was questioned, as it was true. They concluded, *naturally*,' he spat with cutting sarcasm, 'that the money had gone from the drunkard's pocket into mine.'

'But couldn't you have explained how you got that money?'

'God knows, I tried! The trouble was, I'd often stopped at farms and other places, done a day or two's work, and then moved on. Most of the time, I didn't take any notice of the names of the places. The brewery was the only establishment I could definitely name, and I hadn't earned anything there as they'd given me board instead. The police sergeant did contact a colleague in Exeter and confirmed it, but it didn't help at all. I really needed a lawyer, but they confiscated all my money as evidence, so I had nothing to pay one with.'

'But I thought you said you still had some army pay? Couldn't you have got them to verify that?'

'I could have done, but there were reasons why I didn't want them digging up my past. Personal reasons. Nothing sinister, and anyway, as far as they were concerned, I was a stranger, a man travelling the road. Of no fixed abode. I fitted the bill, so I was convicted.'

'What about your family? Couldn't they have helped?'

'Oh, yes, my father would have loved that!' Seth snorted with a hatred that shook Rose. 'He's a wealthy man, doing his level best to rub shoulders with the aristocracy. Our family home is a country house in Surrey with servants, land, two dogs and, of course, horses. But I was always the black sheep. Didn't fit into my parents' high-society aspirations. Among other things, I was in love with a girl beneath my station, as they put it. I wanted to marry her, so my father hurriedly bought me a commission in the army. Often you can be on a waiting list for years, but he had a business associate who had a cousin who was a colonel – you can imagine the sort of thing.

I was only eighteen years old, so I suppose I felt I had to obey him, but when I eventually came home on leave, the girl had disappeared and I never saw her again. I found out later that her parents had been handsomely paid to move away, taking her with them. Anyway, after a couple of years, I managed to transfer into the cavalry so that at least I was working with horses. My father had to pay extra for that, and he'd already had to purchase my promotion to lieutenant as well, although of course my first commission had been sold on. But it was worth it to him to keep me out of the way, especially as my regiment was posted to India soon afterwards, leaving him and my elder brother to climb the social ladder without me being there to spoil things for them. My father wasn't too happy, mind, when the purchase system was abolished and he hardly got any compensation. But at least when I got my captaincy, there was nothing to pay and it was keeping me thousands of miles away.' He paused for breath, sighing heavily. 'But I'd never been happy in the army. Not being aristocracy, I was an outsider in the officers' mess. I didn't hold with the ridiculous shenanigans they got up to, and I never had the money to live up to all their extravagances, even if I'd wanted to. I can't blame them. I know it was boredom, really. We'd been out there four years, just on patrols, so I can honestly say I've never had to kill anyone, thank heavens. The nearest we got to action was a couple of months on exercise. It was soon after that I resigned my commission, made my way back to Bombay and found a ship I could work my passage home on. I never told my parents, although I expect it got back to them eventually. As far as they're concerned, I've disappeared off the face of the earth. And that was another reason why I couldn't tell the police about the army.' He bowed his head, lowering his eyes before looking up at her again darkly. 'I'd been travelling under a false name to make sure my family could never trace me. My real name's Warrington. Captain Seth Warrington of the 15th The King's Hussars.'

'Good Lord.' Rose blinked her astonished eyes at him. ''Tis a lot to take in.'

'Yes, I know. But for God's sake, please don't tell a soul. I can assure you, though, if you were to look up my army record, you'd find in it nothing but an exemplary career. My only fault,' and here he smiled wryly, 'was that I was known not to be as ruthless with my men as perhaps I should have been.'

Rose chewed on her fingernail, and then stroked Amber's head again as she considered the thoughts that swirled in her mind. 'So the victim, the drunkard, I assume he survived?'

'Oh, yes. Mainly due to my own actions, the physician in question testified at my trial. If he'd died, I'd probably have found myself swinging at the end of a rope. Mind you, sometimes I wonder if that wouldn't have been the best thing,' he added, muttering under his breath.

Rose was appalled. 'No. Don't you dare say that. We should never give up hope.'

'And what hope should I have?' He exhaled heavily, and dropped his head back, his eyes closed. 'I was an idiot to run off like that. I'd worked all through the winter in the quarry, and then nine months clearing prison farmland, soaking wet as we dug drainage ditches, and then harnessed to chains dragging out boulders. I'm sure you've seen it often enough. You'd treat animals better. So I'd done the worst part. If you work hard, you can earn marks towards your ticket of leave. Reduce your sentence by up to quarter, so my twelve years could have been cut down to a mere nine. The warder by the tunnel, he's in charge of me. I'm lucky in that, at least. He's a good sort. One of the few. Not that they're allowed room for much compassion. The authorities are pretty hard on them, too, or so I gather. Anyway, I worked hard, and he awarded me maximum good marks. And because I'd behaved myself, I was considered trustworthy enough to be transferred to working with the animals. With the mist coming down, the land parties weren't allowed out. But the animals still have to be fed, and when the mist became so thick and the warder nearest me was busy taking a swig from his hip flask, well, I suddenly thought I might never have such a good chance again. It was a split-second decision. If I'd stopped to think, I wouldn't have been such a fool. So now, if I'm caught, I'll be flogged for my troubles and lose all my good marks. I could even have another five years added to my sentence.'

Rose had listened pensively, her lips puckered. 'But surely, if you can prove you're innocent—'

'If you can't prove it when you're on trial, you don't get another chance. I couldn't have a lawyer to gather any other evidence on my behalf, but I was allowed to cross-examine the witnesses. But the victim, Jonas Chant his name was, he stuck to his story. Well, he would, wouldn't he? If I were convicted, he'd get his money back. Except that it was *my* money. The real culprit still had *his*. I pointed out that he couldn't possibly have known what his assailant looked like. It was dark, and he was four sheets to the wind. Christ, *I* didn't recognize *him* in the dark! But he swore blind it was me. And the chap who'd fetched the policeman, I asked him if he actually saw me attack him, and he admitted he hadn't. He just saw me going through the devil's clothes. I was only trying to get to his wounds. But none of my arguments did any good. The jury was convinced, and that was it.'

Rose had pressed her hands together as if in prayer and rested her compressed lips against her joined forefingers as she mulled over what he had told her. 'What if you could find the elderly couple? If they testify they saw the real attacker run off, and you coming to the rescue, surely that would prove your innocence? And maybe someone else at the inn saw something. Someone behaving suspiciously. As if they were intent on following that devil out into the street. And what if you could retrace your steps, find some of the other places you worked and prove you'd earned that money?'

'No.' Seth turned his head towards her and gave an indulgent smile, though a deep sadness glimmered in his eyes. 'It's too late. Much as it would be my dearest wish to clear my name. I'm afraid that once you're convicted, that's it. There's no way you can appeal against your sentence, even if you come up with indisputable new evidence.'

Rose flicked up her head, her chin set stubbornly. 'That's insane.'

'It's the law,' Seth murmured as he snapped a blade of straw and twined it tightly about his fingers.

'Then the law's an ass.' To her amazement, she heard Seth chuckle, but then they both fell into a ponderous, contemplative silence. Rose really could not believe – could not accept – the injustice of it. But the fact that Seth was being so open about everything that had happened only served to increase her trust in him. 'Are you absolutely certain there's no other way?' she asked as her angry frustration broke the surface again.

Seth cocked one ironic eyebrow. 'Well, I believe there's something called a royal pardon. Still makes it sound as if you're guilty, though, doesn't it, even though you have to prove yourself beyond a shadow of a doubt? But it's so rare as to be virtually impossible, and it takes a massive amount of power and influence, not to say money to pay High Court lawyers and everything else that's involved. You're trying to overturn a jury's verdict and a circuit judge's sentence, after all. So I haven't a cat in hell's chance of that, have I?'

Rose sucked in her lips. Charles had money, and he knew people in high places. But she might as well try to jump the moon as ask for his help. He had always made his opinion of Dartmoor's convicts abundantly clear.

'The best I can hope for,' Seth went on, 'is that I'm not discovered here until I'm able to leave. And I can't thank you enough for all you've done for me.'

'And . . . what will you do then?' Rose questioned him, shying away from the sadness that gripped her heart at the thought of his leaving.

'I met someone while I was being held in the police cells in Tavistock. There was a street brawl the night after I was arrested, and I ended up sharing a cell for a couple of days with a fellow who was waiting for a coroner's court hearing. The case against him was thrown out, but when I was brought before the magistrate, I was spirited away to Exeter to await the next assizes. The prison there was rife with illness. I never had a day's sickness in the army, but in there, conditions were so bad, I ended up with what they said was pneumonia, not that they cared too much. My chest has been a bit weak ever since. Anyway, I'd struck up quite a friendship with this chap, and I think he'd probably help me to get away. Maybe get on that ship to America. Ironic, really, that I ended up serving my sentence back here on Dartmoor. I served my initial period in Millwall, you see. They send you somewhere else for nine months' solitary to break you down first. It doesn't even count towards your sentence. Anyway, after Millwall, I could have been sent almost anywhere for my sentence proper, but I suppose robbery with violence made me one of the worst felons in the land, which is why they sent me here. But this other man, he was a local farmer. From a place called Peter Tavy. On the moor somewhere, he said. Do you know it?'

Rose nodded. 'Vaguely. I went there once with my father on business. En route to Mary Tavy where there's a huge mining agglomeration called Wheal Friendship. Used to be copper back along, but it's been arsenic for many a long year. My father were manager of the gunpowder mills near here, and we used to supply them.'

She glanced across at him, and caught the arresting clarity of his hazel eyes. 'You were very close to your father, weren't you?' His voice was faltering, sensitive, and with no one to confide in for so long, Rose felt an overwhelming urge to weep, to allow the great, suppressed emotion of her grief to escape in a gushing torrent.

'Yes.' She scraped the simple word from her throat, surprised at how near she was to sudden tears. But they had been talking for some time, and she must have Seth hidden again before Ned returned. 'This farmer, what were his name?'

'Pencarrow. Richard Pencarrow. I can't be sure, but I reckon he'd help me.'

He stopped as the cough irritated his lungs again and he struggled to stifle it. Rose frowned. He had been secreted in the stable for just about a week, with at least another five to go before he could walk out of her life. The weather had turned cold and dank again, and if it worsened his cough and he couldn't smother it he would be discovered in no time.

Rose tried to conceal it, but fear churned uneasily inside her.

Twenty-One

With Charles away, it was a case of dreaming up errands to despatch Ned upon. Rose had instructed Cook and Patsy to spring-clean the house from top to bottom so that everything would be in order when the baby arrived. It was unlike Mrs Chadwick to order them about, but it was probably the growing burden of her pregnancy. She spent hours out with the puppies, Cook grumbled mildly, but at least once she had issued her instructions for the day she let them be.

Not so Ned, whom she was for ever sending all over the place. Often to Tor Royal for extra butter and cream, and she never complained if he dallied an hour with the comely dairymaid there. And one day, Rose had declared a desperate craving for some bananas, if you please! If Ned couldn't find any in Tavistock, he was to take the train to Plymouth, where he surely would! Rose had said it didn't matter if he took all day! But while he was out, Dr Seaton had come to check on her health, and while he was there, he was able to re-plaster Seth's ankle in complete secrecy.

Seth's presence had given Rose a purpose in life, something to spur her into action every morning instead of wandering aimlessly about the house. She lived for the moment when it was safe to enter the loose box with whatever provisions she had purloined for him, relishing in the subterfuge she had engaged upon. She couldn't wait to take up her position sitting on the bale near Amber and her pups, facing the open top half of the door so that she could see anyone who approached and warn Seth to hide himself. She bathed the shot wounds in his shoulder regularly, and there were at last signs of improvement. His cough, too, seemed to have eased, a huge relief as it could so easily give him away, and despite the continuing cold and rain, his health appeared to be a little better.

'When's the baby due?' he had asked amiably.

At just over two weeks old, the puppies were finding their legs and beginning to stumble away from their mother, tippling over quite comically. Amber watched over them indulgently, retrieving them in her soft mouth if they wandered too far, and Rose found she could spend all day being entertained by their antics.

She looked up. Seth was laughing softly as the tiny runt of the litter had toppled on to her minute snout, but in an instant was valiantly heaving herself on to her wobbly legs once more. Seth's generous mouth was stretched with amusement in the near beard on his strong jaw, his face for once quite relaxed, and with his light hair beginning to grow from its convict cut, Rose's heart seemed to trip over itself for not the first time and she allowed the feeling to lap innocently about her tangled emotions.

'Eight weeks.' She smiled a little ruefully, for it seemed a long way off, and she didn't want to contemplate a time when Seth would no longer be a part of her life and she would have to endure her future as Charles's wife.

'And . . . are you looking forward to it?'

'Why, yes.' She shook her head, as it was a strange question, asked in an even stranger tone of voice.

'And your husband?'

'Oh, yes! I think he's always wanted a son.'

'But . . . every time you speak of him,' she heard Seth's quiet, intense voice, 'you seem to . . . I don't know . . . close up.'

Rose lowered her eyes. She couldn't fathom why, but she somehow felt compelled to answer him. As if it would ease the terrible ache inside. 'I thought I loved him,' she barely whispered. 'I *wanted* to love him. I still do. 'Tis why the child's so important.'

She didn't see Seth flinch. 'I'm sorry. I shouldn't have asked. I hope it all works out well for you.'

She braced herself to glance at him again. 'Thank you. I'm certain it will. We've been married little less than a year, so there should be *some* hope for us.'

'You weren't married, then, when we first met, if you can call it that?'

'At the tunnel, you mean? No. I thought back then that my charmed life would go on for ever. But it doesn't, does it?' she sighed sadly.

'No.' Seth's eyes had narrowed and he stared ahead at some unseen spot on the opposite wall, his face set. 'I was really happy, wandering around the countryside and taking each day as it came. Enjoying my freedom from the army. And then look what happened.'

Rose put out a hand and squeezed his arm, her fingers somehow tingling as she touched him. He brought his eyes to rest on her, and she saw the hurt in them.

'I still can't believe it, you know. I still keep thinking that I'm going to wake up and find it's all been a terrible nightmare. But it hasn't, has it? And now I shall probably end up paying dearly for trying to escape.'

'But you might make it away. And if you are caught, they might be lenient. After all, you did save a warder's life.'

'If that's what I did. And I hardly think they'd take that into consideration,' he said with a bitter grunt. 'Some of the other inmates did take exception to what I did, though, and landed me in the infirmary.'

Rose winced as she nodded. 'Yes, I heard. The warder. He's my friend's father. He told me. Or at least, he told Molly and she told me.'

'Really? There's not much escapes you, is there, Mrs Chadwick?'

Rose smiled back. 'No, I suppose there isn't. 'Tis because of Gospel, I reckon. I ride all over the place on him. At least . . .' She faltered, pulling a wistful face. 'At least, I did until Charles stopped me. So I know everyone hereabouts, and they know me. I've lived here, or at least over at Cherrybrook, for so many years.'

'He's a magnificent animal. Your Gospel, I mean. I'd love to ride him.' But the sudden excitement on his face died in an instant. 'But I'll never get to, will I?' he murmured.

And Rose turned away, choking on what she knew was the answer.

Her feet were leaden as she dragged herself across the yard a week later. The pain in her heart was unbearable. She wanted to cry, to scream, to lash out against the invisible force of fate that was tearing her to shreds, since there was nothing she could do but accept the inevitable.

'A telegram came earlier,' she told Seth, her voice broken

and dejected. 'Charles is coming home. He'll be here tomorrow night.'

Their eyes met, clinging to each other, recognizing with appalled compassion what it would mean to them. Seth scrambled to his feet, taking Rose's hands as she stepped towards him, but his own words sounded strange. Detached. 'You knew he'd be coming home soon. He *is* your husband.'

'Yes, I know. But I don't want him to come back. Not ever. I wish to God I'd never married him!'

She stamped her foot, flicking her head so that her hair whipped across her face. Seth smoothed it back. Softly. And then placed his hands firmly on her shoulders.

'You don't mean that, Rose.'

She reluctantly raised her eyes to his face, but in her own anguish, didn't see the torment etched in his features. She drew in an enormous breath, trying desperately to calm herself. 'No, I suppose not. But our marriage was a mistake and . . . Oh, Seth, I don't know what to do.'

'There's nothing you *can* do. Have your child. Make the very most of your life. Be a good wife and mother. Your husband can't be *so* bad.'

Rose blinked at him, her mouth working desperately. How could she tell him how Charles treated her in bed, like a possession, never imagining that she yearned for comfort rather than fear in his arms? 'No, I suppose not,' she answered instead. 'He just always wants everything to be the way *he* wants it.'

'Don't we all, in our own way?'

She gazed up at him, at his understanding smile, his honest, intense eyes beneath his mildly raised eyebrows. All she could see in him was goodness and compassion and suddenly all her suppressed emotions erupted in an unstoppable tide. And it seemed so natural when Seth drew her against his chest, tucking her head beneath his chin. She closed her eyes, allowing herself to breathe in the closeness of him, his strength. Dear Lord, she was going to miss him so much.

''Tis going to be really difficult when Charles gets back,' she said, tearing herself away. 'And 'twill be so much more dangerous for you . . .'

Seth sighed weightily and bit on his lip. 'If it wasn't for this wretched ankle . . . I wonder if I got away at night. They're not looking for someone with his leg in plaster, after all.'

'No, but they are still looking. And you wouldn't get far. And even if you made your way to find this Richard Pencarrow's farm, Peter Tavy's probably ten miles by road. And that's literally going right past the prison gates. You'd need to make a detour of miles, and the chances are you'd get lost on the moor, not knowing it at all, and at night in the dark . . . No. 'Tis probably safer you stay here.'

'But what about you, Rose? If I'm caught here, you're deeply implicated.'

'Oh, you let me take care of that,' she smiled reassuringly, though in truth, she had no idea how . . .

They made the most of those last few hours, talking as if there was no tomorrow. Which for them, there wasn't. And never could be. She told him of her father's accident and how she had tried in vain to secure a new home for herself, for Henry and Florrie until the only answer had been to marry Charles, which she had believed would bring them all happiness. And Seth told her about the army and his time in India.

They talked on, unaware for some time of the quickly passing minutes, relishing the ease which comes to two like-minded people, until they suddenly realized Ned would soon return with Charles. It was like a final farewell, and yet not, for it would be another two and a half weeks before Seth could limp out of her life.

Rose kept delaying the moment of departure, whispering to the mound of straw so that anyone who saw her might have had a doubt as to her sanity. And when she finally lumbered to her feet and walked away, her heart was wrenching in strange, unwanted pain.

She heard him coughing as she crossed the yard and her stomach clenched sickeningly. The days since Charles had returned had been a torment to her. She had hardly been able to come out to Seth at all, and yesterday she had been unable to bring him so much as a drink of water. This morning, though, she had a mug of hot, sweet tea in her hand, which she knew Seth would devour like a man lost in the desert. But the sound of his cough froze her heart with fear, for if she could hear him, so too could anyone else.

She flew into Gospel's loose box, almost tripping over the

puppies, much to Amber's indignation. Seth wasn't even covered properly by the straw, but was lying on his front, half propped up on one elbow as he struggled against the violent, uncontrollable coughing. Rose was on her knees beside him, but her hand on his shoulder only distracted him for a moment before a fresh spasm gripped his lungs. Dear God Almighty, what was she to do? The harrowing cough was clearly agony for him, and when he finally managed to subdue it and drew the back of his hand over his mouth, it came away streaked with blood-stained spittle.

'Drink this,' Rose said, horrified, as she pushed the mug into his hand and instinctively put a supportive arm about his shoulders. She could feel the searing heat coming from him, the brutal trembling that shook his body, and her forehead pleated in dread. Seth tried to take a breath to drink the tea, but only succeeded in spluttering into it and spilling some down his front. She steadied his hand, and as the hot liquid soothed his throat, she felt him relax against her.

'It feels . . . like pneumonia again,' he managed to rasp.

'Then you must give yourself up.' Her heart flooded with the empty numbness of acceptance, as if she had known all along that this would happen. But why now, when Seth was so near to being able to make his escape? It was as if the cruel hand of fate had been teasing them, deceiving them, only to hurl them back into the quagmire of despair at the last minute.

'No. I've got . . . to get to Richard's farm.'

'But, Seth, you could . . . you could die.'

'I'd sooner take that chance.' And he collapsed into another choking fit of coughing. 'I just can't face . . . another ten years . . . maybe more . . . in that hell-hole . . . for something I didn't do,' he gasped. 'If I give myself up, I'm no coward but . . . I won't be flogged when I don't deserve it. Oh, God, I'm so cold . . .'

Rose watched, her heart in savage pain, as he tried to slurp at the tea between rattling breaths. If only Dr Seaton were due to check on her pregnancy, but he would not be coming again for several days, and Rose Maddiford, whose indomitable spirit had always fought back, had fallen into a yawning chasm of despair. There was nothing she could do. All she could think of was to fetch a glass of water so that Seth could take a good dose of laudanum. With any luck, the drug-induced sleep might also suppress his racking cough. And give her time to think.

In her headlong anxiety, she didn't see Ned Cornish stand back from the tack-room door at the opposite end of the stable block. His blinkered mind had only been on one thing lately, seducing the dairymaid at Tor Royal. He'd managed to get his hand up her skirt, and was convinced his aching, throbbing member wouldn't be far behind. But the master's coming home had thrown a spanner in the works. Rose hadn't sent him on one of her fool's errands since her husband's return, and now his free hours that he normally relished – as although he had nothing to do, he must remain on duty in case he was needed to tack up one of the horses at short notice – had become a frustrating burden to him as he dreamt of what he *might* have been doing. Slowly, his half-witted brain became curious. It hadn't struck him as particularly odd the way Rose had been . . . yes, getting him out of the way, he was sure of it now. She had even been neglecting that bloody nag of hers in favour of the two dogs and the litter of mongrels they had produced between them, constantly crossing back and forth with a drink in her hand and extra food for the bitch. But, surely the dog couldn't eat so much. Surely there was something else going on?

And then he heard it. Someone trying desperately to muffle a grating, vicious cough. And if he wasn't mistaken, it sounded like a man.

Ned's eyes widened, then narrowed into cunning slits as his mouth twisted into a sly smirk. There'd been that escaped convict, hadn't there, disappeared into thin air. Well, he hadn't disappeared at all, had he? He was hiding in Gospel's bloody loose box. And Rose had been looking after him! Typical of her! She was known to have some sympathy for the bastards banged up in the prison, and how far had that sympathy gone? When Ned thought of the years Rose had tried his patience, and he'd never had so much as a willing kiss out of her! But what had she given to that bugger out in the stable?

His face twitched with seething rage. With hatred. But for once he checked himself. If he went charging into the stable, the criminal – well, he could be violent. And though Ned would enter into fisticuffs with anyone provided he knew it was a sure assumption he would easily win, he was bright enough to consider that the felon might well be stronger than he was!

No. He would make sure of his facts and then go quietly and politely to the prison. Oh, yes, he'd get his own back on Rose Maddiford! And besides, the statutory five pounds' reward for turning in an escaped convict – the equivalent of six months' pay – would be more than recompense.

Rose was lying on the bed, supposedly taking a rest. But in actual fact she was trying to clear her head of the shock of finding Seth so ill, and force her brain into thinking up a solution. Dr Seaton was not due for several days, but she must invent some excuse for Charles to send for him urgently. She could say that she was bleeding. Just a little. Yes, that would surely bring the doctor at once.

She was just getting up to put her plan into action when she heard the commotion coming from the stable yard. And she knew. For ten seconds, she stood like a granite pillar, the sound of heavy boots and men's raised voices burning into her ears. Oh, no. Her heart stopped beating. Guards. The Civil Guard from the prison.

She found herself retching. But there was no time for that. If there was anything she could do . . . She ran down the stairs, one hand clamped over her mouth to retain the bile that scorched into her gullet, the other clutching at the banister to support her drooping body.

She blundered out into the yard, heedless of the penetrating drizzle, and stopped dead as several pairs of eyes turned upon her, Ned's face in a leering snigger, the guard she recognized as the sergeant suffused with an expression of callous satisfaction, and then Charles . . . He gazed at her, his skin pale from anger and disbelief, and in his eyes such disdain and contempt she might have died on the spot. Not a word passed anyone's lips, each figure a sculptured statue, until angry shouts, the clatter and crashes of a violent struggle, the enraged bark of a dog, drew their attention to the loose box, and the two guards who had remained in the yard raised their Sniders and trained them on the door.

Rose felt she would faint, as if some huge hand had closed about her neck and was wringing the life from her. She stood, quivering with dread, as two burly guards emerged from the stable, Seth held securely between them as they dragged him over the cobbles and then wrenched him upright as they came to attention before their sergeant. Seth's face was bloodless, his broad forehead bedewed with feverish sweat and embellished with a gash from the struggle. He was attempting to resist even now, but it was hopeless, and when the sergeant spat at him with a taunting jibe, he defiantly drew himself up to his full height and stared resolutely ahead.

'You've led us a merry dance, you *scum*!' the sergeant snarled, and with a malevolent cry drove his fist into Seth's stomach.

The barb pierced into Rose's side and she turned away, grasping on to whatever was at hand, which happened to be Charles's arm. She heard even *him* wince and for a fleeting instant their eyes met in horror before they both looked back. Seth had collapsed on to his knees, locked in a heaving convulsion of coughing. The sergeant sneered down at him, his face a pitiless mask of spite. Seth lifted his head, still spluttering and fighting for breath, a streak of blood dribbling from the corner of his mouth down into the thick stubble on his jaw. He just managed to rasp something that Rose didn't catch before the cough overtook him again.

The sergeant's lip curled implacably. 'Innocent be damned! I suppose that's what you told Mrs Chadwick here, and her being of a kind nature and in a delicate condition, she fell for it, poor lady! Well, laddie, you'll be well flogged for it, mark my words!'

The sergeant's obvious relish plunged a crucifying pain into Rose's flesh, tearing her heart from her chest. Her legs buckled beneath her and she clung to her husband, burying her face in his shoulder, and miraculously his strong arms came about her, buoying up her frail body.

'Oh, Charles, I've been so frightened!' she wept against him. 'I didn't know what to do!'

Somehow, from the corner of her eye, she saw the sergeant glance in her direction with what she imagined was the nearest to sympathy he was capable of. He must have heard her words, and some beacon in her appalled, petrified mind told her that if she was to be of any help to Seth, she must fight to establish her own blamelessness.

'He scared me so much, I were too afraid not to do as he said,' she cried hysterically at the top of her voice.

'What I'd like to know, Sergeant, is how the devil he got his leg plastered?' one of the guards demanded with equal malice, and Rose trembled with cold sweat as she thought of the kindness the elderly physician had shown them.

''Twas me.' She stepped forward on uncertain legs. 'I stole the plaster from Dr Seaton's bag when he came to visit me because of the baby.' She hesitated, withering under the sergeant's keen stare. And then – may God forgive her – she jabbed a finger at Seth. ''Twas *his* idea. He told me to do it.'

The pulse was pounding at her temples as the sergeant frowned, but still kneeling on the ground, Seth raised his head, still half choking on the relentless cough.

'I said I'd kill the puppies if she didn't,' he gasped, putting an unfamiliar coldness into his voice.

Across the space that separated them, their eyes met in one last clinging, frantic gaze, and in the depths of his agony, Rose saw some calm and steadfast faith. Some belief in the brief trust they had come to share. Neither of them was aware of the sergeant's uncouth oath. Or the barbaric grunt with which he thrust his boot into his prisoner's side.

Seth had no breath to cry out, but sprawled forward again in a writhing heap, coughing until his lungs would split and blood splattered on to the cobbles before him. And Rose screamed.

'For God's sake,' Charles cried at once, 'do you have to treat him like that in front of my wife! Can't you see how distressed she is? Surely she's already been through enough without you—'

'No need to upset yourself, sir! Just needed to make certain he wouldn't try to escape again. We'll take care of the bastard now, so if you'd just like to take your wife inside. Right, get the cuffs on him, lads. And you, sir,' he said, turning to Ned who was preening himself proudly and clearly enjoying the spectacle, 'if you'd like to accompany us, we can see about claiming your reward.'

Rose watched them all disappear around the corner of the yard, virtually carrying Seth between them, for he hadn't the strength to stand, let alone walk. It was only Charles's arms firmly about her that stopped her from running after them as she battled to swallow down her unleashed, monstrous outrage. She drew in an enormous breath as the futility of any further protest flooded into her heart, the strain of the last weeks suddenly draining the strength from her. And for once in her life, she was ready to submit.

'Come now, my poor darling,' Charles whispered comfortingly into her hair. 'You've been through so much, and we must think of the baby.'

Rose nodded, leaning heavily against him as her legs turned weak beneath her. She tottered back to the house on his arm, and he all but carried her upstairs to the bedroom, calling to Cook to bring up some hot, sweet tea for the mistress. Once in the room, he removed Rose's shoes and helped her into bed. She was pale and shivering, with that vile emptiness in the very core of her she had known once before – when her beloved father had died.

'I'm so sorry, my dearest, that you were subjected to that display of barbarity,' Charles declared as he tenderly returned a stray wisp of her hair to its pin. 'I will of course complain to the governor of the gaol. For his sergeant to behave with such cruelty, especially in front of you, my dear, was unforgivable. Of course it distresses me that the villain had threatened and deceived you, but really, to have treated the devil like that when he was clearly so ill was a crime in itself. Ah, the tea. Thank you, Cook. Now you drink this, and try and get some rest. Would you like me to fetch Dr Seaton?'

Rose had been so numbed with shock that her brain had been unable to formulate any thoughts. Her mind was saturated with her lacerating sorrow at seeing Seth being dragged away so callously, and now she was as malleable as a child as Charles tucked her up in bed.

'No, I'll be fine, thank you, Charles,' she managed to croak. 'I'll just have a little nap. There's no need to call the doctor.'

'As you wish, my dearest.' He bent to place a kiss on her forehead, then drew the curtains before creeping quietly out of the room.

The all-invading silence rang in Rose's ears. She was exhausted, but how could she sleep when Seth would be suffering such agony with only the prospect of the punishment cell and a flogging to look forward to! Oh, dear God, they had been so close to victory! Only another fortnight and he would have been able to make good his escape. She would never have seen or heard from him again, and that place in her heart he had touched would have remained raw until the day she died. But at least she would have known he was safely away. But now . . .

She tossed and turned, unable to get comfortable with the burden of her unborn child. Everything kept churning over in her head, how Seth had won her trust and yet had had such care for her own safety. The blatant lie he had told to protect her, but for which he would surely suffer – if he survived the pneumonia or whatever infection it was that racked his lungs. Oh, poor, *poor* Seth.

Tearing anguish swelled in her throat, forcing tears to her eyes, and she let them fall, soaking into the pillow. Surely she would drown in her own grief. And she felt ashamed that she had said such things about Charles when he had been so furious at the sadistic way the sergeant had treated Seth. In so many aspects, Charles was a good man, and just now he had shown deep and genuine compassion towards the ill-treated prisoner.

Rose suddenly realized that her tears had dried. Her desperation to find a way out of this nightmare was already clawing its way back to determination. Perhaps the answer was in the very place she had not looked. Could she possibly persuade Charles to help Seth? He would be just the man, with connections in high places. Before, she had scorned the idea, but the ugly scene in the stable yard just now had made her wonder.

As she lay in the darkened room, hope began to emerge from her despair like a butterfly from a chrysalis. Her own headstrong will had likely coloured her opinion of Charles, and perhaps she had misjudged him. He would surely not tolerate the injustice that had been done to Seth Warrington. Rose felt stupid, like a petulant child. Now, as she awaited the birth of her own little one, it was time to grow up.

'Did you sleep, my love?' Charles enquired when he stole into the room some time later.

'No, not really,' she sighed, shaking her head. 'I couldn't help thinking about those soldiers and the way they treated that fellow.'

'It was certainly uncalled for,' Charles snorted. 'He obviously wasn't going anywhere. I have already begun a letter of complaint—'

'Charles.' Rose sat bolt upright in the bed, grasping his hand while her brow knitted in painful earnest. 'Charles, I know you have little sympathy for the prisoners here, and I agree that some deserve such harsh punishment. But I'm sure you would deplore such injustice if someone had been wrongfully convicted.'

'Oh, Rose, my dear, you don't mean to say that villain—'

'Charles, please, listen to me!' Her voice rose to a shrill crescendo as her heart began to beat wildly. 'He told me such things . . . It really is possible that there is evidence, witnesses, that could prove his innocence. Surely, as good Christians, we cannot allow such a miscarriage of justice? Please, I beg you, couldn't we look into it? See if there is anything to be done? He never threatened to kill the puppies, you know. He said that to keep me out of trouble!'

'I've no doubt that was his story—'

'Please, Charles! I know you can help him! It needs someone like you . . .'

She held her breath, almost hysterical, her cheeks blushed a beautiful peach and her lovely lavender-blue eyes glistening. Charles hesitated, his lips pursed, and then he smiled.

'For you, my darling Rose, I will do anything, you know that. You are my dearest wife and soon we will have our son to love and to cherish. Tomorrow, you will tell me all that you know of this fellow's case, and I will see if there's anything I can do. I just wish you had trusted me in the first place.'

He looked so forlorn, so hurt, deepening Rose's shame. 'I should have done, Charles, I realize that now. And I'm sorry. I behaved like a child. Can you ever forgive me?'

'Of course, my dearest, lovely girl. When I look at you—' He broke off, his eyes softening. 'I understand. It's your delicate condition. Tomorrow, I promise, I will listen to what you have to tell me. But tonight I wish to dine in peace and quiet with my beautiful wife.'

His expression was so intense, so caressing, that Rose felt her heart soar. 'Charles, I know we've had our differences, but . . . can we make a fresh start?' she questioned, joy blossoming inside her.

'Yes, a fresh start.'

He took her hand, brought it to his lips. Oh, what a fool she had been! Yes, Seth had reached into her soul, touched her heart. But that was all a dream, a fantasy. Life wasn't like that. Life was down-to-earth. She had married a good, dependable man, not perfect, not a hero. And tomorrow he was going to help someone she thought he would despise. She had been so wrong about him. A warm contentment lulled her heart as she returned her husband's smile.

For tomorrow was another day.